MW01199114

VAMPIRE VINTAGE BOOK ONE :
BELLADONNA IN HOLLYWOOD

ALEX SEVERIN

Copyright © 2011 Alex Severin

ISBN: 1477414436
ISBN-13: 978-1477414439

"We are all in the gutter, but some of us are looking at the stars."

- Oscar Wilde

This book is dedicated to my Mum & Dad, K, Mike, Carol, Quita, and Jenise & Scott, with my love and thanks that you are all part of my life and are with me every step of the way.

Without you I'm nothing.

- Alex Severin

CONTENTS

ACKNOWLEDGEMENTS

I would like to thank the following writers whose works inspired and instructed me in my research for this book. I thank them sincerely for their painstaking research, tangible passion and dedication to their respective subjects. There are also a few websites and movies that were invaluable for inspiring authentic scene setting, tone and vernacular of the day.

David Stenn (Runnin' Wild : Clara Bow)

Arthur Lennig (The Immortal Count : The Life & Films of Bela Lugosi)

Mick LaSalle (Complicated Women : Sex & Power in Pre-Code Hollywood)

Paula S. Fass (The Damned & the Beautiful : American Youth in the 1920s)

William K. Everson (American Silent Film)

Edward D Wood Jr. (Hollywood Rat Race)

The Hollywood Sign Trust - www.HollywoodSign.org

The Dirty 30s Sourcebook - http://www.paper-dragon.com/1939/

The Internet Guide to Jazz Age Slang - http://home.earthlink.net/~dlarkins/slang-pg.htm

Wikipedia (for historical dates & other info) – http://www.wikipedia.org

"Cocaine Fiends"[1935] Willis Kent Productions

"Reefer Madness" [1936] George A. Hirliman Productions

"IT" [1927] Paramount Pictures

"Dracula" [1931] Universal Studios

COVER CREDITS

COVER DESIGN -
Alex Severin

IMAGES -
'Portrait in Noir Style. Diva' -
by RetroAtelier (iStockPhoto.com)

'Hollywood Sign from the Griffith Observatory' by
Harbor12 (Creative Commons License via
Commons.WikiMedia.org

Photoshop Moon Brushes by ObsidianDawn.com

FONTS -
Market Deco, Deco Tech & Riesling via DaFont.com

CHAPTER ONE – THIS IS HOLLYWOOD

HOLLYWOOD, CA – NOW

Lust hung heavily in the air as he smoldered his way through another song. Drums like a heartbeat throbbed behind his voice and distorted guitars screamed like the adoring crowd.

The warehouse was packed, wall-to-wall, the air wet with excited sweat, the crowd exhaling their desire for him into air that smelled like sex.

Belladonna grinned grudgingly and shook her head as she watched him preach to his disciples. Not much had changed in the eighty years that Belladonna had been a vampire.

Vivant still needed an audience.

And that audience was still on its knees, vibrating with lust so fierce you could almost touch it, taste it.

Men and women wanted him, needed him, just like they always had. And some would even die for him.

Looking at the people in the crowd reminded Belladonna that fashion never changed all that much over the years. Most of them looked as if they'd just stepped from the corroding celluloid of a silent movie, black-eyed and pale and at odds with the colorful world around them.

It was pointless trying to hide; Vivant would have known she was here long before she crossed the threshold. No one could successfully sneak up on him.

Belladonna wondered why he had never left Hollywood for any significant period. He'd arrived here from eastern Europe and not left for more than a few weeks at a time in more than a century.

But it was a foolish question. She knew the answer. It was the reason she was standing there at this moment.

Because *this* is *Hollywood*.

And there's no place on earth quite like it.

Hollywood is where the widest dreams can come true and heart's desires are crushed. The place where legends are made and souls are lost.

It's where fantasies can become a reality and reality can turn into a nightmare.

Hollywood is love and hate. Euphoria and despair. Good and evil.

And it is a place where there is *always* hope. Hope that maybe, just maybe, you are *the one*. Hope that maybe someday it will be *you* sitting in the back of that long black car sipping ice-cold Cristal from platinum-rimmed flutes, giving head to the top box office star of the year, instead of parking his Limousine.

And Hollywood is where that *might* just happen. There's always a chance – no matter how small, how miniscule, that it *could* happen.

Because *this* is *Hollywood*.

That's why everybody always comes back.

And why some never leave. Can't leave. Won't leave.

She smiled. Sepia-toned memories invaded her, things she hadn't thought about in years, but she was glad she remembered them.

She was home again. Not that she had been gone for long.

And she was in love again.

With Hollywood.

CHAPTER TWO : BELLADONNA IN THE ROSE CITY

OREGON BOONIES, 1929

The farmhouse was silent save for the frequent creaks and groans the old place made as the night cooled its timbers.

The Philco 70 radio crackled at her as the transmission of The Shadow rounded off the Detective Story Hour on CBS for the night.

She waited patiently in the dark until she heard the wall-shaking snores of her father as she lay in bed, fully clothed with the covers pulled up to her chin.

Her muscles burned with tension as she lay there, eyes wide open, barely daring to breathe for fear of discovery.

Her mother was a light sleeper, but, fortunately, the mere creak of a floorboard was unlikely to rouse her from her room; she would figure it was her son, Cal, coming home late from the local illicit still, full of moonshine and stolen kisses.

But her father - he would spring out of bed at the slightest sound and snatch his Springfield 30.06 rifle from the corner. He'd cuss the air blue then be chastised by his wife for his language in front of the kids, even if one of them *was* full of illegal booze.

Belladonna rose from her bed and crept along the hall deliberately, slowly, expertly avoiding the floorboards she knew creaked and cracked under foot, just in case.

She hoped she did not bump into her big step-brother on his way in. He would surely make so much noise upon seeing her sneaking out so late that the whole household would be roused from their beds.

A few years ago she'd encountered Cal in the middle of the night on her way to the kitchen for a glass of water. He'd just discovered the joys of moonshine and wasn't yet used to it.

He grabbed her and tried to dance with her, singing a bawdy, inappropriate old song about a milk maid and a bull. He twirled her around and around until she was laughing and giddy.

Unfortunately, Cal lost his balance and plowed into his mother's small, but prized collection of miniature teapots. The loss of her collection devastated her - only three pieces had remained intact.

Since that day, each birthday, holiday, and anniversary, she received miniature teapots from family members and now had a respectable little collection again. They weren't worth much, but she loved them.

Morag would never allow Cal to forget he was the murderer of the teapots and reveled in reminding him often.

If Cal did indeed roll in half-cut and start making a fuss, Papa would bolt out of the bedroom, his gun trained on them, mama would be fretting in case he shot one of the children by accident.

Quita, little sister, would be sleepily rubbing her eyes wondering what all the commotion was about.

And then, inevitably, Belladonna's secret would be discovered – her plan to sneak off to Portland to see a stage production of *Dracula* - and everybody would try to talk her out of it.

This would be her one and only chance to see the play - it was a special, one-off performance that had been commissioned by an extremely wealthy Portland businessman for his daughter's sixteenth birthday.

Belladonna couldn't let anybody talk her out of this. She couldn't let that happen under any circumstances. She knew that this was the beginning of her destiny. Nothing could be allowed to stand in her way.

She left a note on the stove so they would know where she went.

Belladonna shut the door behind her and stood still, waiting for Cal's staggering footfalls in the dirt.

All was quiet.

The only thing stirring was the country night life – the snort of horses in the barn, the solitary moo from a cow in a far off pasture, the hoot of an owl, the distant scream of a coyote.

She chose each step carefully, walking lightly over the stony dirt track, holding her breath. She expected to hear someone call her name and ask her where she thought she was going at this time of night.

Once she cleared the property line, she took off at speed. She knew she would have to walk at a steady pace to make it to the next town in time for the bus to Portland.

If she missed it, she'd be out of luck. There wouldn't be another bus for days.

But she would not miss it. Even if she had to run all the way, run all night. This was something she had to do. This was her rite of passage, the step that she knew would take her from her prolonged girlhood and into being a woman.

She had to swallow her fears, silence them. She needed to prove to everybody she knew that she was no longer a little girl and that she had long since become the woman they did not want her to be. She had to show them that she did not need mama or papa or Cal by her side to hold her hand anymore.

She needed to show them that she was all grown up, that she was not the same age as little Quita, and that she was no longer *Lil' Bell*.

The bus ride to Portland was uneventful most of the way there. But the closer it got to Portland, the more people crammed on. By the time they were almost there, Belladonna had given up her seat for a little old lady and was now being jostled and shoved by the other travelers standing in the aisle.

She felt like she'd been sitting on the bus forever and that she was never going to get off it.

As the bus emptied slowly, she was pushed aside by people with no manners, people who did not say *excuse me* or *sorry* when they bumped her or shoved past her. Belladonna thought they were very rude and wondered how they'd been brought up. She would never behave that way.

She hoped that the people in Portland would be a little more friendly than the passengers on the bus.

As she stepped off the bus Belladonna felt like Jonah being swallowed up into the belly of the whale. She felt so small. So insignificant. Again pushed around, this time by people on the street, Belladonna had never felt more like a little girl than she did now.

She felt tiny in this great big city, overwhelmed by its size. And there were so many people, people all around her pushing her out of the way. She wished that mama or papa or Cal was beside her to hold her hand at this moment.

She was vulnerable and she looked it too. Her huge dark eyes were full of moist innocence and her naturally rouge-colored lips - lips that had never been kissed – quivered with emotion as the sights and sounds of the big city threatened to swallow her whole.

Portland was fast. People walked fast, they talked fast. Everything was big and loud. Everything was frightening.

It wasn't *really* all that big or even all that fast, but for somebody from such a small place it *was* big and it *was* scary. Papa loved how small and wildly rural Independence was and always called it "a one horse town - and the horse just died."

Belladonna was giddy with anticipation, nauseous with apprehension and excitement, both churning around together in her stomach.

She felt sick as she thought about her mother and how she would probably still be crying, blaming herself for her daughter running away to the city.

She was so afraid her family would disown her, cast her aside, look at her differently now that she had made a decision for herself and left home, even if only for a short time.

She only hoped that they would allow her to come back. She hoped they would not think differently of her, that they would not treat her with any less love and affection than they had. She didn't want to stay in the city, she just wanted to visit, just wanted to see what it was she came here to see.

She was here with a purpose, on a mission - Belladonna was in Portland, the great big city, to see *him*. She was there to see Bela Lugosi perform as Count Dracula on stage. She had listened to him play the part of the Transylvanian vampire on the radio and had held on to the thrill he made her feel.

She would curl up by the fire with a crocheted blanket around her shoulders, made by her grandmother's twisted arthritic fingers which always looked to Belladonna like knotted, gnarled tree branches in winter.

She would listen to his velvet voice, her eyes wide and dreaming of what his face would look like. She was sure his eyes would be red as rubies, his hair black as night sky, his skin paler than moonlight.

Belladonna was madly in love with the man who played *Dracula*, even although she had never laid eyes on him.

But soon she would. Soon she would be sitting in the audience looking up at the stage, looking up at *him*, gazing into the eyes she just knew would hypnotize her. She would hear, in the very same room as she sat, the voice that made her sigh, the voice that made her dream of things she had never even imagined before.

She would be in the same room as the man who had taught her how it felt to be a woman, and helped her shake off the last vestiges of being *Lil' Bell*.

CHAPTER THREE : WIDE-EYED IN THE DARK

As Belladonna stood in line she trembled as she listened to the excited whispers of the other theater goers. They were mostly young girls and older ladies, chatter amongst themselves about how many times they had seen the stage production of *Dracula*, and how many cities they had visited to see Bela play the immortal vampire Count.

One girl flushed ruby red as she told her friend about sneaking in to Bela Lugosi's dressing room in Los Angeles; she stole a kiss from him. She also stole a lit cigar, perched precariously on the edge of his dressing table as she ran for the door.

And there were more stories Belladonna overheard, each one more elaborate than the last.

One told how she knew a theater manager on the east coast and was introduced to Bela Lugosi after a performance.

Another claimed her father was a top Hollywood producer and had been taken to dinner by Lugosi.

And one, a beautiful city sophisticate told the whole crowd...

"Hah! That's nothing – he asked *me* to marry him!"

The crowd giggled, some nervously, some embarrassed by their own tall tales, knowing that everybody knew they were telling little white lies.

The doors opened and a collective gasp ran through the crowd of Dracula's disciples.

There were beautiful young girls all around her, their faces painted like china dolls and wearing the latest fashionable clothes.

Although her beauty surpassed all the other girls in line, Belladonna felt inferior beside these modern city girls.

Her simple dress, hand-made by herself, felt awkward and shabby in comparison.

She felt naked; she wore no make-up on her face, no jewelry dangled from her ears, nor clung to her neck or her wrists. She felt every inch the rube from the country and suddenly despised who she was.

Now, standing in line with these beautiful, fashionable young women, she felt like nothing more than a country bumpkin who deserved their scorn.

But she took note of what the young girls were wearing, paid close attention to the way they styled their hair and how they made up their faces.

Some girls ahead of Belladonna in the line snickered about her behind palm-shrouded lips, laughed about the dress she wore, the way her hair was styled, screwed up their faces at her ample breasts.

"Such a wheat!"

"So unsophisticated!"

"Doesn't even wrap her chest"

She'd never heard the term *wheat* before but she was sure she knew what it meant.

That'll be another word for a country bumpkin, I'm sure.

But Belladonna didn't really care what they thought - she was just here to see Bela Lugosi, and she knew she would never see any of these people again.

But the next time she visited a big city - and she knew there would be a next time - she would not look like a girl who stepped straight off a bus from the country.

INSIDE THE THEATER...

Belladonna sat rigid in her seat, tapping her foot on the floor. Her stomach was knotted with nervousness, her mouth dry, tongue sticking to the roof of her mouth.

She let out a tiny squeak as the house lights dimmed and the murmurs of conversation in the audience ceased.

The room was silent.

Then the quiet was broken by the sound footsteps treading the boards behind the blood-red velvet curtain.

Belladonna trembled with anticipation. Only moments ago her breathing had been rapid but was now stuck in her lungs making them burn.

She let out the trapped air and gasped for more; those around her glanced sideways at her, raising eyebrows, looking at each other with slanted smiles.

The air was charged with excitement and several young girls in the audience also gasped as the curtains parted slowly.

A young girl, no more than sixteen years old fell into a dead faint and was carried off by two burly ambulance men. They waited at the back of the theater each performance for the inevitable fainters.

The papers hyped it all up - Lugosi's performance was so terrifying that it made women pass out.

But the medics knew otherwise. They knew it was not terror that made these women – young and old – flush at the cheeks and tremble. It was simple lust. It was overwhelming desire. Crippling need.

She waited patiently, her eyes scouring every inch of the stage, oblivious to the other characters, the other actors, waiting, waiting, for that moment when he stepped on to the stage...

And then – there he was. Right there in front of her.

Another three females fell limp to the floor with heavy sighs.

Belladonna thought she was going to die.

Her heart felt like it had stopped in her chest.

Her breath froze in her throat.

Her eyes were wide, drinking in the sight of him for the very first time.

Belladonna was entranced by him.

His eyes.

Oh, my God, his eyes...

They were even more fierce than she had imagined them, they were more hypnotic than she had dreamed they would be.

And in that very instant of breathless awe, Belladonna was in love.

And then he spoke…

"I bid you welcome..."

And she caught his eye. Lugosi looked straight at her, a look that seemed to see *inside* her. She made a little startled noise in her throat, her eyes growing ever wider with disbelief that he was looking at her.

Lugosi grinned at her as he exited the stage, a knowing, confident grin that told her he knew what she was thinking about him as she sat there in the darkened theater staring up at him on the stage.

He knew what they were all thinking. He could feel their desire filtering through the ether to him. He could hear their sighs and gasps.

He felt invincible when he was on stage. He felt as if he could take on the world, as if nothing on earth could touch him.

Being Dracula made him feel immortal.

And while he was on stage, sweating under the lights and feeling the waves of adoration reaching him from the audience, he could forget the crippling agony of his old war wounds that sometimes morphine could not even touch.

Belladonna felt blackness creeping behind her eyes as she willed herself to breathe again before she lost consciousness.

But it seemed she had forgotten how. She tried to inhale, tried to open her mouth and gulp in precious air but she could not.

A young man sitting next to her nudged her in the ribs and she sucked in a huge gulp of oxygen just in time to banish the blackness.

Her eyes were fixed on Lugosi the whole way through and he kept looking at her for the duration of the performance, his eyes saying more to her than the learned words he was reciting.

She thought she knew what he was trying to tell her – that they would meet again at another time, meet again in another place under different circumstances.

From that moment forward, Belladonna was forever changed. She was no longer a child. She had felt something stir inside her, felt something spring to life, grow.

Bela Lugosi planted a seed that would soon to burst into bloom.

And as the final curtain closed with a swish of red velvet and the uproarious applause became excited chatter amongst the patrons, she knew that she had been reborn.

Belladonna knew that this night would transform her life. Nothing would ever be the same.

Belladonna did not receive the tongue-lashing she imagined she would get when she returned home from Portland.

Everybody told her she was all grown up now and she could leave home if she wanted to, but she would always have a place on the family farm.

Their reactions disappointed her a little - she wanted to be a rebel, wanted her parents to try and stop her from leaving the house, to tell her off and yell at her.

She wanted, just once, to know how it felt to be a bad girl. She wanted to know how it felt to be chastised for being the errant one, just for a change, instead of *Good Li'l Bell*.

Belladonna was different now, changed. She was not the girl who had left home for the big city. Something had happened to her as she sat there in the darkened theater.

Her fascination and infatuation for Bela Lugosi had become something more. She watched him as he spoke his black velvet words, entranced by his face, hypnotized by the eyes she had only ever dreamed about seeing.

His voice seemed to reach out for her, glide over her skin like an intimate touch.

Back home and in her room, radio on and listening to the sound of his voice again, Belladonna could now see his face when she closed her eyes, could see his hypnotic stare.

She felt the tide of her blood rise, throbbing inside her like never before, and found the rhythm of her own hips as she sweated in the dark.

He had helped her on the arduous journey to being a woman.

He made her feel things she had never felt, want things she had not experienced, things she knew nothing of before.

Suddenly she wanted all of these things, needed them.

Now, she wanted much more of him than just his deep seductive words. She wanted to feel more than the touch of her own hand and the sound of his voice.

She was restless now. Always restless. Had been since the day she got back.

Her life on the homestead had always been enough before. The farm and her family had always been her life, her whole world, and until *that* day she had never felt more than a fleeting desire to explore the rest of it.

But everything changed as she sat there wide-eyed in the dark, listening to that voice, watching *that* face, *those* eyes.

1931

Tod Browning's DRACULA – The story of the strangest passion the world has ever known!

Belladonna couldn't believe her eyes as she flicked through *Photoplay* magazine.

There it was in black and white – the announcement of the motion picture *Dracula* to be directed and produced by Tod Browning, and starring Helen Chandler and Edward Van Sloan, with Bela Lugosi reprising his smash hit stage role as the immortal Count.

Belladonna squealed. She dropped the magazine as if it were on fire and singeing her fingers. She picked it back up, squealed again, then hugged it tight to her chest.

"A *Dracula* picture! A *Dracula* picture! I don't believe it!"

It was scheduled for release on St. Valentine's Day.

But it would be months later than the February release date that it would finally reach Independence, via the traveling movie theater. If she waited for it to come around.

Belladonna would not be waiting patiently for it to come around *eventually*. She wanted to see it right away. She wanted to see it as soon as possible. She would be there, in Portland again, waiting in line on the day *Dracula* opened.

She *had* to see it on the first day. *Had* to.

PORTLAND, OR – 14th FEBRUARY 1931

The excitement this time was unbearable. Her stomach churned and her knees were weak as she stood in line once again outside the same Portland theater as before.

She couldn't even imagine what the movie would be like, how wonderful it would be, how incredible he would look up there, larger than life on the silver screen.

And this time, none of the girls in the line snickered at her. They looked at her with awe. They looked at her with envy in their eyes and she loved it.

This time she was dressed in the latest fashion – and not one of them could tell she had designed and made the dress herself.

Her hair was perfectly styled and her face exquisitely painted with rouged cheeks and stained lips.

She was a vision – like a movie star. They could hardly bear look at her, but they could not avert their gaze.

She willed the doors to open so she could get inside to take her seat, wait, in delicious agony, for Bela to walk on to the movie screen, for *Dracula* to begin.

She loved that first shaft of light that shone from the projection booth; it beamed brightly and glittered with sparkling dust.

And she loved the noise the movie projector made - the mechanized clicks, the whir of celluloid, and the snap and slap the film stock made when the reel came to an end.

The title card appeared...

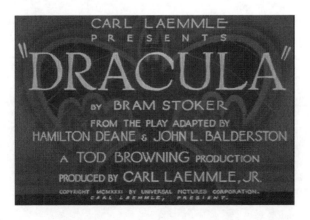

The music swelled – Tchaikovsky's *Andante* from the classical ballet, *Swan Lake*.

Belladonna could hardly stand the anticipation any longer. But she still read every word in the credits, as always.

She needed to know all the details whenever she watched a film – the producers, director, writer.

And the cast list – she read it from the bottom up. Her heart skipped a beat just reading his name on the screen. *Count Dracula...BELA LUGOSI.*

Then...

The Carpathian mountains appear. A carriage races along the precarious passes.

The passengers inside are jostled to and fro by the rickety wheels on the rough, stony mountain road.

They arrive at a small roadside tavern and are met by locals, pleased to see tourists stepping from the coach.

But their enthusiasm turns to fear when one of the passengers announces that he is not staying the night – he must carry on to the Borgo Pass where he will be met by another driver at midnight.

That driver will take him on to Castle Dracula.

The locals are horrified. One old woman crosses herself. The inn keeper tells Mr. Renfield that the locals believe vampires live in the castle and that the Count and his three wives drink the blood of the living by night. Of course, the sophisticated Englishman is amused by these uneducated and superstitious foreigners.

He insists he must carry on and turns to get back on the coach. An old lady stops him, puts her crucifix around his neck and asks him to wear it...for his mother's sake.

Then...

In the vaults deep beneath Castle Dracula lie dusty old coffins. A lid creaks open and is slowly lifted by the pale hand of the Count.

And his beautiful, alabaster-skinned wives rise from their rest, ready and eager to feed.

And there he is - larger than life - on the screen, clad in black from head to toe, his dark cloak wrapped about him.

Belladonna draws in a breath, her eyes widen. A tiny squeak of excitement escapes her throat and she is in thrall to him once more.

Her heart hammered in her chest, her wide eyes consuming each flicker of light and shade, the thick gothic atmosphere made a little surreal by the placement of armadillos and giant-rat-like possums among the dirt and the cobwebs.

She was wide-eyed and breathless in the dark once more.

This was it. This was her dream. This was romance.

And then he spoke.

"I am...Dracula. I bid you welcome."

The wolves howled on the hillside beyond the old castle walls. Dracula stops to enjoy the sound.

"Listen to them...children of the night. What music they make."

Belladonna's eyes closed momentarily, as if she was in ecstasy, as he spoke. She sighed as she listened, his voice like a lover's caress on naked skin.

Dracula walks up the stone staircase, magically passing through a gigantic cobweb without disturbing the painstakingly-spun silks. A huge spider, maker of the web, scurries up the castle wall.

"A spider spinning his web for the unwary fly. The blood...is the life, Mr. Renfield.

Count Dracula leads Mr. Renfield, the unsuspecting law clerk from across the water up to his chambers. Count Dracula has laid out a cold supper for the hungry traveler.

He uncorks a bottle of wine.

"This is very old wine. I hope you will like it," he tells Renfield.

He pours the dark potion into a fine goblet.

"Aren't you drinking?" Renfield enquires of his host.

"I never drink...wine," Dracula tells his guest.

Belladonna sighed long and hard. She knew what she had to do. There was no other way. There was nothing else in the world for her, no other path she could take in life.

She had made up her mind. In an instant her heart was consumed by one desire.

Belladonna was going to Hollywood to become an actress and star in a movie opposite Bela Lugosi.

Morag was worried about her daughter. Ever since Bell had come back from Portland for the second time she was different. Even *more* different than the first time. There was a glint in her eyes that shone like stars. She knew that her daughter was keeping something from her. She *knew* it.

She'd asked her time and time again what the matter was but Belladonna would always reply with the same answer.

"Nothing, mama. I'm fine."

And she would smile her disarming smile, the smile that rendered anyone and everyone unable to keep a furrow in their brow or a scowl on their face. And mom would walk off, smiling for a while, believing the lies her daughter told.

Deep down, Morag knew that something wasn't right. She also knew by the ache in the pit of her stomach, that at some point Belladonna *would* tell her what was wrong. That worried her so much more than not knowing.

Belladonna was working hard, harder than she ever had, and she was always a grafter. But now she took on any job she could. She mucked out stables and milked grumpy cows, broke her back harvesting fruit by hand, and baked scones and oatcakes, made fresh preserves and pickles to sell at market in the next town.

Morag knew that the revelation was coming soon

Belladonna came to mother and the look in her eyes made Morag's heart sink and her shoulders slump before she even opened her mouth.

She knew she was about to hear something she would rather not hear at all. This was it – the day she had been dreading.

"I'm leaving home, mama. I'm going to Hollywood to be an actress."

Morag stumbled dramatically and Belladonna rolled her eyes, thinking that maybe her mom should come with her and be a movie star too.

But it was no act – the statement made her feel weak at the knees, made her guts turn somersaults inside her, her innards gripping and spasming as if they were trying to break free of her body.

Her mother pleaded with her not to go; Portland was one thing, Hollywood was quite another. She'd heard stories about it, how people are chewed up and spat out and used and abused by unscrupulous men who prey on young, impressionable girls like her.

Hollywood was a place for women of ill repute, a place for drunkards and the drug addled. To her mother, Hollywood was the modern Babylon, brimming with sin and sinners.

Belladonna was angry with her. She was treating her like a child again, the same way as she had always treated her.

She knew now that her mother would have loved it if she had come home from Portland with a sob story and never wanted to let go of her apron strings again.

"Mama, I have to do this. I have to. I'm not doing it to hurt you. I love you, you know that. But no matter how much I love you, and papa and Cal and Quita, I still need to do this. I'm a big girl now. I'm all grown up."

Morag couldn't speak. Panic held her throat and it took every ounce of will she had to keep on breathing. But even if she could have spoken, she had no idea what to say to Belladonna.

She did not see a beautiful young woman standing before her about to embark on the adventure of a lifetime.

She saw a little girl, her little girl about to put herself in harm's way.

And there was nothing she could do about it.

She was at a loss for words, her fears and her anguish robbing her of the ability to express herself.

But this was more than being afraid for her daughter as she ran off to the big city. Much more. This felt like she was losing her child. This felt like Belladonna was dying, like she was never going to see her again.

There was nothing Morag could say or do to dissuade her from heading to Hollywood. Belladonna knew her destiny lay within the spotlights and the glamor of the place they called Hollywoodland, and beneath the sign which said the same.

CHAPTER FOUR :
BELLADONNA IN HOLLYWOODLAND

Belladonna sat on her tiny suitcase in the blistering heat. It seemed like she'd been sitting there forever with her knees almost touching her chin as her shoulders slumped and her head pitched downward.

The heat had been increasing by the minute; the temperature now at a blistering 110 degrees as she sat there, far from shade, her café latte skin exposed to the merciless heatwave.

Belladonna had inherited some of her father's coloring and skin tone - with a little extra cream. He was of mixed race – an eclectic blend of Mexican, Latgawa Indian, Scottish and Irish. He would joke with her that there wasn't really any white blood in the family because the Celts – the Scots and the Irish – were the Mexicans and the Indians of Europe. But she did not yet know how much of her father's volatile blood ran deep in her veins. Belladonna was unaware of the spitfire she was to become.

Sweat began to pour from her and run down the cleft of her back and between her ample breasts. Behind her knees and the bends in her arms were hot and wet, and the soles of her feet slid and slipped inside her dainty sandals. She wiggled her dusty toes and made a face as grains of sandy dirt made their way between them.

She wondered, sitting there in the dry heat and dust of the Oregon boonies if she was really doing the right thing.

The doubt set in - she'd never been away from home for more than a few nights to stay with her grandmother or her aunt or a friend in her entire life. Barely had a day passed that she did not see her mother, her father, her sister, or half-brother. Belladonna wondered just how she was going to get by without them all around her as her protectors.

But suddenly, all fatigue and weariness, all trace of reticence fled from her body as she saw the bus off in the distance. It shimmered like a jewel in the heat haze as it inched toward her.

This rickety old vehicle was going to take her far away from the one-horse town she grew up in, and deliver her to her destiny in the City of Angels.

By the time the bus creaked open its rusty doors to let her and the other frazzled passengers board, Belladonna was soaked through and covered from head to foot in dust.

The bus ride from her tiny hometown of Independence, Oregon, was long and uncomfortable, but she sat there with a smile on her face all the way. She bounced up and down with the motion of the bus as it dragged itself over rough, uneven roads, which at times were little more than well-traveled dirt tracks.

She didn't care that her pretty summer dress was saturated with sweat now and clung to her curves like a second skin. She was oblivious to the fact that people were staring at her because her nipples were hard and showing through the delicate fabric of her dress now that it was wet and had become semi-transparent.

It didn't matter to her that beads of sweat ran down her scalp and made the nape of her neck itch, and the scratching had knotted the underside of her hair.

She didn't even mind the foul stench emanating from the bacteria-infested fat rolls of the morbidly obese man taking up an entire seat to himself in front of her.

Not even the tiny, yapping dog that pissed on the cloth bag at her feet, which contained her few valuable possessions, could erase the smile from her face.

Belladonna didn't care about anything at that moment. Not a thing in the world could bring her down or wipe the smile from her lips, a smile that showed a stunning set of perfect white teeth.

She was on her way to a new life - a life that would be extraordinary and was waiting there for her beneath the sign that said HOLLYWOODLAND.

Belladonna reached into her purse and fondled the edge of her well-worn paperback copy of *Dracula*. If it hadn't been for that book, if she hadn't fallen in love with the romance of the vampire, she would never have been inspired to go see the stage version in Portland and she would never have fallen in love with the star of the production - Count Dracula himself - Bela Lugosi.

If none of those things had happened she would never have been sitting on the bus and on her way to Hollywood to become an actress.

She *had* to land a part in a Bela Lugosi movie.

It would all be so perfect - she would find a part in a Bela Lugosi picture and he would fall in love with her at first sight and he would sweep her off her feet and they would live happily ever after.

She knew that her dreams were going to come true. She knew that an incredible life lay before her.

But Belladonna's destiny was one even she could never have imagined.

Hollywood could smell innocence. And Belladonna gave off the scent in abundance.

Belladonna was little more than a girl in a woman's body - a *desirable* woman's body. Her inexperience of life and her naiveté made her irresistible to almost everyone. Her purity was like an aphrodisiac, her innocence arousing to the predators all around.

But it didn't take long for her to get wise to the games in Hollywood. It didn't take long for her girlish qualities to fade to black.

The spectacular innocence that made the predators salivate, that made their eyes sparkle, and their lips curl into knowing smiles would one day be no more. And when that happened,

Belladonna would become just like all the other would-be starlets – worldly wise and jaded.

From child-like bumpkin who was taken advantage of, to wily, suspicious, and distrusting, took only a matter of weeks for some in Hollywood.

Belladonna had taken a little longer; she simply refused to believe that everybody in this beautiful town was on the make and up to no good, no matter how many chewed up and spat out neverweres told her so.

But the experiences she had each and every day were rubbing off on her. She could not carry on with the denial for much longer when all she could see around her was dirt and degradation.

She wondered how *anybody* ever *made it* in Hollywood when the shysters seemed to outnumber the legitimate producers and directors by several-to-one.

But the change came. One day she woke up and looked at the world through newly-jaded eyes.

Now *she* could smell innocence on other suckers who flocked toward the bright lights and the big city and the lure of fame and fortune.

Now *she* smiled sadly at the pretty young things who came here like sacrificial lambs by the dozens every day.

Now *she* understood that look she'd seen thrown at her a thousand times since she'd been here.

And all of these new, young hopefuls would soon know how that sad smile felt on their own lips one day. Soon.

They came in their hundreds every month. Some days, she could look down from her balcony and see hoards of them, all the same, all blonde and pale and stinking with inexperience. hey would stand there on the street, their bodies vibrating with excitement to be in Hollywood, believing they were standing on the brink of their own stardom, gazing up at the huge white letters on the hillside.

And someday, all of them would know what it felt like - the realization that they were not going to be a star.

But what was worst about the whole thing, the whole place, all the people here, was nobody would ever leave. Nobody wanted to return to whence they came with their tails between their legs and choruses of a hundred-fold *I told you sos*.

No matter how hard the knocks, no matter how sleazy the so-called producer, no matter how difficult life became, so many stayed. Or died here.

It had been a particularly bad day for Belladonna; she was exhausted and her high heels made a metallic dragging sound as her fatigued muscles failed to lift her aching feet off the sidewalk.

But *the show must go on - this next stop could be the one*, she thought. She knew she had to carry on, carry on through the fatigue of her spasming muscles, through the heat and the dirt.

She had to get to the next appointment, no matter what.

She was light-headed from lack of food. She'd skipped breakfast that morning to save money, then missed lunch because she had to hang around an office reception all day waiting to see a casting director.

"Sorry, doll; but I'm in the market for a skinny little blonde thing right now, not a curvaceous brunette. Damn shame," the casting director told her the instant after he laid eyes on her.

After waiting for more than three hours, their conversation lasted no more than a few seconds. She thanked him, but he didn't wait to shake her hand or throw her a smile, instead she said "thank you" to the slam of his office door behind him.

These days, not being at least leered at by a casting director or a producer seemed like an insult.

The plain Jane behind the reception desk smirked, eyes sparkling with delight behind her bottle-end spectacles at Belladonna's dismissal by her boss.

The secretary watched her all the way out the door; Belladonna felt her eyes on her. The blood rose in her veins, throbbed in her temples and flooded her cheeks with red heat as she heard a snicker issuing from the sneer on the frump behind the desk.

Belladonna turned around, grinned one-sided and looked her up and down. She didn't need words - one glance from her obsidian eyes and the flash of contempt across her full red lips was enough to make the secretary feel as ugly on the outside as she was on the inside.

Belladonna had mastered that withering look now. She had seen it thrown in her own direction often enough when she arrived here, by those who envied her pristine beauty, those who could no longer get away with saying that they were in their first flush of youth, even if they really had been only a short time ago.

The life they had chosen – the life they craved, longed for – had robbed them of their looks and their youth, many of them their dreams. And some of them, their life.

Belladonna felt better for getting one over on the nasty secretary, but the humor she was in right now was foul and she was in no mood for more hours sitting around in a stifling windowless hallway in the heat.

But the next appointment was one she simply could not miss. The next appointment *really could* be the one that would change her life.

The next appointment was the one she had come here for in the first place. This casting was for a movie that might just be Bela Lugosi's next - that was the word on the grapevine, at least.

His face was plastered all over billboards everywhere and he was riding high on the current success of the film version of *Dracula*.

Belladonna adored him - and she was desperate for him to adore her too. She could not imagine ever being with any man but him. She had never even dreamed of being in another man's arms or feeling the heat of another man's lips on her own. It was all about *him*.

She couldn't even imagine going through an entire life and not knowing him. She was certain that they were meant to be and that she was put here on this earth to worship him.

He was all she wanted. Her dream was that he would take her away to live in a fairytale forever - that dark, mysterious, experienced man with the black velvet voice that made the hairs on the back of her neck stand on end and her knees tremble violently.

Listening to him made her smile, made her close her eyes and picture his distinguished features – his regal nose, his hypnotic eyes, his dimpled chin.

She wanted this part badly. She knew that she was right for it. She knew she could play the part. She simply *had* to get it. She thought, fleetingly, that she might even kill for it.

The lobby was filled with young women, some hardly shy of childhood, some barely acquainted with their teens, and chaperoned by fading beauties they called *mother*.

Those mothers had wanted the same thing for themselves, but failed, and now wanted to live that life, vicariously, through their unwilling offspring.

Some girls ran in floods of tears from the office, with red-faced mothers pulling them by the arm, suddenly aware of how young their daughters were again.

Some walked quickly with their heads down, wondering how many of the girls standing in line knew the type of movie they were waiting to be cast in.

Belladonna was the last in line. By now, she knew that this movie had absolutely nothing to do with Bela Lugosi; *Bela would never be involved in Burlesque movies!* she thought.

But she went inside the producer's office anyway. Belladonna wrinkled her nose as she inhaled the scent of the fat man's body odor. The stench of stale sweat, cigar smoke, coffee breath and unwashed hair filled the office, and Belladonna instantly felt dirty just having the air in the place surround her skin.

"Come on in. You're just what I'm looking for, sweetheart. Stick with me and I'll make you a star," he told her.

Belladonna knew what this man wanted from her. He wanted the same thing most of the other casting directors and producers and whoever else that told her *I'm in pictures; I'll make you a star* wanted.

Belladonna wondered how anybody ever got cast for a part in a movie; there seemed to be more charlatans than actual movie people in Hollywood. She wondered if she'd interacted with anybody who really was what they claimed to be in all the time she'd been there.

Now, with another disappointment to slap her in the face, and the fact that this dirty old man wanted her to take her clothes off in front of a camera adding insult to injury, she was growing more bitter by the minute.

And then, the final straw was stacked.

The stinking old man reached out and fondled one of Belladonna's large, round tits, grabbed her hand and forced it down the front of his pants.

She felt something slimy under her fingers, and squealed at the veined firmness of his cock on her palm as he rubbed her hand over it.

Belladonna was enraged by him and yanked her hand away. She swiftly kneed him in the groin, dropping him immediately to the floor, and fled from his office.

She was furious and marched along the sidewalk. She'd stood in line there for hours on end, waiting around for what seemed like forever. And for nothing. Again.

Belladonna was sick and tired of the people in Hollywood. It saddened her that such a glamorous and exciting place - the place she had dreamed of since she was a little girl - should be populated by so many who tarnished it. The drunks and the losers, the cocaine fiends who howled in the dark streets at night, the fallen women who stood in the back alleys and the no goods who handed over cash to them for a few minutes of emotionless sex.

And there were those so bitter and twisted that they hated the town itself, despised the very streets they walked on when they found they were not paved with gold after all.

And even more disconcerting – and downright puzzling to Belladonna – were the people who *had* been a success, the people who *had* been the talk of the town, and lauded and applauded; some of *them* also hated Hollywood. Some of *them* also despised the air they breathed and the earth underfoot, just because it belonged to Hollywood.

Hollywood was the stuff of dreams, the place to come to make those dreams a reality.

She didn't understand their attitudes at first, couldn't imagine how anybody could hate this beautiful town, but now, a matter of a few months later, she could appreciate how those people felt.

The shine had begun to wear off.

Belladonna sat alone on the balcony at her tiny apartment. None of her roommates were home. They were probably out doing what she had been doing all day - pounding the pavements and running out of hope. She pulled the blanket tight around her shoulders against the chill of nightfall and inhaled deeply on her cigarette. The smoke stung her throat as it passed the tender spot, which had been home to a lump of emotion for the past two hours. Her face was still puffy from crying and her eyes were rimmed with red.

She shook her head and smiled sadly. She was bitterly amused by the profound changes in herself that had began just weeks after her arrival. She laughed mirthlessly as she visualized the shocked look she would see on her mother and father's faces if they were watching her sitting here in her underwear drinking booze and smoking cigarettes in full view of the street below.

She sat there on a metalwork chair in a pair of black silk French kickers and matching black lace camisole. Her silky thighs were kissed by a snap of black suspenders; she smoothed her hand along the back of her stockings and stretched her leg out to admire the contours beneath the dark silk. She stood up and checked her reflection in the glass of the balcony door to see if the lines in her stockings were straight even although nobody would be seeing them.

It didn't matter that she was stunningly beautiful - it was Hollywood, beautiful women were a dime a dozen. She laughed bitterly at herself; she had truly thought she was special, thought that she was going to *make it*, become a glamorous movie star and marry Bela Lugosi and live happily ever after in a fairytale castle.

Belladonna started to cry again, even as she still laughed at her own naiveté. But her mirth tasted bitter like the homemade red wine that stained her lips near black. She swallowed down a full goblet of the booze in an attempt to dislodge the raw emotion constricting her throat. Belladonna didn't even care that a group of women were looking at her from the street below and could see that she was sitting there in her underwear.

They probably think I'm a whore. So what? I feel like one. What's the difference?

She picked up her glass, filled it with the blood-red wine and raised it to them in a toast.

"To Hollywood!" she shouted down at them from the balcony. "Don't you just fucking love it?"

The women below carried on walking by Belladonna, voicing their outrage, hands on hips and heads shaking in disbelief at her impertinence and her foul language.

Belladonna didn't care anymore.

She knew now that she would not land a part in a Bela Lugosi movie. She should have known there was something amiss with the so-called movie producer she met earlier. She was an expert on Lugosi and devoured every magazine article and newspaper feature about him. She knew he was about to begin filming *Fifty Million Frenchmen* for Warner Bros., and that was to be followed by *Women of all Nations* for Fox, whose cast included a little known actor named Humphrey Bogart.

And she knew that he was in demand. She should have known this movie had nothing to do with him and that his name being attached to it was only a ruse. But in its desperation her hopeless heart ignored what her gut knew.

Her plans were ruined now. Lugosi vehicles were cast for months ahead. Famous leading ladies and on-the-rise starlets were falling over themselves to be cast in his movies. He was all booked up from now until doomsday and she would never be able to get near him.

In just four months, Belladonna had gone from being a bright young thing full of hopes and dreams, to being jaded and cynical. She had gone from a fresh-faced, clean living virgin, to being a heartbeat away from prostitution and alcoholism.

But each day she hung on. Each day she tried harder to steer herself away from the life that would be easier than the one she had chosen.

Four months ago she was an innocent young girl covered in Oregon dust. Now she was a bitter woman of the world. Any remnants of child-like innocence that remained within her voluptuous curves had been ripped from her the first time her legs were forced apart on the casting couch.

Although her experiences in Hollywood had left her stunning face and body unscathed, inside was a different story. Inside, Belladonna felt used and dirty. Inside, Belladonna was filled with anger and bitterness toward her fellow wannabe starlets and the loveless movie industry. But, even after all, she was still in love with Hollywood.

She couldn't help but fall in love with the town all over again each day she woke up under its skies and saw the gigantic letters that stretched across the hillside - *that* sign, the icon that read HOLLYWOODLAND. Every time she looked at it, she knew that she would tolerate the effluent she waded through each day. It was because of those letters - and what they stood for, what they meant - money, fame, glamor, adoration, - that she was here.

And the billboards that stood on every street reminded her of why she was here, why she stayed, and why she wanted to remain. She'd been there for such a short time and been treated nothing but badly since she set foot on California soil, but this place was in her blood. It would be forever. To cure herself of her addiction, her passion for it, she'd have to bleed herself dry.

Hollywood had a hold on Belladonna's heart and she could not, for the life of her, leave it behind.

CHAPTER FIVE : THE VAMPIRE VIVANT

It had been Belladonna's worst day ever. A casting director promised to introduce her to Lugosi if she was nice to him. Belladonna knew what that meant.

She swallowed her pride, knowing that this guy was almost certain to be conning her. And she knew he was conning her as soon as she was finished blowing him. He burst into raucous laughter as his semen dribbled down her chin, its heat melting the red lipstick that stained her full lips, making her look like a vampire.

His words echoed endlessly inside her head...

...Why the fuck do all you brainless sluts believe this bullshit...you can't act to save your life but you give good head...stupid cunt...

She could still hear his laughter. She could still *feel* his laughter. It was like a physical blow, like a blade, forced in up to the hilt, twisting in her gut.

Her body ached all over, and her leg muscles felt tight enough they may snap at any moment. She'd been walking fast for a long time, her high heels making the sinew in her calves taut, strained, but she did not slow her pace.

Belladonna raged about her misfortunes at the hands of Hollywood men. She balled her fists at her sides, her long nails digging into her palms. She talked loudly, unashamed, her need to vent greater than her need to claw back some of her dignity.

Belladonna was unaware that she was being watched as darkness fell across Hollywood.

Vivant was *always* searching. He'd searched the world over more than once. He'd searched through time, through centuries. And still he searched.

It was not an easy task to find someone worthy enough to share an eternity with. He had made some poor choices over the years, ones that turned out to be costly to him. He thought back to his time spent in Bohemia in the late 19th century. He had fallen in love with the city of Prague with its colorful, hospitable people and breathtaking Gothic architecture. Vivant made it a point to walk by the *Orloj* every day, the astronomical clock that graces the southern wall on the Old Town City Hall in the Old Town Square. It was his daily ritual to see the mechanical figures of the Apostles come out, and the skeletal figure of Death strike the hour.

Vivant had taken many foolish risks in the past and barely escaped with his life. He'd been loose with his tongue on occasion, boastful of his own unusual condition.,

He'd even had an angry mob or two at his door with flaming torches and vile tongues, ready to drive a wooden stake through his heart. Even old vampires can be careless on occasion.

Of course, he was never caught. He could move so fast he snuffed out their torches and left them scratching their heads, looking at each other, bewildered.

But, thankfully, people were more cynical these days. Nobody believed in vampires or anything remotely supernatural, not *really*. There was interest in it, even obsession with it, but seldom real, unshakable belief.

The masses in modern day America were too sophisticated, too educated. He was a long way away from uneducated and superstitious European peasants. And that was fine with Vivant. He was vain and loved to be the center of attention, and being here in Hollywood was the perfect cover. And he played the part of the beautiful, strange club singer so well.

He's so pale. Hot dog! Isn't he the bees knees! He looks just like a vampire!

His favorite time in America, apart from now, was in the Wild West when he made the trek on the Oregon Trail from Missouri. He lived, for the most part, a normal, ordinary life amongst other normal, ordinary folks. And he loved it. It had been a long time since he could do that. Young modern America was a wonderful place for him. But times changed and people changed. One year to the next, sometimes one day to the next.

And he'd been a little forlorn lately. Until he laid eyes on Belladonna.

The streets in this part of town – and she had no idea where she was right now – were deserted.

The vampire Vivant stood high above her, balanced on top of a massive *Dracula* billboard. A wicked grin spread across his face as he watched Belladonna argue with the night.

This one has a fire inside! My God, I want her.

Belladonna stopped and turned to look at the billboard. Her eyes were filled with tears, the hurt, anguish, clearly visible in her dark irises.

She looked long and hard at the image of Lugosi on the billboard until the vision of him was completely obscured by tears.

She didn't even see Vivant descending from above, and was unaware of his presence until she felt his hot breath on her throat, and his arms enfolding her, pulling her close to him.

And she didn't resist; whatever this was, whatever this stranger was going to do to her, she would let him do it, and hope that it was severe enough that she would not wake from it.

The last thing she had seen was Lugosi's face before the tears filled her eyes; his image still burned there.

Then the pain hit her, pain so severe her knees buckled and the stranger had to hold her tight to keep her upright. But the pain was welcome. It felt *good.* The pain was cleansing. It seemed that the chemical rush of endorphins and adrenaline charging around her body in response to the pain were purging all the dirt and the humiliation from deep within her veins, and allowing it to run out of the gushing red wounds in her throat.

And then the ecstasy hit her harder than the pain.

In that moment she felt more alive than she had ever felt in her entire life. It was pleasure that transgressed the sexual and the physical. It was a pleasure than invaded not only her body, but her mind, her heart. It was a pleasure that took hold of her soul.

The vampire didn't let go. He moaned loudly as he fed on her, pulling her ever closer to him as if he were trying to seep inside her body to become one with her. But that was how it always made him feel. For those moments when the blood flowed over his lips and slid down his throat in waves of wet heat, he was madly in love and filled with devotion.

Belladonna lost consciousness with a gasp in her throat as the vampire Vivant scooped her up into his arms, effortlessly, and disappeared into the darkness of the Hollywood night.

Belladonna stirred as Vivant gently laid her on a decadent four poster bed. She sighed as she felt the cold kiss of the crisp black silk sheets on her skin, and against her hot cheek. Belladonna's eyes remained closed and she seemed to fall into a deep, desired sleep.

Vivant knew she would sleep for a while and he wanted to be here when she awoke. He pulled a book off the bookshelf - one of his favorites - *The Misfortunes of Virtue* by the Marquis de Sade. He had read it many times but he never, ever grew tired of it. There were very few books that captivated him in this way, but the few that did he took with him everywhere.

He smiled as he opened the worn cover, the spine making a delightful cracking noise as the book opened. The very things that would make a book collector pale were the things that made him love his books even more.

He didn't care too much for brand new books and bought most of them in second hand stores. As he looked at their shabby appearance he knew that they had been read and enjoyed, knew that they were loved.

He knew that tears had been shed over their words and laughter had been shared over a humorous quote, or a beautiful line recited by one lover to another led those lovers to bliss.

Vivant chose a random page and began to read from half-way down...

...I think that if there were a God, there would be less evil on this earth. I believe that if God exists here below, then either it was willed by God or it was beyond His powers to prevent it. Now I cannot bring myself to fear a God who is either spiteful or weak. I defy Him without fear and care not a fig for His thunderbolts...

He grinned his wicked grin to nobody, content to be alone with his books and watching over Belladonna. Now and then he would glance up from the text and look at her. He'd never seen such a beautiful face.

Not even the angelic statuary in Italian cemeteries were as beautiful as she. Not even the great works of art of the old masters could compare. He thought back to 1820; he was there the day Louis XVIII was presented with a statue recently found in Greece, the *Aphrodite of Melos*. The King paid the handsome sum of 6000 francs for the sculpture.

She was beautiful. The embodiment of female perfection. Belladonna was even more beautiful than the world famous statue now known as the *Venus di Milo*. Not even the ageless piece of art could match her.

Belladonna's beauty also deserved to be preserved like the works of art he had seen in his life. She deserved not to age, not to see her skin slowly slide off her bones with the passing of time. She deserved not to lie in the ground until her skeletal remains had been picked clean by the ravenous life in the earth.

Vivant was captivated by her. The pink blush on her cheek, the soft, blood-red lips, and the scent of innocence that came off her skin was like expensive perfume to him, a rare and heady aroma.

He watched her eyes fluttering rapidly beneath her silky lids. Her brow furrowed; Vivant knew that hunger was stirring inside her and soon she would awaken.

And when she did awaken, she would be changed, different. From the moment she opened her eyes she would know that she was not merely human anymore. She would know beyond a shadow of a doubt that she was not the Belladonna who had lost consciousness on the street just hours before.

She would feel something rise in her blood, something stir deep within. There would be pain, and there would be desperate need. There would be confusion too; she would not know at first what it was she craved, what she needed. But even alone, a fledgling vampire will find its own nature and do what comes instinctively.

But once she fed, once she had felt the hot flow of human blood straight from a vein pumping down her throat in time with a thundering heartbeat, she would know the true meaning of ecstasy. She would know what it feels like to be truly satisfied.

Belladonna would no longer be just a beautiful girl - a common commodity in Hollywood. When she awoke, she would be an extraordinary creature.

While he was waiting for his new conquest to awaken, Vivant thought he would have a nosy in her handbag. Sometimes you could find extremely interesting things in a woman's purse.

He rummaged. He didn't dump out the contents and just look at it. He liked to take his time, took each item out as his hand found it, like a Lucky Dip at a carnival. There were the usual things – lipstick...compact... wallet...comb.

"Boring...Boring. Bo...hello?"

He felt what he knew was a book and pulled it out. He grinned. It was Belladonna's old, beat up copy of *Dracula*. He laughed loudly, truly amused at the irony.

"Fuck Dracula. Vivant's here now. In the flesh," he said, leaning over Belladonna's sleeping form and grinning at her.

Vivant had not been this excited over a companion since he and Valentine first met all those centuries ago in Russia.

She reminded him of Valentine; he had been young, hungry and raging too when he found him. Vivant adored him immediately and knew they would be together for for lifetimes.

He smiled at the memory, then his face hardened as he remembered how Valentine had betrayed him.

He wondered where he was, what he was doing. But Vivant was powerful enough that anytime he wanted to, he could find out where Valentine was and pay him a visit.

Nobody – not even another powerful vampire – could hide from the vampire Vivant.

He didn't even jump when Belladonna woke up screaming; he'd been through this many times before.

She knew her pain must have *something* to do with the man beside the bed, but she had no recollection of him doing anything to her, never mind biting her neck and sucking her blood. She was curled up tight in a fetal position, cursing the air blue at the pain slicing through her innards, and the nausea that had a strangle-hold on her gut.

"You did something to me! What did you do to me?" she demanded.

Her screeching immediately irritated him. Vivant hated being yelled at.

"Don't shout so! That's enough to deafen a mere mortal," he paused and scowled at her. "What did I *do* to you? I gave you something nobody can buy. I've been offered money by the million, by the billion, for the gift I just *gave* you."

Belladonna couldn't even scream anymore. She was stunned into silence by her pain, although she would have loved to beat Vivant to a pulp with her bare fists for making her suffer this way.

"Please. Please, help me," she begged, her eyes moist, filled with anguish.

"Alright, then; are we calm now? Are we done shouting and screaming like fish wives at the docks? It's quite simple; there's just one thing that you must do to end your suffering. This one thing alone can take away all your pain. And I promise you, you will never, ever feel pain like this again."

"What is it? What do I have to do?" Her voice was breathy and weak.

"All you have to do, Belladonna, is drink some of my blood."

"Drink some of your blood? Oh, my God. What are you talking about? You're insane if you think I'm gonna do that, mister. Find somebody else to play your sick little game with!"

"This is no game, Belladonna - it's life. *Your* life now. Well, sort-of life," he told her with a grin on his lips.

Belladonna's face was contorted with pain and confusion.

"I don't understand. *My life now*? What does that mean?"

She was sobbing violently now and Vivant smiled as he watched her face, enjoying her vulnerability. He knew she was an innocent. Although she showed the world a sophisticated exterior, and gave the impression she was a woman of the world, she was really no such thing.

Vivant could smell the scent of her pure soul coming off her skin. He could smell it all the way up on top of the billboard as she marched angrily down the street. She was like a rare, expensive delicacy that made him salivate in anticipation. Innocent blood had a special potency to it and it was hard to come by these days, especially in a such a notoriously debauched city as this one.

The combination of the fiery temper she had not long discovered she had, and the innocence that shone from her, was an irresistible and thrilling combination to Vivant. Even being used and abused by the morally corrupt had not blackened her beautiful soul, nor tainted her blood.

Belladonna closed her eyes, concentrating hard on dealing with her pain.

Vivant slowly removed his shirt, and without his gaze leaving Belladonna, he reached for an ornate trinket box that lay on the nightstand. The lid of the box was encrusted with dark jewels that glittered in the flickering candlelight.

She was aware of him moving and watched as he removed a straight razor from the box. He opened the blade and looked at Belladonna, watching intently for her reaction. She didn't care what he was going to do with the blade and he was disappointed that there was no fear in her eyes.

She didn't care if he took the blade and drew it across her throat and she bled to death there on the spot. At that moment, all she wanted was for the pain wracking her entire body to stop.

Belladonna watched, wide-eyed, her pain momentarily forgotten as Vivant drew the glinting blade across his own throat. He sighed as it slid effortlessly through his flesh, gliding across the surface of his skin. He closed his eyes and smiled, enjoying the sting of the cold steel.

His blood began to flow in a steady stream down his torso.

"Drink it," he told her. "If you drink from me, I can promise you an extraordinary life. And I can promise you the pain will end and you will never feel it again. Drink my blood, Belladonna. That's all you have to do."

"And if I don't?" she asked.

"You will die. And you won't come back. Don't take too long to think about it, darling. if your heart stops before you drink, it's lights out."

The pain swelled inside her again and she did not hesitate. She pulled him to her, her arms wrapping around his waist as her tongue made contact with his scarlet flow.

The ecstasy was almost too much for him to bear. She sucked hard on his hot wound, her pain instantly diminishing, piece by piece as she drank his blood. Strands of pleasure rushed through his veins as his blood was drawn from them, feeding his new-born vampire companion.

And then her pain was gone, and in an instant after the beat of her heart and Vivant's merged into a single throb, it was forgotten.

Everything had changed. She knew that nothing about her life would ever be the same again.

She stopped. Stood silent, quiet. She looked confused.

"What is it?" Vivant asked.

"My heart. I can't feel my heart beating. It stopped!"

She began to flap and panic, pacing rapidly around the room like a caged animal.

"It's alright. You just died, that's all."

Belladonna laughed hysterically.

"I *just died* - that's *all*?"

Vivant rolled his eyes, as if dying and still being able to walk and talk were commonplace.

"The *human* Belladonna just died. Wait for a few seconds," he said.

"Wait for what?"

"Just wait. You'll know," he paused, then, "Should be right about...now."

No sooner had the words left his lips that Belladonna drew in a sharp breath.

"It started again!" she shouted. "But...but..."

"You thought you wouldn't have a heartbeat if you were dead, yes?"

She nodded, her hand pressed to her chest feeling her own heartbeat, loud and strong inside her.

"Oh, no, not at all. Our hearts beat harder and faster than any other creature," he said, crossing the room to her and pulling her close. He whispered in her ear. "There's nothing on earth that can feel what you will feel, that can love the way you will love. Your heart has a million times the capacity of a human heart...and all the time in the world to use it."

And from that moment she knew she was different. The way she heard was different. The way she saw the world was different. The way she felt inside her own skin was different.

Belladonna, just a pretty girl among many pretty girls, was now an extraordinary creature - the vampire named Belladonna. Vivant knew that a legend had just been born.

Vivant stood and admired his protégé. She did not return his smile.

Despite now being pain free, she was not grateful to him. A storm brewed behind her eyes and the grin on Vivant's lips soon faded, the muscle tension transferred to a now furrowed brow. She knew instinctively that her new heart also had a bigger capacity for hate.

"What's wrong?"

"What's wrong? You're asking me what's wrong? I want to know what you did to me!," Belladonna screamed at him.

"I told you – I gave you a gift that money cannot buy, something no one can have unless I want them to have it. As I said, I've been offered obscene amounts of money, offered all the wealth I could possibly imagine, in exchange for what I just gave you as a gift."

Her rage lessened and was replaced by a melancholy expression as she thought back to the pain.

"I've never experienced pain like that in my life. Please, you owe me this much, tell me what you did to me. And before you answer," she fixed a cold stare from her near black irises on him, "I don't believe in vampires."

Vivant laughed at her, his mirth instantly fueling her rage once more.

"Belladonna, just because you don't believe in something, does not mean it doesn't exist. Let me show you something."

He put his arm gently around her shoulders and leaned in to her, spoke in a whisper.

"If you were anything other than a vampire now, would you survive this?"

Before she could ask what he meant, Vivant plunged his hand into her chest cavity, through her ribs, splintering them with the force of his blow. He ripped her heart from her chest, the movement so fast that the organ was before her eyes, still beating, spraying her own blood into her face before she could scream.

She looked at him in disbelief.

My heart is in your hands.

My heart is in your hands.

She kept repeating the phrase like a mantra in her head. Vivant heard her thoughts. A hateful grin, full of confidence, arrogance and ego slithered across his lips.

"Did you ever doubt that it would be?"

Vivant casually threw her heart in the air repeatedly as if he was tossing a piece of fruit before devouring it. He placed her heart back in her ruined torso. Belladonna gasped, shocked and frightened not only by the fact she'd just had her heart torn out and lived to see it, but that her body was repairing itself before her eyes. She watched in fascination as the severed aorta and pulmonary artery found their way back into her heart. The remainder of her ribcage grew new bone from the ends of the fractures, and her sinew - the torn ligaments, tendons and muscles, and the nerves, veins and capillaries knitted themselves back together again.

"So, what are you then, Belladonna, if not a vampire? Is there another being you know of that could survive what you just survived?"

"You're a...a...," she could not find the word.

"I'm a what...a monster?"

"How could you do that to me?," Although her voice wavered with a slight vibrato of emotion, she was determined that she would not cry in front of him. She would not give him any more of her power. She could see that he thrived on the emotion of others, that he derived a thrill, an exhilaration from the distress he caused.

But hate the fact as she did, she knew that she needed him. She knew she would have to be nice to him, she would have to tolerate his smugness and his selfishness and his arrogance.

She knew nothing of what she was. She was completely ignorant of her own new form; if she had any vulnerabilities in her new state, she did not know of them as yet.

If there were things that could harm her in the world, she would need to find them out.

She needed to know, now that she was a vampire, if any of the old myths and legends should be heeded. She must find out if she could be killed by a wooden stake through the heart, or if a face-full of holy water would make her skin combust and slide off her bones.

She wondered if she would really have to sleep in a coffin and she would be extremely displeased if she could never again touch or look at the crucifix her mother had given her as a child, and now hung in her tiny room over her bed, just like it had all through her childhood.

"I can see you have questions, darling. I know you must be very curious about everything. I understand - I've been there, after all. It was a very, very long time ago, but I remember. Anything you need to know, I'll answer you as best I can."

Belladonna tried hard not to narrow her eyes at him, and hid the contempt that made one half of her mouth want to curl up in a sneer. But she controlled it. Instead, her lip just twitched.

She could see right away that one of the old vampire myths wasn't true - she could see her own reflection in the mirror at the other side of the room.

Vivant knew that she would stay with him; he accepted it would be for selfish reasons on her part, but he would work on her. He had not chosen a plan of action yet. He was undecided whether he would beat her into submission and subservience with cruelty, or whether he would woo her, make her fall in love with him. He desperately wanted her to love him.

He despised not being loved. Vivant felt that everybody should love him. He was beautiful, he was rich, he was immortal. He could bestow the gift of eternal life. He was talented in every facet of what he chose to do at any time and could learn new skills in a heartbeat. He spoke several languages. He was sophisticated. Vivant had nothing but contempt for those who did not have the intelligence to instantly adore him.

Vivant had fallen in love with Belladonna the moment he saw her stomping down the street arguing with the night air. But she was full of fire, full of life. He knew that he would need time for her to trust him. It may take even longer to make her fall in love with him. He knew that he would need to control his flow of information so that she did not learn too much too fast and desert him.

But he knew he would have to decide quickly which route to take. He grinned at his own thoughts – making her fall in love with him would be so much more of a triumph.

There were so many things to consider. He knew from experience that she would not be the same person once bullied into submission and therefore the possibility existed that he may not love her once that happened. But if he left it to chance, allowed his own personality to persuade her, then she may not ever feel the same way about him. It was very hard for Vivant to believe there was *somebody* in the world who *possibly* may not love him. He had people swooning at his feet every night on the club circuit where he sang to people and made them fall in love.

Vivant and Belladonna stood looking deep into each other.

Vivant was thinking what he could do to make her stay. What he could do to make her love him more than anybody else had ever loved him. He was thinking about what he could do to make her stay forever.

Belladonna was thinking about how soon she could get away from the monster that had turned her into a vampire. She was thinking what she could do to have her revenge on him. But first, she needed the power of his knowledge.

At that moment, for very different reasons, both of them needed each other.

At that moment, neither one of them trusted the other.

Vivant knew what he wanted; he had never shied away from taking anything he had ever desired. He wanted Belladonna and if she didn't want him, then he would try to make her stay. He had given her something incomparable, given her the greatest gift that money could never buy.

Belladonna knew what Vivant wanted from her. Rage swelled inside her as he came nearer and nearer. Her skin crawled as he wrapped one arm around her waist and grabbed her face with the other and forced their lips to collide violently.

Man-sex-pain
Hard-cock-bleed

Belladonna made a noise of protest as he kissed her and slid a hand down her thigh and hoisted up her skirt. She felt his lips curl into a smile as they were still pressed to hers as his fingers glided with ease into her Judas-cunt, already slick and ready for his attention. She cursed herself for her arousal, knowing he would view it as a victory, see it as her being already conquered without so much as one battle fought.

Belladonna felt the swell of his cock growing ever harder against her pelvis. She hated herself for longing to feel it inside her, but she did, she wanted it more than she'd ever wanted anything. She wanted him inside her despite her past experiences with men, with sex, and all the pain that had come with them.

Belladonna had never known sexual arousal that ended with mutual pleasure. She had never made love. Each time she was in the presence of a hard cock, she was either running from the clutches of the over-amorous owner or slapping his face in disgust. But on more than one occasion she had not made it out the door. She learned what it felt like to be impaled without the benefit of first being aroused and made ready. But one of her rapists had been a gentleman, at least, and spat a wad of phlegm on his own hand and lubricated his cock with it before forcing it into her.

But this was different; Vivant was a perfect fit, and Belladonna's eyes rolled with the immediate pleasure that engulfed her. He bit into the delicate skin on her neck, drawing blood. He suckled the flesh wounds made by his lethal fangs, a deep and violent kiss. Belladonna felt more pleasure than she knew was possible and wondered if she would be able to bear it without dying or going mad.

She twisted the cool black silk in her fists as they writhed together, emotions soaring and crashing down, both of them tormented by what they felt, what they experienced. This was a man she knew she could love and hate in equal measure. She wanted to love him and at the same time she wanted to kill him. Vivant's feelings were entirely mutual.

They were perfect for each other.

He could hear every thought that ran through her mind. He could hear her saying that she loved him, that she hated him, that she wanted to be locked together with him forever and that she wanted to rip his head off with her bare hands. Instantly he had brought out the beast in her.

Vivant towered over her, his hands restraining her wrists. He tried to make his face as stern as he possibly could to make her see as well as feel his domination. But it was useless. He could not hide what he felt for her, and that fact angered him. Belladonna wrapped her legs around his back, desperately pulling him deeper into her dripping sex, needing to feel him as far inside as was physically possible.

And as they came, both of them looking deep into each other's eyes with a potent cocktail of love and loathing, of passion and hatred, Belladonna could hear each thought in Vivant's head too.

At that moment there was nothing in the world that could possibly tear them apart.

But as Vivant was making love to her for the first time, Belladonna's thoughts turned elsewhere as a moment of epiphany made her gasp. A familiar face filled her head, the last face she saw as a human; it called out to her in those dark silken tones. The thought did not please Vivant and it made him want to hurt her. Belladonna was a vampire now and she knew that she had a gift she could bestow upon anybody she desired - a gift that money could not buy.

She was quiet. Sheepish, even. A little ashamed at the abandon she had felt while they made love. And she was angry at how easily she had given herself to him. But she could not hold on to that anger for more than a few minutes at a time.

This was bliss – sitting here in the slight chill of the night air, high up on top of the grandest hotel in all Hollywood, sipping fine vintage Champagne. She watched the sparkle of stars in the black sky like the bubbles bursting in her glass.

It was beautiful. She had never seen anything like it it real life. It brought to mind the *Hanging Gardens of Babylon* that Nebuchadnezzar II had built for his homesick wife. Belladonna had seen drawings of them in an old encyclopedia her dad bought her when she was a little girl.

There were fragrant plants she had never smelled nor even seen before, great trailing vines like the succulent tentacles of some great forest beast. Gigantic ferns and impossibly colored orchids some redder than blood, some more purple than amethysts.

There were trees so huge that she wondered why they didn't fall through the ceiling and crash through the rest of the building's floors.

Vivant smiled and explained he had a team of the best engineers in the country reinforce the roof so he could have them here.

She was in love with the beauty of this enchanted garden.

And she knew she was falling in love with the man beside her, the man who had made her a vampire. And for that, she hated herself.

Belladonna excelled at being a vampire. She stalked her prey like a born predator. She could coax even the most faithful of men into a dark alleyway with the promise of her charms.

She was a fast learner and soaked up each piece of knowledge Vivant imparted to her. But he was sparing with his knowledge; he made her work for each morsel of information he shared with her, and made sure that she showed her appreciation.

Although she had strong feelings for him and knew she was falling in love with him despite her better judgment, his demeanor, his personality, his attitude, his arrogance, his sarcasm, just about everything else that made Vivant Vivant, she despised. Mostly. Sometimes she grudgingly admired him. And sometimes he drove her mad with desire.

She hated the way he fussed over his clothes like a woman. Each outfit had to be perfection. A spec of dust or a stray crease was enough to send Vivant into apoplexy.

She grinned as she watched him during a fitting for a new suit. She knew something that would make him utterly insane. She knew something she could do to make him absolutely hate her to the degree that he would actually want to kill her with his bare hands. She knew something that would enrage him beyond compare. Even his beloved Valentine running off and leaving him, something she knew still aggravated him immensely when he thought about it, would pale into insignificance in comparison.

Belladonna had the notion that Bela Lugosi would make a spectacular vampire. He looked right, he sounded right. He had the perfect hypnotic stare to disarm and distract, the voice to soothe his victim before going in for the kill to drain the blood.

The thought of an eternity with her idol, the perfect vampire, the perfect man, the perfect lover, made her gaze dreamy and far away as if she were staring at something distant only she could see. And the thought of how Vivant would react made her grin; it was a grin that would rival the wickedness she so frequently saw on Vivant's lips.

Vivant absolutely detested Bela Lugosi.

She could have the man of her dreams and fantasies, eternally, and pay back Vivant for his cruelty to her and to everybody else he had ever encountered.

Two birds with one stone.

ON THE RADIO...

...I am...Dracula. I bid you welcome.

...Listen to them...the children of the night...what music they make!

...A spider spinning his web for the unwary fly, the blood...is the life, Mr. Renfield.

Belladonna sat listening, enthralled by Lugosi's voice, as always. She had a dreamy look on her face and she was imagining the words being whispered directly in her ear, and the spine-tingling sensation of his hot breath on her neck, and the scent of blood in the air around them.

Now that she had tasted it, she had a whole new appreciation for *Dracula*. And an all-consuming passion for Bela Lugosi.

She gasped, carried away by her fantasy, hungry to find him and to make her dreams a reality.

Vivant walked past her with a sneer spread across his mouth. He was unable to hide his contempt, or his jealousy.

Vivant knew, no matter what he did for her, no matter how benevolent a mentor, or how considerate a lover, or how wonderful he was to her, he knew that he could never compare to the fantasy of Lugosi she kept inside her heart.

But he was sure that if she ever did catch up to him, she would be greatly disappointed to find out that he was *only* a man.

"But *such* a man, Vivant. An exceptional man. An extraordinary man," she told him as she read his thoughts.

He cursed himself silently for letting his guard down and allowing his emotions to lower his defenses which were always running at the maximum.

He hated Belladonna at that moment, hated her for being the object of his affection, for making him feel the way he did, for being able to make him feel like he was second best. Vivant had never felt that in his entire existence.

He did not understand why she felt the way she did about somebody he considered beneath him. Vivant held actors in no higher regard than whores. Long ago, he remembered, anybody and everybody who were above paupers thought of actors as vagabonds in costume, nomads who roamed countries, had no homes.

What does she see in him? He's just an actor. The modern day equivalent of a court jester or a courtesan. He couldn't possibly give her the things I have given her. Can he give her immortality? No. Can he take away her human inevitability of sickness and death? No. Is it possible that he could save her from the ravages of age and the changing of her firm, pink skin into hanging, colorless flesh? No, it is not. He can never give her what I gave her. She'll be forever young and beautiful, eternally in the first flush of her womanhood. I made her eternal. And he's just an actor. An actor who pretends to be what I am.

Vivant paced the floor, hands behind his back and a serious expression that did not suit his beautiful face. Due to his youthful looks, when he scowled he resembled a petulant child pouting because he didn't get his own way.

It made him insane to watch Belladonna sitting listening to Lugosi in a radio play, her distant, dreamy expression leaving nothing to the imagination what she was thinking.

He wondered if he might have Belladonna's undivided attention if Bela Lugosi was not a famous movie star. And he wondered if she would look twice at him if he walked past her in the street without the benefit of being a movie star. He liked to think not.

Fucking B-picture hack

Belladonna scowled at him, again hearing his thoughts about Lugosi.

Vivant desperately wished that Bela Lugosi did not exist.

He knew she was planning something. He knew without a doubt that she was forming a scheme by which to capture her idol and make him a vampire. He only hoped that she would fail, that she would take too much of his blood and kill him before she gave him some of her's, or that she would give him too little and he would die anyway. She couldn't possibly know how much was enough and so he must keep her from gaining that knowledge. There were few other vampires around but there *were* some. Any one of them would be able to tell her what she needed to know.

Vivant had to keep her away from other vampires…and away from Bela Lugosi.

Belladonna had to find out where Lugosi lived. That would be the place he would be most relaxed, unguarded.

ON THE RADIO...

…Say, this story is a real pain in the neck!…Today in Los Angeles, Bela Lugosi, Count Dracula himself, was awarded American citizenship. The fang-tastic actor is holding a private reception at his home in the Hollywood Hills. Welcome to America, Count Dracula!…

Belladonna clapped with delight - he was to be a permanent fixture in Hollywood now - an American citizen. She knew that he must love Hollywood as much as she did. She looked forward to talking about it with him.

She knew she could find him; she had an idea of the general area he lived in. She knew it was a big house in the Hollywood hills. But she didn't need directions. She knew she would be led to him by her instinct, by her love for him. She knew that she would be able to find him if she wandered through the darkened city and let her nature seek him out.

She walked. Searched. Listened. A hundred conversations filtered through the darkness to her.

Somebody was sitting alone, crying.

A girl. Young, naïve, more than likely not long off a bus from the country, just like her. The girl sobbed, her heart breaking.

This isn't fair. I don't deserve this. No man will ever want me now.

Then she heard the metal clatter of a gun barrel against teeth, the click of the pistol's hammer being cocked, the bang as she pulled the trigger. There was a wet slap as blood and brain tissue painted the wall behind her.

Belladonna closed her eyes tight as if she was there at the scene of the suicide, watching the young girl blowing her brains out.

She hated being an aural witness to the fears, pain and torment of others. She hated having to listen to the personal anguish of so many people - sometimes many at once.

Unfortunately, the troubled mind shouted louder than the joyful heart.

She wished she could shut out the noise sometimes, enjoy silence. She longed for it, to sit in absolute quiet, alone, and hear nothing but her own thoughts in her head. That was another thing she hated Vivant for - stealing her ability to sit quietly and think.

And then she heard it - *that* voice. Although he was singing and she had never heard him sing before, it was unmistakable. There was nobody in possession of a voice quite like it.

As he sang, a vibrato of emotion crept into the song. She imagined the tears that were in his eyes as he thought about the home he could never return to whilst he sang songs of it in a foreign land.

She swallowed hard, fighting back her own tears. A swell of emotion thudded in her chest. She could not talk, or breathe, or even move for a few moments. She was overwhelmed by her own need, by the enormity of what she felt for this man.

Vivant kept his distance but never let her out of his sight. She was much too wrapped up in her quest to find Bela Lugosi to sense Vivant following her. He made a low growling sound in his throat as he eavesdropped on her thoughts. His jealousy made him want to rip his own heart out of his chest so he did not feel the pain she was causing him anymore.

Belladonna moved with purpose now; not only did she know her beloved Bela was close as she heard his voice, but she *felt* that he was close.

She began to tremble, and her breath came in short, shallow gasps.

Finally, she came to a stop outside a house. Only three guests remained, sleepy-eyed, ready for the party to end but having more fun than they were currently capable of.

Bela was still on his feet, wide-awake and full of energy. Belladonna crouched in the bushes near the front window and had a good look around the living room. Her eyes widened as her gaze rested on a portrait on his wall. The painting was of a naked woman, stunningly beautiful with flaming red hair. The woman looked very much like Belladonna.

"You dark horse," she said, grinning. The woman in the painting had to be a lover. She imagined the woman in black and white, just like the movies and she realized instantly who she was. She was *The 'It' Girl*, Clara Bow.

She watched as Bela walked over to the bar to make himself another drink. He picked up a room-temperature beer, opened it and let the top fall, roll off the counter and land on the floor. He followed it, and as he bent down to pick it up near the window, Belladonna's face was no more than inches from his. She held her breath, formed her mouth into an 'O' and widened her eyes as far as they could possibly open. With her little black kiss curls caressing her face and her impossibly huge eyes, she looked like Betty Boop, desperately trying to evade the clutches of yet another devious villain.

Bela emptied the warm beer into a tall glass then poured himself a whisky chaser. He dropped the small glass of Scotch into the beer and drank down the foul brew with hardly a pause. He closed his eyes and shuddered once the drink was mostly gone. He hated the taste, but it did what he required it to do - help kill the pain of his old war wounds, fast. Sometimes, Morphine and Demerol just weren't enough.

After what seemed like an eternity, the remaining guests left the party. Belladonna was starting to feel burning pains in her calves from crouching in the same position for so long in her high heels.

Bela's guests bid him goodnight and staggered merrily down the street, where they all tumbled into expensive chauffeur driven cars.

They attempted to sing the old Hungarian folk song he had tried to teach them earlier. Belladonna covered her mouth to stifle a giggle as she listened to Californian accents struggling with the Hungarian words, of which they could remember only two or three Unfortunately, the tune was entirely lost to them.

Bela waved from his front doorstep as his guests left for their own homes. He shut the door and was all alone now in the quiet of his house.

She watched him as he drained the last of his drink. Bela's face changed; the distinguished lines deepened, his lips were pulled taught by the tension in his face. His vim and vigor had been mostly an act for his friends. It was was how he *wanted* to feel. He held his hand out and managed to catch the edge of the bar to steady himself.

Belladonna instinctively reached out for him, her face painted with concern. She knew he was in a great deal of pain and all she wanted to do was take that pain away from him, see the tension drain away and the cheeky smile that belied his fifty years come back.

I can take away your pain

Lugosi turned his head toward the window and peered into the darkness outside. He shook his head and began to pour another drink.

I can take away your pain, Bela. I love you

He hurried to the window as fast as his pain filled legs would carry him, flung it open and called out.

"Who is there? I heard you speak."

Belladonna froze, unable to talk or move.

She knew there was nobody else here with them. Bela had heard her thoughts.

Belladonna found her courage and sprang from the middle of the bush she crouched in.

"Mr. Lugosi! Don't be afraid. I...I just want to talk to you."

He stepped back from the open window, startled at the appearance of a young woman from the middle of one of the bushes outside his window.

"My goodness; I thought you were Clara for a moment. What are you doing out here? Who are you?" he asked.

Belladonna closed her eyes momentarily, unable to stem the shudder that shot through her body as he spoke to her. When she opened her eyes he was grinning at her and she used every shred of willpower she possessed to stop herself from fainting.

"Where are my manners?" He disappeared, then she heard the turn of a key in the front door lock.

Belladonna waited for the door to open, her legs shaking so violently the metal tips on her high heels beat out a rhythm on the path.

And there he was, in the flesh. Right in front of her, so close she could reach out and touch him.

"Just talk, please," she told him.

Bela laughed. He was tired of telling people he never drank…wine, and opted for an appropriate line from the book instead.

"Welcome to my house! Enter freely and of your own will, and leave something of the happiness you bring."

Bela smiled and bowed, gestured for her to enter.

Had he been entirely lucid, he would not have let a strange woman into his house in the middle of the night. But this had been a special day - his first as an American citizen and the reason for the day's over-indulgences in food and drink and sentiment.

Belladonna perched herself on the edge of a chair, muscles rigid with tension. Her heart hammered against the inside of her chest so violently she thought it was going to burst through her rib cage and land at Bela's feet.

"So, what can I do for you, young lady?"

She couldn't speak; she'd waited so long for this day that now it was here she was tongue-tied. There was only one thing running through her mind and she knew she couldn't stop herself from saying it once she found her voice again.

"I love you," she said.

Lugosi raised an eyebrow at the bold young woman who looked just like his beloved Clara Bow. He looked sad for a second, remembering the disturbing news he heard only a few weeks ago. Clara had been admitted to a sanatorium, a necessity for treatment of her ongoing *problems and afflictions*, they'd been described to him as. But he knew all too well what that meant. She had feared it her entire life. It had infected her grandmother and her mother, Sarah, and she knew she it was creeping into her too. Clara had fought her mother's madness her whole life and suffered relentless insomnia ever since the day she woke from sleep to find her standing over her with a butcher knife. Sarah told her she was going to kill her because it would be better than watching her run off to Hollywood and become a *hoor*.

And her nervous state was always made worse by her own dark thoughts that she had killed her own mother by choosing to be an actress. But Sarah did not live to see her daughters success and her rebirth as a legend.

Bela tried to rid his mind of his sombre thoughts about his darling Clara, and turned his attentions to his guest.

Lugosi didn't know what to say. A stranger in his living room just told him she loved him.

Women had screamed it at him from audiences before, frequently. They accosted him in the street yelling it at the top of their voices. They sent him letters scented with fine perfumes and gifts of candy in heart-shaped boxes. They sent him bottles of his favorite Whiskey, cans of Toltott Kaposzta, a Hungarian favorite of stuffed cabbage, containers of Eros, the fiercest variety of paprika, to make his beloved Goulash, and packages of Erdélyi, a Transylvanian Salami procured from Hungarian and Romanian delis in Southern California.

Some fans, ones with money and connections, even imported specialist foods for him from the old country, and items were even sent to him from his home town of Lugoj. The generosity of his fans always amazed him. But he had never had to deal with such a fan in his own home in the middle of the night. He wondered what sort of gift she had for him; they *always* had a gift to give. Suddenly, he was uneasy.

Although she was stunningly beautiful, Bela felt that there was something not quite right about the woman in his sitting room. She was *too* perfect. Her beauty seemed almost exaggerated, her skin was flawless, her lips and cheeks perfectly ruddy, and her huge, dark eyes sparkled unnaturally.

She was like a perfect version of his troubled Clara. Although she unnerved him, he did not want to be rid of her. He wanted her to stay. He was fascinated by her and even although he was potentially in danger, he did not care. His curiosity out-weighed, and out-argued his reason and rationale.

Vivant scowled in through the window. One side of his lip curled up into a feral snarl. He heard what she said to her idol, and her words were like a physical blow to him. He clutched at his gut as if trying to pry out the pain of her words.

"I have something to give you, but only if you want it," she told him.

"My, you are a mysterious young lady. What is it? You have a gift for me?"

His voice, no matter what he was saying, made excitement fizz inside her.

"What would you say if I told you I could take away the pain you suffer?"

He frowned, but smiled soon after.

"I would say you should keep on talking."

"I can. I can take your pain away. I can make it so you will never suffer pain like that again, you will never suffer illness..."

Lugosi raised his eyebrows.

"...and you will never die. I can make you immortal, Bela."

"Ah! You are a vampire! Well, I am Dracula! I am already an immortal so I shall bid you a goodnight."

Lugosi ushered her with a gentle, but firm hand toward the door.

Belladonna stopped in her tracks and put her hand on his face.

"I'm not insane, Bela. I'm telling you the truth. Let me show you."

Lugosi stood watching her as she slowly removed her jacket and her blouse. He didn't move; his thoughts were filled with the possibility that she may be utterly insane, but also with his astonishment at her devastating beauty. He was, after all, a full-blooded, passionate man. That alone kept him rooted to the spot, waiting to see what she was going to do next.

Belladonna stood in front of him, stripped to the waist save for her bra.

She braced herself, still unsure if she would be able to do it the same as Vivant had. She plunged her hand inside her own chest and ripped out her heart.

"Look, see? I *did* tell you the truth, Bela. I would never lie to you."

Lugosi stood, speechless, looking at a half naked woman in his living room holding her heart in her hands, dripping red gore all over his floor.

His face was splattered with her blood. It crossed his mind that this was some sort of magic trick, perhaps an elaborate practical joke being played on him. He wiped his fingers over his face collecting some of the red substance. He licked it off, expecting to taste the sweetness of a red-dyed sugar syrup, something, anything but blood on his tongue.

He gasped as he tasted bitter metal. His face contorted as he stepped back from the young woman holding her heart in her hands. The warm substance on his tongue was undoubtedly blood.

"You can live forever, Bela. You and I can be together for eternity."

He'd heard declarations of undying love from fans before. He'd had many women tell him he had *stolen* their heart, and that he had *won* their heart, or *broken* their heart. Many had told him they would *give* him their heart. He never expected that someday, one actually *would*.

Bela was sickened and horrified by what she had done; but he knew that she was not a mere human – she *couldn't* be. She stood there still, blinking, breathing, talking, whilst she held the seed of her own life before her..

He did not know what to say, or even how to react. Regardless of the horror he had just witnessed, there was also the possibility, since he was looking at her, still standing and talking to him, still conscious and breathing, that she was telling the truth and she could indeed make him immortal.

"This is insanity," he said. But still, he did not want her to leave.

Vivant decided it was time to step in. He couldn't risk her bringing Lugosi over. Everything would be lost to him if that was allowed to happen.

Lugosi looked puzzled as a man seemed to just materialize out of the air and appeared next to Belladonna.

"For goodness sake, Belladonna, put that away," he said with a smile.

Belladonna's face immediately flushed with anger at Vivant's appearance, knowing that he had followed her, and maddened by the fact that she had not been aware of it.

"What are you doing here?" she asked, her rage clear to him.

Vivant ignored her and began to talk to Bela Lugosi.

"Mr. Lugosi, please, I must apologize for Belladonna's behavior in your lovely home. Forgive her - she's not very well."

"Not well? I think what I just witnessed goes beyond being unwell, Mr?... what is your name?"

"Just call me Vivant."

"Vivant, I don't understand. Who *are* you? *What* are you?

"What am I? You of all people should know what I am! I am a vampire and I have offered you the gift of immortality," Belladonna told Lugosi.

Vivant made a circular gesture at his temple and flicked a sideways glance at Belladonna. Lugosi nodded; he understood.

"But what about the..."

"An elaborate trick; she has quite a talent for it."

Vivant grabbed Belladonna by the back of the hair and the two of them disappeared.

Lugosi looked into the spaces the two of them had occupied. He thought momentarily that perhaps his beverage of choice was making him hallucinate. Or maybe his pain, or both.

"A bad bottle of beer, perhaps. Or the excitement of the day," he told himself, trying to rationalize what he had just seen. "A trick of the eye."

But the sticky red pool on his floor was no illusion. It was real. He could see it, feel it. He had tasted it. No sleight of hand or magic trick could make him do that. There was a puddle of congealing blood on his living room floor.

Belladonna's blood was on the carpet, his shoes, his trousers. Her blood was on his skin. Her blood was in his mouth.

He was sure, no matter how excited he had been earlier, or how bad the beers he drank had been, that he cold not hallucinate the taste of blood in his mouth.

Bela Lugosi had just encountered two vampires in his living room. And he knew it.

"I fucking hate you!"

Belladonna screamed at Vivant, her words strangled, forced through raw, constricted vocal cords. She balled her hands into shaking fists at her sides. Every muscle in her body knotted with rage at what he had done to her in Bela Lugosi's house.

"You don't own me!"

Belladonna spat as she spoke, eyes wide, feral, her anger bordering on insanity. She could never forgive Vivant for this affront.

Vivant looked at her, expressionless, unimpressed and unmoved by her tantrum.

"Are you quite finished? Good. Let me tell you something, you little idiot. I *do* own you. I own the exclusive clothes you're so fond of. I own the expensive jewelry you weigh yourself down with. I own the imported French perfume you drown yourself in each night like a Parisian whore. I own the ground you walk on and the air you breathe. I own the fucking flesh which covers your ungrateful bones. If it wasn't for me, Belladonna, you'd be selling that tight little cunt of yours for 50 cent tricks on the Strip by now. You were a heartbeat away from it when I saved you."

Vivant's sharpened words were like a stake through her heart and wounded her.

"Stupid slut."

Belladonna was stunned into silence by the force of her rage. She was stricken that Vivant would talk to her the same way as the sleazy, dirty old men in Hollywood would talk to her, belittle and humiliate her in the same way that they did.

She stuttered and blinked rapidly, trying to force her words out past the fury gripping her throat.

"Don't call me that!"

Belladonna looked around the room desperately searching for something to hurt Vivant with. She knew that she could not kill him, but she *could* hurt him. She wanted to hurt him so badly that he would *wish* he could die from it.

She wanted to flay him, strip off his skin and rub salt into the wounds. She wanted to watch Vivant bleed and suffer, listen to him beg her for mercy and hear his screams.

And it had to be dramatic. It had to be loud. It had to be unmissable and unmistakable. Then she remembered - Vivant's sizable collection of firearms. He'd not soon forget that - being shot with one of his own precious guns.

They looked at each other; Vivant's smirk withered when he saw the manic grin that bloomed on Belladonna's lips. She turned away from him, the grin bursting and becoming a giggle drenched in madness.

She ran to the cabinet where he kept his collection and before Vivant reached her, her new-found supernatural speed had allowed her to fill the magazine with rounds; he heard the click of the clip as she slid it into the butt of his favorite pistol; a Russian Tokarev.

"Belladonna, please, be careful with that - you might hurt yourself."

She laughed at him.

"Actually, I'm very proficient with all kinds of firearms, Vivant. See? You don't really know me very well, do you? When I was a little girl, me and papa toured state and county fairs all over the west coast with our Wild West Trick Shot Show. I could shoot a single hair off the top of your head , blindfolded, one arm tied behind my back with any one of these guns."

Vivant looked at her, slack-jawed. He didn't know if she was telling him the truth or not.

"And I know where to shoot you to cause the most pain."

Vivant used his speed to pick up another one of his guns, a Luger pistol, load it and step back, his sights trained on her.

"So, now what? You shoot me and I shoot you back? We can't kill each other, Belladonna."

She grinned at him, her face becoming an eerie sight. The hair stood up on the back of Vivant's neck as he looked at her.

"No, but I can shoot you full of holes just to watch you bleed."

Now it was Vivant's turn to grin eerily.

"My God, I'm so glad I chose you. I knew you had a fire inside you that nothing can extinguish. You didn't even know what a firecracker you were, did you? You should thank me, sweetheart, I set you free."

And with that, Belladonna cocked the pistol, squeezed the trigger and unloaded her clip into him. She shot him in both hands, in the gut, the groin, the knee, the shoulder, between the eyes and the final shot she let fly straight into his heart, just like Cupid's arrow.

He shot back. Round after round hitting her, blowing holes in her killer body.

And Vivant fell even more deeply in love with her. The pain swelled in him, his entire being ignited in agony.

But almost too soon his wounds began to heal and within the space of less than a minute, he was once again untouched, new, all trace of the agonies of moments before, gone.

And she was healed too. Now unscathed after suffering multiple gun shot wounds.

It wasn't enough for Belladonna. She was even more enraged now than she was before. He'd enjoyed it. He loved the pain. He reveled in it. If shooting him couldn't hurt him to the point where he screamed in agony, she wasn't sure there was anything that *could* hurt him.

In her anger, she reloaded the clip, strode over to Vivant and unloaded each round into his head. She watched, fascinated, as the back of Vivant's head burst open; skull fragments and gray matter rained onto the wall wall behind him. She went to the wall and picked up a chunk of his brain.

"Ewww."

She flicked it off her finger and giggled as it slapped against the window pane and rolled down, leaving bloody streaks in its wake.

She looked back at Vivant. And for a moment she felt panic. He looked dead. His eyes, usually so full of expression and mischief, eyes that usually glittered and glinted with life and with passions were empty. Dark. *Dead.*

And then that spark came back into them.

He tried to speak but his brain wasn't fully recovered yet; he sounded retarded and she laughed at him. She could see *that* - the fact that she had laughed at him, and not that she had shot him in the head at point-blank range and sprayed his brains all over the wall - enraged him. He waited until his brain was fully repaired before opening his mouth again, so profound was his vanity.

"That hurt, you fucking tart!"

This time, there was a look in his eyes that she could not interpret. He knew from the look on her face she was confused by his expression and he smiled at her.

"What?" she asked him.

"Now I know."

"Now you know what?" she asked.

"Now I know how much you love me."

Belladonna rolled her eyes.

"No, Vivant, now you should know how much I hate you."

"No, no, no. You can't possibly hate somebody as much as you hate me, without loving them even more."

"I think you must be brain damaged. Must still be a loose piece of gray matter floating around in there out of place if you think I just shot you in the face because I love you."

Her blood rose as he gave her his special look of condescension that always made her crazy.

"Sweetheart, you don't have to pretend with me - it's OK, really it is. I know how irresistible I am."

Belladonna turned away from him, aware that any response, any twitch of her eye, any curl of her lip or sound from her throat would be interpreted by Vivant in any way he pleased. And then it dawned on her - that perhaps he was right. Perhaps he *did* make her so crazy because she loved him so much.

No, no, no, no, no! Don't listen to him, I'd know if I was in love with him or not!

"But you *do* know."

In her confusion and anger she'd let her guard down and allowed Vivant to read her mind. She cursed silently at herself for forgetting.

"Why won't you just let me go, Vivant? Why? Why do we have to be here, together, hating each other and fighting with each other every day? Why?"

"Who's stopping you from leaving, Belladonna? Are you chained? Do I keep you locked up in a dungeon? You are free as I to come and go as you please. You are not my prisoner. You are here because you want to be here - and for no other reason. And don't ever think I can't hear each and every thought in your pretty little head. No matter how well you think you're cloaking your thoughts, I can always read them."

He was lying to her but the look on her face told him she wasn't sure if what he said was true or not. There was no way she could know for sure.

And then it hit her; Vivant, as cruel and as vindictive as he was, must feel the same way about her as he thought she did about him. By extension of his own logic, it had to be true.

He heard the thought.

And he was furious.

His own medicine was bitter and stuck in his throat.

Nobody, throughout all the years, the decades, the centuries he'd traveled, had ever infuriated him the way Belladonna did. He had never encountered anyone who could make him lose his cool the way she did. No one had ever aroused such enormous passion inside him, made him feel love and hate and desire and made him spit venom, all at the same time. Finally, Vivant thought, he may just have met his match.

CHAPTER SIX : FINDING BELA

Belladonna walked alone through the darkened city. It seemed that Hollywood never quite slept, that Hollywood was never quite silent.

She walked the path that led up Mount Lee. Even although she had been here for months, she had not yet visited those big white letters which rested upon the hillside and read Hollywoodland.

To touch them now, amid the surrealism that was her life, and even in this land of make believe and lies, it would make her feel real again, human again. The sign was something solid, something tangible in a world she increasingly felt was ethereal.

She had to find him. She had to see Bela again. She had to make sure he knew she was not insane. She needed him to know that she was not the lunatic that Vivant portrayed her to be.

She wanted to sit down with him and just talk, tell him about herself, tell him all about what had happened to her, tell him all about what Vivant had done to her. She had to make him understand, make him believe that she really *was* a vampire, and not a lunatic.

Belladonna walked. She thought. She wondered if Bela would believe her, or if he might think her even more insane once she told him the whole story. But she had to take that chance. She owed it to herself, and to Bela.

She found the house again easily, barely even thinking about the route she was taking there. She was instinctively led to him, like she had been the last time. Once again she stood outside his window, looking in, watching Bela Lugosi.

Bela's head was lowered and his face was masked with sadness. He was staring at a photograph. With her vampire vision she could see tears welling up in Bela's eyes as he studied the photograph.

He closed his eyes; his grip around the picture loosened and it fluttered to the floor. Belladonna recognized the woman in the picture immediately – it was Clara Bow. His tears spilled over and ran down his cheeks. Belladonna felt a lump form in her throat and swallowed hard against the pain of her emotion as she watched the man she loved weep over another woman.

She entered the house and stood in front of him as he still cried for Clara. He was unaware of her presence, wrapped tightly in his own grief.

"Bela," she said.

Bela looked up, slowly, unstartled by her presence. It was as if he had expected her to be there, as if he knew that she was coming.

Belladonna was surprised that he didn't jump at her appearance. Suddenly, she was lost for words; all the things she wanted to say had been forgotten. Now, she just stood there, slack-jawed, looking like the mental case she feared he already took her for.

Bela smiled through his tears.

"I knew you would come back," he said.

"You did?"

"Yes, I knew it. I knew we would see each other again."

Once again Vivant stood outside Bela's house, snarling into the darkness. His blood rose and slammed into his temples, his perfectly manicured nails gouging the flesh from his palms, blood trickling down through his fingers and dripping from his knuckles.

You fucking ungrateful cunt. I give you everything. Everything!

"You don't deserve immortality. You don't deserve anything!"

Vivant realized he was shouting now and that Bela and Belladonna were standing staring out the window. Vivant entered the house. There was only one thing left to do - to confront both of them.

"Why do you do these things to me? Why? I give you everything! Is there a thing in this world you could possibly want that I've not given you? Is there?"

Vivant was screaming at her, incensed at her betrayal.

"Yes, there is something I want," she said.

"Then what is it? What?"

"I just want him," she said, looking at Bela the way Vivant hated to see her look at him.

Vivant was struck mute by his rage. Belladonna's eyes shone; she knew that Vivant was in absolute agony, knew that the blood inside him effervesced with rage.

And now she knew how to hurt him. This hurt him more than any physical blow ever could. Wounding his ego, his pride, letting him know that there was somebody else she desired more, wanted more, loved more, had a bigger place in her heart than he, was more than Vivant could bear. Even if it wasn't entirely true and she was lying to herself as much as she was lying to him.

It was incomprehensible to Vivant that someone, anyone, could find another being more attractive than himself. Especially a *human*. It was unheard of for him to be on the receiving end of such dismissal. It made him so angry he wanted to kill her and Bela Lugosi.

But he also loved her and he knew that he could not live without her. That revelation to himself just made him more enraged. There was nothing he could do or say to salvage his pride.

Vivant vanished into the night so fast even Belladonna didn't see him move. He was just gone.

"Is he your..."

"No, he's not. He's my nothing. The only thing we have in common is the fact that he turned me into what I am," she said.

Bela smiled knowingly at her.

"No one could hate so completely without loving in equal measure, Belladonna."

"Why do people always say that? That's what *he* says. I don't love him," she pouted at Bela, pursing her lips like a spoiled little girl.

"Belladonna, I'm long enough in the tooth to know something about being in love. Sometimes it feels like the opposite. I know this, believe me. I know how it feels to resent the one you love for the way they make you feel, for the way they have power over you, and because you know that you would do anything for them. I know how that feels. Truly."

"I don't love him. I don't."

She spat the words at him, tiny droplets of her saliva sprayed his face and he blinked as they hit his eyes. All he did was smile at her. He knew being told that would just throw fuel on her anger.

Belladonna's huge black eyes filled up with tears and her bottom lip began to quiver with emotion. The sight of her tears were like a blow to him and he covered his heart with his hand.

"Come to me," he told her and held out his open arms to her.

She threw herself into his embrace and held him so close and tight that he winced. And she cried, tears of longing, tears of frustration, tears of joy and love and hate and resentment.

It felt so good to be held by him.

Oh, my God, he's holding me! I'm in his arms. I'm in Bela's arms.

He closed his eyes as he held her. She even *felt* like Clara, but the notion was fleeting. His thoughts were not of Clara now. All he was thinking about was the strange and beautiful girl he was holding.

But what if she is insane? What if she wants to kill me?

Belladonna stood back from him. She looked hurt.

"Kill you? You think I would ever hurt you? I'd rather die, right here at your feet, than hurt you, Bela. I love you. All I want to do is be with you. And take your pain away."

"You can hear my thoughts?" he asked.

"Yes, I can hear your thoughts. It's just something we can do."

"We? You mean...vampires?"

"Yes, Bela; vampires."

A little shiver ran through her body as he said the word. His heavily accented pronunciation turned it into a three-syllable word that came out as vam-piy-urs.

She knew he was pondering his next move. He was torn. She heard the turmoil inside him. He wanted her but he was also afraid of her, afraid not for his safety this time, but afraid that she may actually be what she said she was. The implications of it – no more pain, eternal life, never dying – were of such gravity he had to sit down again.

He knew what she meant when she said she wanted to be with him. He knew she meant *forever.*

"I know this isn't easy to take in. I'm not used to it myself, yet," she smiled at him, trying to put him a little more at ease. "I know you'll need time to think this over. There's no rush. We have all the time in the world."

Bela looked up. She was gone. But he knew, even although he was panicked at first, he called after her to come back and not leave him. Although she did not return he knew that he would see her again. He knew the strange little girl named Belladonna would come back to him again soon.

"Vivant!" Belladonna screamed his name. "Vivant! Where are you, you pretentious little bastard?"

Belladonna waited for his reply. None came. Vivant was not at home. He was *always* home when she returned for feeding for the night. Always. The fact that he was not there unsettled her.

Where is he? He's always here Maybe he let me go. Maybe he's gone and he's not coming back.

Instead of thrilling her, instead of the thought that she may be free of him exhilarating her, the thought terrified her to the core.

No more Vivant

The pit of her gut tightened.

No more Vivant

A tiny sound of emotion escaped her throat through nerve-constricted vocal cords.

Her knees felt weak and threatened to collapse beneath her.

No more Vivant.

Her breath stuck in her throat, her lungs burned and suddenly her head was swimming. Belladonna panicked, flapped her arms as she desperately tried to remember how to breathe.

"Miss me?" Vivant was standing behind her, listening in on her torment.

She tried hard not to gasp for air as she began breathing again.

"No. Why would I?"

"You missed me. I heard you - *No more Vivant. No more Vivant*," he mocked her, raising the pitch of his voice and squeaking out the words.

Her face burned with shame. She was angry at herself for allowing him to witness her moment of weakness.

"I'm sorry, darling. I shouldn't have made fun. I'm touched. Really."

He reached out and stroked her blood-rouged cheek with the back of his hand, a gentle, tender gesture, so unlike him she became immediately wary.

Belladonna cast her eyes downward. She didn't know what to say, didn't know what to do. She didn't know whether or not to start another argument like usual or to relent and sit down and discuss how she felt. She knew there was the distinct possibility that she would open up to him and bare her soul, only for him to ridicule her mercilessly. That was what she fully expected from him.

She decided a change of subject was the safest move.

"Where on earth have you been?" Belladonna asked.

"Oh, I'm sorry; I didn't realize I needed permission to leave the apartment," he said in his usual bi-polar bastard way, turning on her after a moment of such tenderness.

"I didn't know where you were. When I got back you were gone. I just wondered where you went, that's all."

"I had some business to see to. I took my lawyer out to dinner. Italian. The food, not the lawyer; he's Jewish. They had the most exquisite seafood linguine – touch of butter, fresh cream and a dusting of saffron threads. It was divine," he said.

"What?"

"I said I had some business to..."

Belladonna cut him off. She heard very well what he said.

"I heard you. You ate? Food?"

"Well, of course I ate...Oh, my God!..." Vivant started laughing, clamped his hand over his mouth.

"We can eat?"

"I'm sorry, Bell. I didn't tell you that, did I?," he asked, his words muffled by his hand. He knew that he had not told her.

"We can still eat food and you didn't tell me?"

"Oops."

"You bastard!"

Belladonna looked around the room for something to hit him with or throw at him. Nothing stood out as particularly useful. She looked down at her own fist. Before she could talk herself out of it, she took a swing at him and planted a smack squarely on his mouth.

"You can't hurt me, sweetheart; I'm indestructible," he said with a satisfied smile, that was momentarily missing one of his front teeth. Before his smile straightened again, his tooth had grown back, the blood dried, then vanished.

"Maybe I can't hurt you, but punching you in the kisser sure felt good!"

Vivant was always amused and strangely aroused by Belladonna's violence. She was pretty as a picture, sweet-voiced and doe-eyed, but she would shoot him in the face or smash his skull open in a heartbeat. He loved that about her.

"You want me to take you out to eat, darling?" he asked.

"No, I do not."

"Why not?"

"I don't want to go anywhere with you, you pill!"

She turned her back on him and folded her arms, pouted like a spoiled little girl. He loved that too. It was so adorable to him.

"Oh, come on, now; I didn't do it on purpose. It just...slipped my mind," he said.

"Slipped your mind?" she asked, incredulously, without turning around, just turned her head and looked sideways at him.

"Yes, it slipped my mind and I'm sorry, alright? Come on; I'll make it up to you."

He held out his hand to her but she didn't move.

"Come on. Let Vivant make it all better."

He took her hand and kissed it, made an exaggerated pouty bottom lip and sad eyes at her. She grinned in spite of herself and allowed him to lead the way.

Belladonna was happy and giggly. The act of eating food instead of drinking blood had made her feel just like an ordinary, every-day person again, just like everybody else in the restaurant. She liked that feeling. She felt like her old self as they sat and ate a meal together, talking, laughing – just like all the other patrons of the restaurant. They were like any other young couple in love.

But Vivant was about to spoil the whole evening with his next question.

"Have you decided then?" he asked.

"Decided what?"

"Have you decided which one of us you want?"

"I don't know what you mean."

"Well, you can't have us both, Belladonna. You have to choose between us."

"I can't choose. I won't."

"You *will* choose. You *have* to. Don't be such a greedy whore."

"Don't call me that! Why do you always say things like that?" she asked him, her face flushing red again, this time with anger, not shame.

"What else would you call a woman who wants to keep two lovers; Clara Bow? Mr. Lugosi must like loose women, eh?"

"You bastard. How dare you talk about me that way, or about Clara Bow. You don't even know her. She hasn't done anything that everybody else isn't doing. She was just honest about it."

"Actually I do know Clara Bow, as a matter of fact. We were lovers, way back. Before she and Bela, actually, shortly after she arrived in Hollywood. Anyway, all this is beside the point. You have to choose. End of story. I'm a selfish beggar; I don't share my toys with others."

Belladonna's jaw fell open.

"Your *toys*? Is that what you think of me? I'm a *toy*, something to be played with for your amusement?," Belladonna's voice became increasingly louder and vibrated with emotion.

"Oh, calm down. It's just a turn of phrase. Don't evade the issue. You need to make a decision. Now."

"I have to go," she said.

"Belladonna, no! Just make up your mind once and for all."

"I think maybe you just made it for me."

Vivant reached for her and grabbed her by the wrist, pulled her around to face him. She struggled against his grasp. All she wanted to do right now was to get away from him, be alone with her thoughts without him eavesdropping on each and every one of them.

He grabbed her by the shoulders and made her stop. He looked deep into her eyes, searching for any indication that she didn't really mean what she just said about him making up her mind for her. And he couldn't read her. She was silent. Like stone. His own tumultuous emotions were dulling his powers and for the life of him he had no idea what was going on inside her head. Vivant was helpless.

At that moment Vivant realized just what he felt for her. He realized with a sharp intake of breath that he loved her, truly loved her, like he had never, ever loved anything before. And suddenly he regretted his ultimatum.

Belladonna found herself alone on the darkened streets of Hollywood, once again. She had no idea what to do. As brutal with his tongue as he sometimes was, as vain and arrogant and egocentric as he was, she couldn't bare to think of life without him. It was somehow imponderable. It was a thought that made her feel sick, made her guts twist and turn inside her when she tried to imagine being without him, when she thought of never seeing him again, never being touched by him again.

She didn't *want* to want him this way. She wanted to hate him. She wanted to despise him as much as he deserved. He was rancid in the heart and she knew that he would never, ever change. He was much too long in the tooth for that. But she couldn't help herself. She *did* want him. But she also wanted Bela, the kind-hearted, deep, passionate man she had fallen in love with while listening to him on the radio. But now, now that she had been in his arms, felt his touch, heard his velvet words spoken in her ear, she wanted him even more.

But Belladonna didn't *know* Bela. Not yet. What she knew was Count Dracula, an image on a screen. What she knew was a darkly romantic fairytale in which Bela Lugosi had the leading role. In truth, Bela and Vivant were more alike than not. He could be controlling too. Unreasonable. Even cruel to the women in his life.

Tears flowed down Belladonna's cheeks. She shook her head, in disbelief at her dilemma, wanting it to just go away, wishing she didn't have to choose between the two men she loved, neither of whom she wanted to live without.

If only I could die I would commit suicide. I know how I would do it too. I would climb up the maintenance ladder of the letter 'H' in the HOLLYWOODLAND sign. I would stand there on top of it and let the wind sway me as I look out over the city I love so much. And then I would close my eyes and I wouldn't feel the hurt and the hatred and the sadness any more. They would all flow from me as I leaned forward and let myself fall from this icon and plummet to my fitting death on the hillside below.

But she knew that she couldn't die that way. She had no idea what, if anything, *could* kill her. But she didn't *really* want to die. She just didn't want to make the decision she knew she would have to make soon.

She hated Vivant for making her choose between he and Bela. She wanted them both for different reasons. Between the two of them they were the best of both worlds, two halves of the perfect man, perfect love and perfect lover, the perfect mate to spend eternities with.

Belladonna had no idea who to choose. She cried harder.

Belladonna walked the streets, alone with her thoughts and the turmoil inside her. Each time she thought of Vivant she wanted him. Each time she thought of Bela she wanted him. Perhaps, she thought, the only solution to her problem would be to walk away from *both* men. Perhaps the only answer was to choose neither. But she knew to have neither one in her life would be a double blow that would kill her, vampire or not.

She decided she didn't want to think about it anymore. Not now. What she wanted to do right now was go to the movies. Here, in Hollywood, that was what she always did when she was troubled. The movies soothed her. Movies were her escape. They were few and far between when she was growing up, but now they were abundant, all around her, everywhere, all day and all night, 24/7.

She could find succor, solace at every turn here. There was a cinema on every corner, billboards all over. She was spoiled for choice. After all, this was Hollywood. This was the town where all these movies were made, the town where all the stars lived. This was the very heart of what she had always dreamed of.

Movies were her friend. They wanted nothing from her, except that she watch, that she listen, and that she love them.

A title card flashed up on the screen...

"IT" is that quality possessed by some which draws all others with its magnetic force. With "IT" you win all men if you are a woman—and all women if you are a man. "IT" can be a quality of the mind as well as a physical attraction." - Elinor Glyn.

It had been three years since Belladonna had seen this film. Originally released in 1927, it had not reached the Oregon boonies until the next year. She loved Clara Bow movies. Everybody told her how much she looked like her.

Belladonna had been entranced by the glamorous womanly version of herself on the big screen and knew, even back then, before she knew that a man named Bela Lugosi existed, that she wanted to be an actress.

It was never any more than a wild dream she used to think of in private moments until *he* came along, but she had always wanted to be like Clara, up there on the silver screen being looked at adoringly by a rapt audience. She wanted to be loved and cherished by legions, like Clara. And she wanted Bela Lugosi to worship her too.

And as she watched Clara on the screen she realized something – everything that had happened to her, everything she had gone through, each experience, each day, every hour, since that fateful night she turned on the radio and heard that voice, was *because* of Bela Lugosi. Each move she made was a step toward him- going to Portland, leaving home, heading for Hollywood - all of it, had been to bring her to *him.*

She could say none of these things about Vivant. He happened across her by chance and stole her life. He gatecrashed his way into her existance. Without a fleeting thought for her, for her dreams and aspirations, without knowing anything about her as a person or about her life, he changed *everything* for her. He changed what she thought was her destiny. He made sure she could never have what it was she longed for, hoped for.

Her head hurt; fast and furious thoughts raced through her mind. She didn't want to think any more. She just wanted to sit here, quietly, not thinking, not feeling anything, except the power of the images on the screen.

Belladonna sat engrossed in the movie. There were a few other people in the audience and some of them did a double take when they saw her. She heard people whispering in the dark. And she heard their private thoughts - *Is it her? No, can't be. It is! It's her! Naw, she's in the nut house, ain't she?* They debated with themselves and each other whether or not she was Clara Bow. She was flattered and irritated at the same time, but mostly indifferent. She was watching *It.* They could just gossip amongst themselves. The movie was more important right now.

Sweet Santa Claus give me him!

She wondered about Clara. Thought how she must be an incredible woman, an exceptional person to capture the heart of Bela Lugosi. And Bela – what a truly exceptional man he must be, to have made a woman who was once America's greatest movie star, loved and lauded and adored by so many, fall in love with him.

But there were things that Belladonna didn't know, things she didn't know about Clara and about Bela. She didn't know that Bela's passions could become obsessive; he still worshiped Clara and he always would. She didn't know that he'd even had a marriage fail because of his obsession with Clara. The marriage was over in four days.

She knew that he still loved her. He'd brought her to tears at the sight of him weeping over Clara's photograph. She could see that he still felt pain at the loss of her love. And she realized that, no matter how wonderful she herself was, or how much she loved him, or how well she treated him, she may never be anything more than a substitute Clara Bow.

Belladonna knew that she loved him enough to give it a try. But she didn't want to live in the shadow of *the It girl* forever.

Belladonna climbed the hillside. She'd been walking for hours since leaving the movie theater.

The early morning dew on the grass soaked her ankles through her stockings making the skin itch beneath the sheer material. She hiked on, listening to the turmoil of her thoughts and the thundering of her heart inside her chest. There was just one place she needed to be right now, one place that would clear her mind and bring her a little calm to the storm that raged inside her head. She needed to be near it. To touch it. The Hollywood sign.

She rested her cheek against the cool metal or the letter H and just breathed. Then the tears came.

She cried, wailed, unabashed.

"What the hell happened to me? What happened to my life?"

She choked out a laugh through the tears and the lump in her throat.

"I should have stayed in the boonies or gone traveling with the Wild West show again."

She wiped her nose on the back of her hand and dried her tears with the sleeve of her jacket.

"I was a dab hand at trick shots. The best. I don't belong here. I don't belong anywhere."

"Yes you do; you belong with me."

Belladonna snapped her head around to see Vivant standing behind her. He looked so beautiful. His concern for her, his fear of losing her had erased his permanent air of arrogance and superiority.

"Where did you come from?"

"I've been with you most of the day. I was in the movie theater too. I knew you'd go there and when I saw *It* was playing. I know that's one of your favorites. You look a lot like her, you know? Have you made up your mind yet?"

"Made up my mind?"

"Well, have you?"

"Yes. I've made up my mind." she said.

Vivant moved toward Belladonna, slowly, almost as if he was afraid of making her bolt.

"Are you going to tell me? Put me out of my misery?" he smiled at her. But his smile faded when she didn't return it. He knew that her decision hadn't gone the way he wanted it to. He knew that Belladonna had chosen Lugosi.

"It's not you. I've chosen Bela.

Belladonna was waiting for Vivant to start ranting and raving at her about how ungrateful she was, what a selfish bitch she was, about how she was betraying him after all he had given her. But Vivant was silent. She cast her eyes downward, unable to look him in the eye. When she looked up again, he was gone.

CHAPTER SEVEN : LOST IN HOLLYWOODLAND

Cal wandered the streets of Hollywood searching for Belladonna's apartment. He kept looking down at the crumpled scrap of paper in his hand as if, somehow, a map of the route he needed to take would suddenly appear. The more he wandered, the more lost he became.

Cal had thought that Hollywood was some sort of a tiny village where movie stars lined the streets and the only cars on the road were stretch limousines filled to bursting with the rich and the beautiful and the successful. But it wasn't like that at all. It was huge and he was lost.

The streets were not filled with movie stars, nor the roads teeming with *only* expensive cars. There were old bangers on these roads too – beat up old pickups driving through what was once sage-brush and sand and a dirt track.

And there wasn't a movie star in sight.

He asked an old man for directions but he was so far away from where he needed to be that he couldn't remember everything he'd told him. He decided to follow them as far as he could remember and ask somebody else when his memory ran out.

His legs ached. This was a worse walk than coming home from the illicit still clear across town back in Independence. He walked until he got to the last direction he could remember.

His head filled with fresh directions, Cal carried on. Much closer now he kept moving even although he was tired and hungry and all he could think of was something to eat and a comfortable bed. He longed for his bed back home. And he was missing mom's cooking already. It had been half a day since the food Morag packed for him ran out and he'd not eaten since. He hoped that Belladonna was home when he finally reached her apartment and would make him a home-cooked meal, just like mama makes.

"Darn it, how big is this town? I musta gone clear across it and back again," he told nobody except the night air. It was rapidly growing dark and he'd been lost enough in the light.

And then he saw the street sign that read the same as his wrinkled piece of paper. Now all he had to do was find the building and the apartment and the first part of his mission would be accomplished.

The harder part would be persuading Belladonna to come back home with him.

Cal eventually found Belladonna's old apartment. All the girls there, apart from the one who had taken her place, knew her and asked him if he knew where she was – none of them had heard from her from her in months. But they'd heard rumors about her.

The girls fussed and giggled around him. They made Cal a meal with what little they had in the kitchen, even although it meant they may go hungry tomorrow. But this was Belladonna's brother, and if the rumors were true – that she was hanging out with the big wigs of Hollywood and dating a major producer who was about to give her a starring role opposite Clark Gable – then perhaps Cal, if they treated him right, could put in a good word for them. Perhaps they could even land a part in a movie if they played their cards right.

They all stood in the kitchen – Rose, Catherine, Anna and Elizabeth. They bickered in animated whispers, fighting over which one of them was going to sleep with him first. Rose argued that she should have first shot at him – she'd been the one to bring Belladonna into the apartment in the first place so none of this would be happening if it hadn't been for her anyway.

But Elizabeth disagreed – she was the closest to Belladonna, and they were both huge Bela Lugosi fans so she should be the one to have him first. The other three thought this hilarious.

"What the hell kind of reason is that for sleeping with somebody's brother, Lizzie? Who cares what movie stars both of you like?" Rose asked her.

"It's a fine reason. Just fine. It's as good as yours," she snapped back at her.

Anna, a little more sensible and a little less of a slut than the other three rolled her eyes at her roommates.

"Maybe you should let the poor guy decide who he's gonna pitch woo with. Really, ladies, you have the morals of alley cats. And if you're gonna throw it around, at least make sure you've got a real good reason to throw it in the first place."

"What d'you mean?" Catherine asked.

"I mean you're all willing to sleep with some guy who just walked through the door on the off chance a rumor or two about his sister *might* be true. Don't you have any respect for yourselves?" she directed the question at all three of her roommates, looking from one to the other, expecting an answer.

Rose was the one who answered her.

"I used to have self respect, but I left most of it on the casting couch."

Catherine sighed.

"And where did it get you? You're standing in the kitchen of a broken down apartment no further along than you were when you got here. How long ago was that, Rose? *Too* long. Time you learned to think with an organ above your waist."

Rose had no reply. She knew that Catherine was right. She'd whored herself to nowhere. All she was known for in the lower end of Hollywood was being an easy lay. Easiest lay in the business. She went to every casting call there was going in her desperation to *make it,* but she knew what all those so-called directors and producers wanted. And she always yielded, she always let them do whatever they wanted to her, just in case.

Nausea suddenly gripped her gut. There was no chance for her here anymore. There was no hope of her dreams coming true, no matter who she slept with and the more she put out, the less her chances became. But she *had* to hope. It was all she had and if she didn't have that she might as well be dead already.

Her face burned with shame. She knew what she thought of other women in Hollywood who did what she did, day in day out. She called those women *whores*.

How can I keep doing this to myself? What am I doing? Why couldn't I see it? Why?

She ran from the kitchen and smacked into Cal who was on his way there to ask if there was any more food. She landed on her ass on the cold kitchen tiles. Elizabeth giggled. Catherine and Anna didn't. They both knew that Rose had just suffered an epiphany and landing on her ass in front of a devastatingly handsome stranger just added insult to injury.

Hot tears began falling from her eyes, the salt stinging her already scarlet cheeks. Her ego was in tatters, her self esteem non-existant. She wondered what had ever possessed her to come to this place. She wondered what ever made her think she could be an actress, knowing that she had no discernible talents apart from lying on her back with her legs in the air.

That's all I'm good for.

I might as well go all out and stand on a street corner with all the other whores. At least it would be a living. At least it would be more honest than pretending I'm not a Goddamn whore.

Cal held out his hand to her to help her up. He was gorgeous – muscled the way most country boys are – in all the right places, with fair skin and blue eyes and a full head of thick, wild blonde hair.

Maybe just once more. For old times' sake.

Rose could always turn over a new leaf some other day. This might just be the one who could help her on her way. Again. And there were so many things she could show this country boy. There was a whole world out there that he knew nothing of and she could show him the sights and the sounds of the big city.

Vivant sat on the end of his bed poking at the floor with the toe of his boot like a sulky little boy. He hated feeling this way. He hated Belladonna for choosing Lugosi over him and wondered what was wrong with him that she had. Women fought over him. Women destroyed their own marriages for the love of him. Women had even died for him. But her – she was different. The feisty little bitch had got to him in ways no other lover ever had. He'd never experienced the things she had made him feel – not even with Valentine. Vivant knew he had met his match, his soul-mate, the one. And he'd lost her. Just like he lost everybody he ever cared for.

"Belladonna, you little bitch."

He smiled, forlorn smile that showed his worldly weariness. He'd done everything. Seen everything. He'd seen ages. He'd seen history. He'd witnessed the rise and fall of empires. He's seen the birth of civilization. All that was left to experience, to cherish, was love. He'd been so long without it that when it came to him, when he scooped it up in his arms that night, he'd not even recognized it. And when he had, it was too late.

As always, Vivant ended up alone. Usually by choice. But this time he'd fought and lost the battle. But what was bothering him was his indecision. He wanted her back, of course, but he could not decide whether or not to fight for her. He had to decide what mattered more to him – his ego, his pride, or what Belladonna wanted.

For some inexplicable reason, Belladonna hadn't thought that there may be a woman in Bela's life. She knew about Clara, of course. But that relationship had been over for some time. She knew about Bela's first wife back in Hungary. She knew how he loved her very much and always called her *baby* because she was so young when they married - just sixteen - almost a child. She knew how she had been from a rich society family and her parents were disapproving of the actor and his Bohemian lifestyle traveling with theater companies, not having a steady job. And she knew he's been very briefly married to an American woman, for a matter of days a couple of years ago. But it didn't occur to her that he was in a relationship, in the here and now, until she saw the young woman in his arms through the window and she stood there, once more, looking in.

She froze. Her breath caught in her throat and her lungs burned.

She watched as Bela kissed the young woman – a passionate kiss between two people very much in love.

Her guts heaved, twisted inside her as if trying to wrench themselves free. She turned away from the scene, nausea washing over her as she clutched a hand to the pain between her guts and her heart.

No. It can't be. It can't be.

Her head was spinning. Everything was ruined now. There was somebody in his life, another woman – somebody he must have been madly in love with to kiss her in such a way. She could see the passion, she could see the love, the bond between them.

She wandered off down the street, staggering like a drunk, ignoring the people passing her and laughing because they thought that's what she was. She didn't even see them. She couldn't see anything for the tears in her eyes.

Everything was ruined now. Her life was in tatters. Her plans to be an actress had been dashed because Vivant turned her into a vampire. And all of her plans for she and Bela to be together, to live happily ever after in that beautiful Gothic fairytale she had all worked out in her head, had turned to dust.

"I might as well be fucking dead!"

She laughed.

"But I can't even do that either!"

She stumbled down the street laughing hysterically.

"I can't even die! Vivant, you fucking bastard! I hate you!"

A curtain twitcher across the street peeked from behind ugly floral drapes; she dialed the operator and asked for the police.

Vivant, just like he'd done all those weeks ago when he first laid eyes on Belladonna, swept down from the night sky and plucked her from the sidewalk. She fought him, kicked his shins as hard as she could, dug her stiletto heels into his legs, elbowed him in the ribs. And she was strong. Vivant felt the blood trickling down his legs from the metal heel tips that had ripped through his flesh.

"What are you doing? Why did you do that? Why can't you just leave me alone?" Belladonna screamed at Vivant, her fury thundering in her chest and her temples. The blood raced through her veins. She wished there was a way to kill Vivant and if there had been she would have done it at that moment.

"Leave you alone? That old hag across the street with the bad curtains was calling the police," he said.

"What? So?'

"Oh, you'd like to be cooped up in the jailhouse for a few days and not be able to feed, would you? And, if your nature got the better of you and you killed somebody while you were in there, how does twenty years behind bars sound?"

"It sounds just swell, Vivant – you wouldn't be there."

Vivant dramatically clutched his chest as if his heart was wounded by her words.

"You're just sore because I'm always coming to your rescue, that's all. You just can't admit you need me."

Vivant turned away and grinned, knowing that her fury and exasperation would be written all over her face without even looking at her.

She hated him with a passion. She hated him wholly and completely and wanted nothing more than to hurt him, make him suffer, more than she had before.

But there was nothing she could do to him. Anything she did would last for a few seconds and then he'd be back to his old self again. He was untouchable. She was unable to have her revenge and this fact only made her even more insane with anger.

She was helpless.

Utterly helpless.

Vivant had won the war.

Belladonna was lost. For days she stayed in bed, sometimes crying, sometimes screaming at the walls. This was it – this was her life and it was to last for all time. There would be no end for her, there would be no relief. She would have to suffer through eternity being unfulfilled, living what was laughingly called a *life* and hating every second of it. She had forever to ponder her mistakes and her regrets and no way, ever, of undoing them. And Vivant would be there to sneer and smirk his way through the decades at her.

Belladonna was in Hell.

And Vivant was out there being worshiped, as usual.

STARDUST

Vivant stood in the center of the circular stage looking down on his adoring fans.

Young men and women, not even of age to be in a once-legal drinking establishment were all together too young to be in this one.

They stood gazing at him whilst he sang his own rendition of the ever-popular song, *Stardust.*

> *And now the purple dusk of twilight time*
> *Steals across the meadows of my heart*
> *High up in the sky the little stars climb*
> *Always reminding me that we're apart*

One girl in the front row dramatically raised the back of her hand to her brow before she swooned and landed in the arms of her extremely bemused boyfriend.

> *You wonder down the lane far and away*
> *Leaving me a song that will not die*
> *Love is now the stardust of yesterday*
> *The music of the years gone by*

Daisy stood in the front row, right under where Vivant was singing his heart out on stage.

She was mesmerized by him, staring unblinkingly lost in a world populated by only herself and him.

Her dark eyes bored into him, willing him to look at her – and he did.

She struggled to hold her composure and not pass out. If she lost consciousness she might miss her opportunity to meet him after his performance.

Other girls who had met him in the flesh told her how strange he was, but they couldn't remember what had happened exactly

All of them said the same thing.

She hoped that she would not forget when she finally met him.

Daisy wanted to remember the moment forever.

Thought I dream in vain
In my heart it will remain
My stardust melody
The memory of love's refrain

And he was singing *her* song. It was a sign, she knew it. She loved *Stardust* more than any other song in the whole world.

When she had first heard it there were no words, just a beautiful and melancholy tune composed by Hoagy Carmichael, that made her happy and sad at the same time.

Then a couple of years later Mitchell Parish added the tragically romantic lyrics and she fell in love with the song all over again.

But hearing this song, a song so special to her, being sung differently form any rendition she'd ever heard before, she knew that Vivant was singing it just for her.

A throng of fans ran after Vivant as he left the stage, all hoping that they would be the one invited into his dressing room for the evening.

A bouncer kept the throng of eager groupies at bay, barely.

As he reached the door he whispered in the bouncer's ear.

"I want the one who looks like Lillian Gish."

The bouncer grinned.

"Good choice."

And she *did* look like her. She had a hairstyle that was a decade or two out of date - loose and wild dark blonde ringlets with a little bow on each side. Her eyes were huge, dark, and her mouth was small. She looked like a China doll that would break into pieces if handled carelessly.

She looked much too young to be standing where she was standing, thinking what she was thinking.

The bouncer grabbed her by the arm a little roughly and escorted her into the dressing room.

The rest of the devotees stood looking at her, some with awe that she was *the chosen one*, some of them giving her dirty looks and wishing that she would drop dead on the spot and they would be picked instead.

"Well, hello there," Vivant said.

"Hello. I'm Daisy. I love you.."

Vivant smiled.

"You're certainly not shy, are you?" he said.

"No, I'm not. And you may be thinking that I'm very young, but I want you to know that I'm a woman and I know what I want. I want you, Vivant."

She saw the look on his face. It was a look of slight alarm. She had called him by his real name.

"How do you know my name?" he asked.

"I know more that that. I know who you are. I know *what* you are."

"Oh? What am I?"

"You're a vampire."

Vivant laughed, hoping that his mirth would make her feel foolish and think that she had made a grave mistake.

It didn't work.

"Daisy..."

"Please don't try to tell my I'm wrong. Please don't do that to me. I'm not some silly little girl or one of those over-amorous pansies who follow you around."

Vivant raised an eyebrow.

"Go on," he said. He knew she wasn't done yet.

"I've been watching you for a long time. Most of my life. I saw you kill my sister."

"Wait a minute, you must be mista..."

"Don't."

Vivant decided not to insult her intelligence.

He gestured for her to take a seat and handed her a glass of cold Champagne.

"I'm listening," he said.

Daisy sat down and took a tiny sip of the cold bubbly and told him her story.

Daisy's sister was a bit part actress in one of those old silent pictures Vivant used to be in.

Talulah was seventeen. Twelve years older than Daisy and they were thrown together against their wills. Their father had left long ago, just after Daisy was born – something Talulah and her mother both blamed Daisy for.

Their mother got sick – a complete mental breakdown – and was thrown in an insane asylum.

All Daisy and Talulah had was each other.

Daisy was nothing but a nuisance to her big sister. She would make her stay in the dressing room when she was lucky enough to land a walk-on part in a picture. But Daisy would get bored playing dress-up. She wanted to explore and she would wander off and roam around the whole movie lot.

The studio employees didn't mind – she was a sweet little kid and no trouble at all, but when Talulah would catch up with her she would smack her so hard it would make her dizzy.

"And one night the dressing room door was ajar. We were the only ones left in the building except for the night guard because it took Talulah half and hour to find me that time. I had made her late for a date. I was lying on the dressing room floor – she was beating me. She would have killed me if you hadn't stepped in when you did. You killed her. Drank her blood and then slit her throat just before she died, just so there was enough blood to make it look like a genuine, normal murder. You saved my life."

"That's quite a story, Daisy – I don't recall..."

"Vivant. Please. Don't insult me. I owe you my life."

She told him how she'd had a wonderful life. How she was adopted by a mother and father who could not love her more if she was their own flesh and blood. And she had a sister and brother who also adored her.

But even with all the love and the affection, the wonderful life that she had, something has always been missing.

Tears welled up in her eyes.

"And what's that?" he asked.

"You, Vivant. You. Everything I have, everything I am, I owe to you. And I've never had the chance to thank you."

"Well, I disagree. I think everything you are you owe to yourself. You had a bad start in life. And you overcame it. You give me too much credit – all I did was what's in my nature to do – kill."

She agreed, but told him the fact could not be changed that had he not done what he did, they would not be standing here now arguing the semantics.

He smiled at her. He liked this funny kid. She was smart and bold. Just like Belladonna. He wondered how she might feel sharing him should he decide to take this little waif into their lives.

"I'm getting married in one week. He's a kind-hearted man and he adores me, and I know we will have a wonderful life together," she said.

"So, what do you want from me?"

She looked at him, looked so deeply into him, almost as deep as a vampire can look.

"Just one night. That's all I ask."

He stretched out his hand to her and she took it, he pulled her to him.

"Then you shall have it."

"One more thing. I want you to drink my blood."

That was something Vivant would have no problem doing at all.

He gestured for her to come closer to him. She obeyed and walked slowly across the room, never breaking eye-contact. She was immersed in his intense eyes.

Her heart pounded in her chest and she felt wet heat spreading between her legs.

He grabbed a fistful of her hair at the back of her head and pulled it to one side, exposing her neck.

Her jugular vein throbbed and he heard her breathing begin to labor.

He could smell the innocent blood inside her.

"I love you," she gasped, and pulled his mouth to her throat.

The stab of keen ivory made her gasp; such intense pain for a heartbeat, then the incredible sensation of ribbons of her blood being pulled from her body and into his mouth.

It was like nothing on earth.

And she knew that after this night, she would never experience anything like it again.

A single tear rolled down her rosy cheek and she wished that she could die right now. For she would die truly happy.

She held on to him, so tightly Vivant felt like she was trying to seep inside him.

He felt his own blood rise and pulled back from her for fear of getting carried away and draining her dry.

She was gasping now, her need close to destroying her.

She had to feel him inside her. She needed this. She could not go on and live her neat, sweet little life with Mr. Normal unless she could have this one night, this one thing that was for her and her alone, the thing that would keep her wet and warm at night for the rest of her life.

She was weeping, her body shaking with desire.

And Vivant didn't have the heart to deny her.

She did not resist him undressing her and didn't try to hide her nakedness. She was beautiful. Young and pink and supple.

And she had waited her whole life for this night.

Vivant inhaled her scent as if savoring the bouquet of a fine vintage wine.

He stopped and looked into her eyes.

"You're untouched."

"Of course I am. I've been saving myself for you."

He mercilessly stabbed into her tight pussy and felt the heavenly sensation of her starting to bleed.

"Waste not, want not," he said and disappeared between the soft pink skin of her thighs.

Her mouth opened. Her eyes widened and she involuntarily arched her back, needing to force Vivant's intimate kiss deeper.

She made no sound. She was mute with pleasure and unable to move anything except her hips which found an easy rhythm quickly.

Vivant was rising as far up to Heaven as she was. The pure, untainted blood of a virgin was a potent drug to a vampire.

He moaned his pleasure and reached up to touch her breasts but found her own hands already playing there.

And then she found her voice. First it was a squeak, quiet, small.

And then as the first wave of orgasm hit her she screamed, her body flooding with sensation.

And then she wanted more.

SNOW BIRD ROSE

Cal's head was spinning. He'd never drank Champagne before. The closest he'd come was some fizzy cider papa had brought home to celebrate the New Year with.

He hiccoughed. He belched. He snorted as the bubbles rushed up his nose. It was nothing like drinking moonshine. He wasn't sure if he liked it or not. But the girls certainly did. And they all showed their appreciation to the couple of swells who had bought it and shared it with them.

"This sure is full of fizz," he said.

"It's Champagne, dummy; of course it's full of fizz!," Rose told him and elbowed him in the ribs playfully. "I got something here that won't give you the hiccoughs or gas, big boy. Wait'll you taste this!"

She looked furtively around the club, wall to wall with flappers dancing manically to bad jazz played by drunken, drugged musicians. The room was filled with laughter, high pitched cackling, low-tone guffawing. Cal thought the revelers in the club were strange. They weren't like any drunks he'd ever seen before. Most of the ones he'd encountered were fucked up on moonshine, passed out in a ditch or throwing up in one. But these people were full of energy. They danced and laughed all night, non-stop. They made Cal feel dizzy.

He protested as Rose tried to drag him into the ladies powder room. He was scared of getting caught and thrown in jail for indecency. Again. It happened to him once, back home. Somehow, one night, he lost his pants on his way home and unfortunately, Officer Schwartz was passing by in his patrol car. It was such back luck – he only patrolled Independence once a month and nothing ever happened. He thanked Cal for being drunk and allowing him to make an arrest.

Men shouldn't go into the ladies room – that's why it's called a ladies room!

But Rose was too strong for him in his tipsy state and she managed to pull him in. She headed for a stall, dragged him by the collar and shut the door behind them.

"Here it is. The stuff I was telling you about. It'll make you feel plenty good, Cal."

"It will?"

"Sure. Sure,"

"How come it does that?" he asked her.

"Aww, gee, I don't know how come, Cal. I'm no scientist - I just know that it makes me feel like I've never felt before."

Cal watched, fascinated as Rose took a folded up piece of paper from her tiny bead-fringed purse. She unfolded the paper, tapped out a tiny mound on the back of her hand and snorted it up her nose. He watched her, fascinated, even although he really had no idea what she was doing.

His brows knitted together in confusion.

He looked at her. She looked back at him, puzzled by his expression.

"What?" she asked him.

"What's that?" he asked back.

"You don't know what this is? Damn, boy, you really are a rube from the country."

"A rube?"

Rose rolled her eyes.

"Are you pulling my leg? You are, aren't you? I knew it! I knew you couldn't be that dumb."

"I don't understand, Rose. What is it? What's the stuff you just sucked up your nose?"

"Jesus; you really don't know?" she asked, in disbelief.

"If I knew I wouldn't have asked. And I'm not dumb. What is it?" he asked her again, a little irritated now.

"It's cocaine. Try some. Come on, don't be a Mrs. Grundy! It makes you feel like you're…uh…invincible. Yeah, that's it – invincible! You *must* try it. Don't be scared. It can't hurt you. It's no worse than the little inhaler stick you like so much. Now hold out your hand."

Cal wasn't sure. He didn't really want to do it, but he didn't want her to think he was a dumb redneck from the back of beyond either. He knew what was on his hand was drugs and he knew they were a bad idea. But she was right about the little stick she gave him – the benzedrine he inhaled made him feel good. And it couldn't be that bad if you could buy it in any drugstore, he figured.

He held out his hand, palm up. She snickered and turned it around and tapped out some more of the white powder near the base of his thumb.

"Now do like I did – just put your nose over it and sniff it up there," she instructed.

"I don't know," he said.

"Don't know what, Cowboy?"

"Don't know if I should do that."

"Don't be afraid, Cal. I wouldn't let you do anything that could hurt you. Honest. It's just like medicine that makes you feel good," she told him.

Cal bit his lower lip, a habit he and his sister shared, and pondered it. He worried what she would think of his if he didn't do as she asked.

Just some rube from the country.

Even although he didn't know what a rube was, he knew that was what she'd think. And he didn't want to be a rube – whatever it was. Then he did it.

He inhaled the powder deeply and stood there, jaw slack and eyes wide, staring at Rose.

And then he smiled.

There was a momentary rush of blood to his head, a fleeting euphoria, and then what she said would happen happened – he felt so good. He felt confident. Invincible.

And all thoughts of finding Belladonna left him. Right now, she was forgotten.

Bela was having a bad day. He'd fallen out with Lillian, his assistant and lover. As he sat alone in his living room all he could think about was the strange girl that had visited him a little while ago and tore her own heart out of her chest.

He'd thought about her a lot. She was incredibly beautiful. She glowed. Her skin had a shine to it like the iridescence of moonbeams, but it was also warm and radiant. And her eyes were almost black, the irises indistinguishable from the pupil. She was ethereal.

A goddess.

Just like Clara.

My God, I miss her.

Bela rubbed at the pain in his legs; the sciatica caused by his World War I wounds tormented him today. He had already taken a shot of morphine, chased with a straight whisky. But he needed more. The pain just wouldn't cease.

Bela picked up his gun, a snub-nose .38 revolver, off the sideboard in the living room. He kept a firearm in every room, fully expecting some day that G-Men from the old country would come looking for him. He was a subversive, a rebel. He fought against the fascism that threatened to take over his country and eventually did. When he left his home he knew that he would never be able to return.

He sat down again and looked at the gun. Stroked the cold metal. He held it to his ear and listened to the metal clicks as he cocked it. Sometimes he thought about using it on himself, but mostly it was for protection. He felt safer knowing there was a gun no more than a few feet away wherever he was in the house.

He longed to see the crazy little girl who bled all over his lounge and showered him with her blood again. He knew wanting to see her was insanity, but he just couldn't get her out of his head.

So like Clara.

"But I'm not Clara. I'm Belladonna."

Bella snapped his head up to find her standing there in front of him, responding to the unspoken thoughts in his head. He stood up, grimacing at the pain.

"I know. I know. I hope you are not offended by my comparing you to her," Bela said, trying to smile.

"A little. But I'll get over it. I just want to be wanted for who I am, not for who I look like. I'm nothing like Clara Bow."

"Oh, but you *are*, Belladonna. You *are* like Clara. Very much," Bela said.

"I am?"

"Yes, you are. She does not, how do you say it – uh, take shit from anybody either?" he said.

Belladonna smiled, a tiny smile, barely there.

"Vivant gave me an ultimatum, Bela. He told me I needed to make a choice. He told me I had to pick you or him and that I couldn't have you both. But I guess we were both getting a little ahead of ourselves. I didn't know that you had a girl. It looks like you two are very much in love."

She cast her eyes down, not really wanting to look him in the eye and unwilling to hear his answer. But she knew that she had to hear it. She needed to move on with her life and she needed to know if Bela Lugosi was going to be a part of it. But she knew deep down what was the right thing for her. She knew that she and Bela were not destined to be together.

"Her name is Lillian. She's from a very well to do old Hungarian family. Her father does not approve of me. He thinks me too old for his daughter. Perhaps he is right. It is like history repeating itself. My first wife was very young and her parents did not approve of me either."

"Do you love her?" she asked, digging her nails into the palm of her hand.

"Yes, I do," he told her.

"Do you still love Clara?"

"I will always love Clara. Always," he said, a slight vibrato of emotion coloring his words.

"Do you think…maybe…" her voice trailed off, not sure if she really wanted to know the answer to her half-asked question.

"That I could love you? Yes, most certainly I could fall in love with you. Perhaps I already have," he smiled, knowing that her heart was breaking at that moment and trying to soften the blow for her. But the words he spoke were true. He did have feelings for Belladonna. Deep feelings he didn't quite understand since they didn't even really know each other. But there was something about her, something that could not be ignored, something that would not leave him from the moment they had met.

He felt the same way the day he met Clara Bow.

"I'm leaving now," she kissed the tips of two fingers and placed them gently on his lips.

The gesture grabbed him by the heart and the tears in her eyes, the sincerity in her gaze, made him wonder if maybe this was the right woman for him. There had only been one other woman in the world that could make him laugh or cry with a look. A woman he would love until the day he died.

And now, there was another one.

Bela pinched away the tears that had began to well in his eyes. He wanted to hold her in his arms, wanted to tell her that he had changed his mind, wanted to press his lips to hers in a passionate kiss.

When he looked up, Belladonna was gone.

Belladonna didn't want to go back to Vivant, not yet. She wanted to delay his inevitable gloating for as long as she could. She was sure he would know where she had been and would have heard everything that had been said between she and Bela.

Because he was *always* there. He heard *everything*, saw *everything*. Wherever she went now, the walls had ears...and eyes.

There was a club run by a local hoodlum she and her old roommates used to go to where they would drink illicit booze. The other girls would allow men to steal kisses, besides other things, for bottles of Champagne they paid a ridiculous amount for. They'd dance the night away. Sometimes they would even get money for dancing with rich older men. Rose would do more than just dance if the price was right.

Belladonna wondered what they were all doing and had a sudden urge to see them. She had feeling that they might be at the club, doing what they had always done, drinking, dancing and trying to find a sugar daddy in case the acting thing didn't work out in the end.

Belladonna walked through the doors of the piano store that was the cover for the speakeasy. The old doorman nodded to her and smiled, opened the concealed entrance. It opened on to a staircase which led to the belly of Los Angeles. There were miles and miles of subterranean service tunnels that connected the government buildings and the big hotels. He had a soft spot for her and gave her a wink.

"They're all here, Miss. Belladonna. Usual spot, having a whale of a time."

"Hello, Frankie. Thank you."

Frankie sighed as he closed the door behind her.

If only I was younger.

She knew exactly where they were and headed for the booth in the corner at the back of the club. It was sectioned off with a red velvet curtain. The noise was deafening as the squeals and laughter of the drunken patrons echoed off the stone tunnel walls.

She pressed on though the throng of bodies, feeling the heat from them as they danced maniacally to blaring bad jazz.

She tutted as she heard Rose's signature giggle and wondered who it was she was hanging on this time and getting to buy her drinks all night.

She pulled back the curtain and almost buckled at the knees.

There was Cal, sitting at the table with cocaine dust all over his face.

Everyone in the booth fell silent.

"Cal!"

"Oops," Cal said.

She turned from the booth and stormed through the red curtain, barged past all the revelers. She pounded on the concealed door after tearing up the stairs. She marched out of the piano store; Cal rushed after her calling her name.

"Bell! Wait! Hold on!"

She marched down the street, ignoring Cal who was running to catch up to her.

"Bell, what's the matter? Aren't you pleased to see me?" he asked her.

"Pleased to see you? What, with you head stuck in a bag of dope? Sure, that's just what I wanted to see!"

"I'm sorry. But it's OK. It's harmless."

"Oh, so, you're suddenly a man of the world and know it all, huh? You know why they call it dope? Because you're a dope if you use that stuff!"

"Aww, come on, Bell. Don't be angry with me. I'm just living a little. This place is amazing! My God, Rose is incredible. She's a real honey."

"Rose is a whore, Cal," she told him.

"Don't talk about her that way. She's not…that." Cal couldn't even bare to say the word.

'What else would you call a woman who takes money in exchange for sex?"

She stood, hand on hip, her mouth cruel as she spat the words at him.

"Well, I'm waiting for an answer. What would *you* call a woman like that?"

"I don't know. She doesn't do that. She doesn't!" he said.

"Christ, Cal, of all the girls in LA you could have fallen for, you had to fall for her. She's no good, I tell you. No good."

She could see the hurt on his face and she knew that he had fallen hard for her. She could kill her for corrupting her brother.

"That no good, dirty…"

"Bell. Never mind all that right now. Where have you been? Mama and papa have been sick with worry. You never write any more. That's why they sent me down here to find you and take you back home. What happened?" he asked.

She laughed.

"I don't even know where to begin. And if I told you the whole story, you would never believe me in a million years. And I'm not even going to try with you in this state. She pulled a small card out of her purse.

"Here. My address and phone number. Come over when you can bear to pry yourself away from *Snow Bird Rose*."

She turned to leave and he stood there looking at the card. When he looked up again, she was gone, as if she'd disappeared into the night.

Belladonna was worried about Cal. Rose was the last person in the whole of Hollywood she would have wanted Cal to get involved with.

Rose was into everything. She'd take any drug or drink she could get her hands on. She went blind for five days straight back in '29 after drinking some bad moonshine. An old friend from back home brought it with him when he moved to Hollywood to be an actor. Rose had written to him and told him what a wonderful and glamorous life she was leading an that he would be seeing her on the big screen real soon. She told him she would never, ever come back east again.

He died in a back alley three months later, selling his ass for drug money.

That was long before Belladonna's arrival, but she was terrified Cal was going to end up the same way. Rose's old friend from back home wasn't the first corpse to turn up around her. He wasn't the last either.

Belladonna got up for her reading spot at the fireplace to answer the loud rap on the door.

"Took me forever to find this place after you ran out on me, sis."

She gestured for him to come in.

She came back into the living room with Cal.

"Bringing your tricks home now, are you," Vivant said.

"Hey, whose the wise guy, Bell?"

"Vivant, this is Cal, my brother," she told him.

"Well, well, well. Pleased to meet you, Cal. I'm Vivant."

"I'd appreciate it if you didn't talk to my sister that way, Mister. She's not like that. She's a good girl."

Vivant laughed.

"You have no idea what the woman standing next to you is capable of, Cal. No idea whatsoever. She's not the girl who left Middle of Nowhere, Oregon a few months ago. Not the same girl at all. Are you, darling?"

"No, I'm not. I'm nothing like her."

"See, Cal, she even talks about the old Belladonna as if she were somebody else."

Vivant looked at Belladonna who was frowning. He could hear her thoughts.

What the hell am I going to tell him?

"Just tell him the truth."

"I wish you wouldn't do that," she said.

Vivant grinned and sat down by the fire again. He was looking forward to this little show. And Belladonna squirming about what she was going to tell her brother delighted him.

"So, tell me, Bell. What have you been up to? Why did you stop writing to mama? She thinks you're dead, you know."

Vivant giggled.

"Shut up, Vivant."

"How is that funny?" Cal asked him.

"You have no idea," he said.

"Sit down, Cal," Belladonna said.

"What I'm going to tell you is the absolute truth, OK? Don't tell me you don't believe me, because every word I'm going to say to you is true," she said.

"OK," he said, frowning, puzzled.

"One night I was walking home from a casting call. I was tired, furious at the way the last casting director had treated me. I was ranting and raving to myself. And Vivant saw me. And he...*changed* me. *Forever.*"

"OK." Cal said, more confused that he had been before she started explaining.

"Vivant is a vampire, Cal. He turned me into one too," she said.

Cal looked at her. He looked at Vivant. A smile started on his lips, slowly growing and burst into a laugh.

"Cal, I told you everything I was going to tell you was the truth."

He kept on laughing.

"Show him," Vivant said.

"Christ, not again," Belladonna rolled her eyes. "OK, there's only one way to prove it so brace yourself, Cal."

Belladonna did her usual parlor trick, she ripped her own heart out of her chest and showed it to Cal.

Cal stared at it. He look at her heart, looked at her and then back at Vivant again. Then passed out.

Vivant tutted and rolled his eyes.

"He's out cold. That must have been quite a shock; he'll probably be out for a while. If he's still alive. Is he still alive?" Vivant asked her.

Belladonna bent down and listened to see if Cal was still breathing. He was. She picked him up and carried him though to the bedroom. Cal was twice her size and it amused Vivant to see her picking him up as effortlessly and throwing him over her shoulder, as if he were a child. She laid him on the bed and gently closed the door behind her.

"Yes, he's still alive," she said, "I hated doing that to him. But there was really no other way to show him. He'd never have believed me."

"I guess not. Not the sort of thing you expect to hear from your sister, really, is it? Were those traces of coke on his face? Looked like cocaine."

"Yes, it was dope. I can't believe it. My own brother's a hop head."

"Well, his sister's a vampire. I'd call that even, wouldn't you?"

Vivant laughed and nudged her in the ribs, but she was in no mood for his jokes. Telling Cal she was a vampire was one thing. Telling her parents was another. She figured the heart trick would probably kill her mother.

'Where did you go earlier?" Vivant asked her, innocently as he could.

"You mean you weren't following me? That would be a first," she said.

"I went to see Bela. Twice, actually. The first time he was passionately kissing a girl in his living room. The second time was to say goodbye."

"Say goodbye?"

"Yes, Vivant, say goodbye. I don't want to talk about it any more, OK. Bela Lugosi is not part of my life any more. He never was. Happy?"

He didn't say a word but he *was* happy about it. Perhaps with Lugosi out of the picture she might come to love him the way he thought she should. The way he thought everybody should love him.

Cal groaned from the bedroom and staggered through the doorway.

"Bell, I'll save you," he said, one of Vivant's guns in hand.

"Cal, no. Don't shoot him. You can't kill him. He's not human. Neither am I."

Cal swayed, his vision blurry, wondering which of the three Vivants in front of him he should aim for.

Cal pulled the trigger…once…twice…three times.

Vivant didn't even flinch as one of the three rounds fired struck him in the face, tearing through his right cheek, shattering his teeth and his lower jaw. He stood there, looking at Cal with a truly one-sided smile.

Cal began to heave, stumbled forward and vomited all over Vivant's shoes.

Now he was angry.

He tried to tell Cal he paid a fortune for the shoes, but his lack of jawbone and support for his tongue made the words sound like an alien language. The sound of his altered voice, the hideous sight of him, appalled Cal and it was more than he could take in one night. He began to laugh hysterically, cry, scream. And then he fell silent, fascinated and repulsed at the same time, as he watched the damage he had done to Vivant's beautiful face begin to repair itself.

He could not avert his eyes as he watched new teeth grow in a matter of seconds to replace the ones which crumbled under the force of the bullet. He was in awe as he witnessed bone and sinew renew and reconnect, the skin form once more over his perfect skull.

"Well?" Vivant asked once he'd finished healing himself.

Cal looked at him blankly.

"W...w...well, what?" he stammered, his voice vibrating with fear and wonder.

"Aren't you going to apologize for vomiting on my shoes? I'm not impressed," he told Cal.

"Your shoes? You want me to apologize for ruining your shoes?"

"Yes, Cal, that would be the civilized thing to do."

Cal looked at him with incredulity. He'd just shot half his face off and wanted him to say he was sorry for spewing on his shoes.

"I'm sorry I upchucked on your shoes," Cal said, waiting for some heinous retribution to come his way for shooting Vivant in the face.

"Apology accepted," Vivant said.

Cal stood open mouthed as Vivant smiled and walked by him and into the bedroom.

Cal looked to Belladonna for some reassurance, some explanation for what must surely be some sort of trickery.

"Now do you believe me?"

He opened and closed his mouth, fish-like and mute, no words tumbling from his quivering lips as his mind raced and tried to accept what he had just witnessed.

"Never mind. Just you get some sleep and we'll talk about this again later, OK?"

"I gotta get home, sis – Rosie."

"Never mind her for one night, alright? We have important things to talk about tomorrow, things that can't be avoided. Don't worry about Rose; I'll call over there and let her know you're OK and you're spending the night here."

Belladonna took his arm and led him though to a guest bedroom. Cal twisted around and looked behind him, staring at the spot where Vivant had stood with his ruined face and fixed it at will, like magic.

Belladonna sat by the fire and rubbed her hands together, enjoying the warmth coming from the flames and the comforting glow of the embers. It reminded her of sitting around the fire at gramama's house. They'd sit up late into the night as the wind howled outside and snow piled itself high on the window sill. Gramama would tell Belladonna ghost stories from her home, tall tales of old Scotland and the spirits and beasties that dwelt there.

She loved listening to her thick Scottish brogue. It was like music to Belladonna, an accent that seemed born to tell stories of ghosts and ghouls and goblins in a far off land she'd never seen.

She wondered if Cal would be able to handle what he had seen tonight. She was worried in case it had ruined his mind, damaged his sanity. She knew he was a strong, healthy man – a strapping lad – but she wasn't sure if tonight – all he had heard and seen – would be just too much for him to bare.

Vivant sat down by the fire and wiggled his jaw back and forth, pushing on it from the side.

"Good as new," he said.

Belladonna eyed him suspiciously.

"Why aren't you ranting and raving like a madman?" she asked.

"Why should I be? They're only shoes. I have dozens of pairs. I mean, I really like these, but..."

"I'm not talking about your shoes! Cal just shot you in the face. Aren't you going to kill him, or something?"

Vivant laughed.

"Kill him? Why on earth would I do that?"

"Aren't you mad at him?"

"No, not really. I probably deserved it. I *did* turn his sister into a vampire?"

"Are you alright? Did that bullet lodge in your brain?"

"Such a kidder. No, darling, it didn't. I'm in rude health, as usual. Apart from being dead, of course."

Vivant grinned at her and she couldn't help but turn her lips up in a slight smile. Sometimes, his sarcastic charm was irresistible to her. She'd always found that attractive; in Vivant, it was divine.

Vivant gestured with a nod for her to come to him. And she did. She sat at his feet resting her head on his thigh and curled her arms around his calves. She closed her eyes and smiled as he stroked her black silk hair and bent down to kiss her ear.

She heard him intake breath as if he was going to say something. She opened her eyes, waiting.

"Were you gonna say something?"

He was silent.

She sat up.

"Vivant?"

She turned and looked at him.

He opened his mouth again and still stayed silent.

"What is it? What are you trying to say?"

He looked at her, searching her face and her psyche with all the powers he possessed, to see if it was the right thing to say, the right time to say it. His min was so full of uncertainty that she couldn't even make sense of his thoughts.

If there was ever a time, it was right this minute.

"I love you."

Belladonna's eyes grew wide, her mouth fell open.

"What?"

"I said...oh, never mind."

Vivant got up to leave, instantly regretting his words, hating himself for letting them slip from his mouth.

"No, wait."

Belladonna grabbed hold of his arm and stopped him from walking away, turned him back around to face her.

"I love you too," she said.

Vivant took her in his arms, held her so close, closer than she'd ever been held before.

"How could you?" he asked her.

"I don't know. I just do."

"Promise me one thing?"

"What's that?" she asked.

"You'll never stop fighting with me. I love our fights – they're spectacular. They're so full of life and passion. Just like you."

"Oh, brother. OK, I promise I'll always fight with you, I'll always hurt you and temporarily maim you with firearms. How's that?"

He grinned at her.

"Perfect."

Cal awoke. He bolted upright. He was drenched in sweat, frightened. He'd had a horrible dream where he'd shot a man in the face and watched the meaty wreckage reinvent itself into beauty.

A chill ran down his spine as he realized that what had happened a few hours ago was not a dream. It was real. And if that was real, if he really did shoot a man at point blank range with a semi-automatic pistol, an injury that would have been fatal to any human barring a miracle, then perhaps everything else that Vivant and Belladonna had told him was also real.

My sister's a vampire.

Li'll Bell's a bloodsucker!

Cal sprang out of bed and chased himself around the room, headless-chicken-style. He stubbed his toe on the dresser, fell over his own boots and got his feet tangled up in his clothes which he tossed onto the floor in a pile when he took them off.

What am I gonna do?

What am I gonna tell mama and papa?

"You really done it this time, Bell. Damn, I wish I had some dope. I gotta have a hit. I gotta have it."

Cal stood still, stopped staggering around and crashing about the room. He crept to the door and listened…

Silence.

He gently turned the door knob, bit his bottom lip as a slight creak escaped the hinges. He started creeping down the hall, tip-toed down the stairs, terrified that the sound would summon somebody, alert them to his presence.

He stopped.

They're vampires. They could hear me a mile away. Idiot.

"I could hear you further away than that, Cal," Vivant whispered in his ear.

Cal screamed like a girl and ran across the room, then ran back, then ran away again, leaving an amused Vivant behind him.

"Don't do that! You almost gave me a heart attack!" Cal yelled.

Vivant laughed.

"It's not funny."

"I'm sorry, but I've been listening to your little inner dilemma since you woke up. I couldn't resist. I'm sorry. Call it payback for my poor, unfortunate shoes."

"Where's my sister?" Cal asked.

"She's, uh, gone to dinner," Vivant said with a grin.

"Gone to din...oh...you mean...?"

"Yes. Don't fret about it. You'll get used to it eventually."

Cal looked at him.

"I'll get used to it? I'll get used to it! I'll get used to my sister being a vampire and drinking people's blood? I don't know where you come from, Mister, but where I come from that's not something you can get used to!"

"You eat meat, don't you?" Vivant asked him.

"Of course I do. What's that got to do with the price of tea in China?"

"There's really no difference. Food's food."

"You're telling me you don't see any difference in me eating a steak dinner and you eating a person?"

"Drinking their blood, Cal. Eating them would make me some sort of cannibal, since I used to be human. Or, technically, a ghoul, since I'm dead. That's quite disgusting."

Cal laughed. He shook his head, in utter disbelief at what he was hearing. He still wasn't one hundred percent sure that all this wasn't some elaborate joke on him.

"Cannibals are disgusting but vampires aren't?"

"That's right. There's no comparison between vampires and cannibals. That's ridiculous! Cannibalism is a savage, brutish tradition. Vampirism is much more refined."

"I must have gone whacky or something," Cal said, more to himself than to Vivant.

Cal sat down. His knees shook and knocked together. He gripped them with his hands to try and keep them still. Beads of sweat began to form on his brow and his skin took on a gray pallor.

"Belladonna said you've picked up a little bit of a habit since you've been in the big city," Vivant said. "Cocaine, was it?"

Cal nodded.

"It's not just cocaine though, is it?"

Cal shook his head.

"Benzadrine?"

Cal nodded, avoiding Vivant's eyes. He was suddenly very ashamed.

There was no point in lying to Vivant; he knew he could read his mind.

Vivant poured them both a large nip of whisky.

"Here; this isn't some gut-rot potion. This is the real stuff. Scottish," he said.

Cal's hands shook as he gulped down the nip. Vivant refilled Cal's glass and sat down.

"So, tell me your story, Cal."

RENTING CAL

Cal and Rose were fighting again. The sweetness of their love affair was short lived. Their romance was no match for each other's insatiable appetite for booze and drugs.

Their relationship was becoming more strained by the day. They were broke and Rose was whoring to make a few bucks just to buy the odd bottle of Bathtub Gin.

But Rose had an idea. She knew a sure-fire way for them to make some good, fast cash.

"We're gonna get thrown out of this dump if we don't pay up on the back rent. You have to do something! We need money, Cal. And besides, snow don't grow on trees, ya know," Rose told him.

"I know, Rosie. I know. But I can't do that. Please don't ask me to do that," he pleaded with her.

"Aw, you're all wet. What's the big deal anyways? Just close your eyes and think of me."

"Oh, my God; I can't believe this is happening to me. How did this happen to me?"

"How did this happen to you? How did what happen to you? You think you're something special, huh? You think you're better than me? Well, let me tell you something, buddy, you're nothing! You're nobody! You're just some stray I took in off the street 'cause I felt sorry for you; how d'ya like that?"

Rose's cheeks darkened as they flushed with furious blood. She was angrier than she had ever been. She was angrier with Cal than she was the day a washed-up Hollywood star spent the whole day abusing her in an hotel room and skipped out on her without paying. She was angrier with Cal than she was the day some low life stuck a gun in her face and robbed her of her whole week's earnings. Her eyes looked dark green instead of pale blue. He'd noticed that they changed color is she was feeling mischievous or lusty or if she was annoyed at something. But he'd never seen them this dark. They were like burnt emeralds, darkest green and her rage sparked behind them.

Rose figured that Cal owed her. She'd been kind to him. She'd showed him life in the city. She'd shared everything with him for the last few months. She'd fed him – food, booze, drugs, sex. They were in trouble now and he ought to take care of her, even if it meant selling his own ass for a change, instead of hers.

She sighed heavily.

"Look, Cal, honey, you get through the first time and you won't think twice about doing it again. It's easy. And think of the money. We can make some serious rubes if you'll just do this. Try it, Cal. Won't you try it, just for me?"

She did her big-eyed damsel-in-distress act. It looked bizarre as she stood there in a tattered night gown, her hair unwashed and uncombed, dark circles under her eyes, like a discarded doll in a dirty playground. But still, it had an effect on Cal and he began to apologize to her, although he wasn't quite sure what he was sorry for.

She had to talk him round. This was their only chance to get back on their feet again. Rose's days of using the casting call to obtain rich movie clients were over. Hollywood knew who she was. They knew she'd been involved in blackmailing a prominent actor a couple of years back. Nobody with any clout would touch her – not even for a half-price fuck. She could set up a John for Cal, by proxy, but she couldn't be directly involved. Blackmailing the actor was the worst thing she had ever done. Up until now.

And she wasn't twenty-one anymore. The toll of her lifestyle, her drug use, the drinking, had all taken their toll on her body and her mind and prematurely aged her.

But Cal didn't see the fine lines around her eyes and her mouth. He didn't notice the dark roots beginning to show since she couldn't afford to go to the salon this month and have them touched up. Rose had been around the block more than a few times and the map of her route showed on her face. He didn't see how dead she was behind the eyes.

And he couldn't see that all she wanted him for was her next hit. If she couldn't whore herself any more, she had to find somebody else to pimp out.

She pouted at him. Fluttered her eyelashes.

"Please, Cal, baby. Won't you do it, just for me?"

He sighed. His shoulders slumped as he admitted defeat, buckling under the weight of her phoney sweetness. He was no match for her expert cunning.

"OK. I'll do it, I guess."

Rose squealed and threw her arms around him, planted a huge kiss on his mouth. Cal just couldn't say no to her. And he knew they needed money – fast. If he didn't do this, there was no way they could make the money they needed in time to save them from getting throw out of their room. They owed three months back rent - $30, and the surcharge for being late to pay – another $5 per missed payment, and an extra buck-a-month for the upkeep of the building. He had no idea where they were going to get almost fifty bucks from if he didn't go through with it. And that was without any money to live on, without any money for food and essentials, like drugs.

As he saw it, if he wanted a roof over his head, food in his belly and coke up his nose, he had to do this. He just hoped that he could live with himself afterward.

Cal stood peering out the window, waiting for his client's car to pick him up. His guts twisted inside him. He was sick with nerves. He was scared of what he was about to do, but he was more scared of being laughed at, of not knowing *what* to do, not knowing *how* to do *it*.

He was scared the man might hurt him. He didn't know how it was going to feel. He was scared that he might die.

"I've got something that'll kill those jitters, honey," Rose said.

Rose took a small square of folded tin foil from her purse and handed it to Cal. He looked at it and then back at her; he had no idea what it was.

She tutted at him and took it back, opened it.

"Know what it is now?" she asked.

Cal cast his eyes downward, embarrassed at what he saw as his own lack of sophistication.

"It's heroin, dummy! You wanna Chase the Dragon with me?"

"Sure," Cal said, with no idea what exactly that entailed. "How did you manage to get it? We're broke."

"Don't ask," she said. So he didn't.

Rose pulled out a lighter that looked like a lipstick - which confused Cal even more until she took the top off - and began to heat the powder. It bubbled and sizzled like melted brown sugar. She took a glass tube from her purse and began sucking up the smoke. She held the smoke in her lungs and a dreamy, relaxed, far away look came over her face as she slowly exhaled.

"I promise ya, you'll feel just swell after a puff or two."

Cal didn't know what to do. He didn't want to do this. He wasn't homophobic – he'd never even knowingly encountered a homosexual – but he knew he wasn't one and didn't want to go out tonight and let some stranger fuck him in the ass.

He didn't want to be obsessed with the drugs she'd already introduced him too. He certainly didn't want to get involved with anything else.

The cocaine was kind of glamorous. Exciting.

The amphetamine made him feel alive, awake, invincible.

But this, this was different. It seemed dirty to him. It was brown. Messy. It wasn't snow white and clean looking like the cocaine. And it wasn't in a discreet little inhaler you could buy for less than a buck from any drugstore, like the benzedrine. He was sure that this one was worse. He had a bad feeling about it. A *very* bad feeling.

But right now he was in such a mess it was either do something to calm down, or take a header out the window and put himself out of his misery.

Cal took the glass pipe from her and sucked in a lungful of the vinegar-smelling smoke. His lungs immediately expelled the smoke in a fit of choking and coughing. His chest was on fire, his eyes watering as he gasped for clean, fresh air.

Rose grinned as she watched his face change from his choking rictus to a serene, peaceful look.

"Wow," was all he said and took another hit.

Cal tried as best he could not to appear under the influence. But the man in the black cap and white gloves standing behind the open door of the Limousine was a Hollywood chauffeur –

he'd seen it all. From A-list stars to uncredited extras and wannabes who almost made it, fall into his car in various states of intoxication.

The chauffeur didn't even blink as Cal tripped over his own feet and fell head first into the back of the Limo.

As they traveled to the Director's home, Cal's thoughts raced. He was on the verge of panic as his fear and apprehension ruined his high and stole his short-lived, drug-induced serenity.

His head started pounding and his guts twisted inside him.

Just think of the money. Just think of the money. It'd take me a year to make $200 back home working the farms. Just think of the money.

But he wasn't *really* thinking about the money. He was thinking about what he was going to have to do to *get* the money.

Do it for Rosie. And for the snow. Gotta get more snow.

And he decided, at that moment, whatever he had to do to, whatever it took to get the money he needed, he would do it. Do it for Rosie. And for the drugs. Mostly for the drugs.

Cal stepped out of the car, but not before finishing the glass of ice-cold Champagne that had been waiting for him. His first mouthful was too big a gulp and the bubbles stabbed his brain.

He walked the thirty feet from the secluded drive to the front door like a condemned man.

He looked back at the chauffeur still standing by the car and wondered if he knew what he was here for.

The driver knew, of course. It was not the first time he'd dropped off a friend for his boss. But he figured it was none of his business what he did in the privacy of his own home. He paid well, treated him kindly, and didn't look down on him. It was a pity he couldn't say the same for any of the other Hollywood types whose employ he had been in.

There was one star – an Oscar-winning actress - who used to whack him over the head with her purse if he spoke out of turn, or if his collar wasn't quite starched to her satisfaction.

He despised her and he refused to ever pay money to see one of her films. In fact, he wouldn't even watch one if he could see it for free. She was mean, rude, arrogant and paid shit.

The day he handed her his resignation, he considered telling her exactly what he thought of her. That was until she handed him an utterly glowing reference that couldn't have been more flattering if he'd written it himself. So, he decided to take the reference and run, keep his mouth shut. He was lucky to have any reference at all from her, he thought, never mind such a useful one. And he knew that if he did pop off at the mouth and tell her what he thought of her, she was influential enough, and vindictive enough, to make sure he would never work in Hollywood again. She wasn't worth destroying his own livelihood for.

Nope, none of my beeswax what the Mr. does. He's a swell guy. Real swell.

Cal tapped gingerly on the ornately carved front door, half-hoping that his knock would not be heard and no one would answer. But no answer would mean no money. No money meant no drugs, no apartment, and ultimately, no Rosie.

He rapped again, a little louder this time.

Cal heard footsteps on a tiled floor. Someone was coming.

His heart hammered in his chest. His mouth was dry and it was difficult to swallow. He ran his fingers around his shirt collar which suddenly felt tight.

The door opened. The man standing before him was not what he expected.

He was young. Very, very handsome, with a mop of floppy blond hair slicked back but too unruly to stay in place.

He held out his hand. Cal shook it.

"You must be Cal. I'm James. You can call me Jimmy. Everybody does. Come on in."

Cal stepped inside. He could smell the incredible aroma of some exotic dish cooking in the kitchen. It filled the air with a tantalizing scent that made his nose tingle and his mouth water.

"Ever tried curry, Cal? I love it. My chef is Indian. From Bangalore. He's the most wonderful cook. You hungry?"

Cal nodded and smiled. He realized that he was no longer afraid.

Cal and James sat at the table in the kitchen and waited patiently for Sanjay to dish up his ethnic delights for them.

"I despise formal dining. I'd much rather sit here in the kitchen. It's much more personal. The kitchen is the heart of every home, don't you think, Cal?

"I sure do. My family always sit and visit around the kitchen table," Cal said. "It's where our whole family lives, right there around the range. Always smells so good. Mama bakes her own bread and biscuits, cookies too. God, I love those cookies. She doesn't make them so much any more though, not since things went so bad and we're pretty much flat broke most of the time. We're kinda lucky though. All them poor Okies from the midwest, they've got nothin'. There's folks that are starving to death, right here in America! I would never have thought that would happen right here, in the greatest country on earth."

"I'm sorry to hear that. Things have been pretty bad for a long time. Hey, maybe things'll change though, huh? About time they did. It's funny though, the worse the economy gets, the poorer people get, the more they spend on motion pictures. Hollywood is booming."

Sanjay placed a sliver-domed serving dish on the table, followed by another and another. As he lifted the lids Cal smelled aromas like he'd never experienced before. The cook smiled as he dished up his delectable food, knowing it was so good is boss would be very pleased with him, as would his guest. He loved it when they initiated a virgin into the virtues of his Indian culinary delights.

Cal stared in awe at the strange food in front of him. There was an array of forks, knives and spoons arranged around his place at the table and he waited for James to pick up his cutlery first, just in case he picked up the wrong one and made a fool of himself.

James laughed.

"Damn. I never remember which fork is which or if I should be using a spoon. In fact, I really don't much care. Let's eat! And you can use any piece of silverware you want to, Cal." James winked at him.

Cal laughed and picked up the nearest fork and began to eat. His eyes grew wide at the explosion of new flavors bursting on his tastebuds.

"Good?" asked James.

Cal nodded in the affirmative but didn't stop eating to talk. James laughed, understanding, and went back to his own delectable plate.

James motioned for Cal to sit down on a plush, blood-red velvet sofa. He handed his nervous guest a huge brandy glass with a small snifter of liquor. Cal watched James as he rested the glass in the palm of his hand and swirled the dark amber liquid around, held it to his nose and inhaled the heady bouquet. He closed his eyes and savored the aroma.

"A fine brandy, Cal. Drink. Tiny sips."

Cal did as James had done and swirled the brandy around the glass and sniffed. He'd never tasted brandy before. It smelled intoxicating. He tipped the glass to his lips and took a sip.

"Hoo, boy! I bet it wouldn't take too much of this stuff to get a fella real drunk."

James laughed. This young man, so genuine and unpretentious, so *unHollywood* and totally unaware of his own innocent charm, was a breath of fresh air in his life.

Nobody ever seemed to talked to him without an ulterior motive. They were always, wannabe stars looking for a fast way into the industry, trying to sleep their way to the top. All he'd ever seen them doing is degrading themselves and ending up in the gutter. Although many made it following that principle, there were a thousand who did not for for each one who did.

"So, what brought you to Hollywood, Cal? You're not from around here," James asked.

"Up north, Oregon. Mama and papa sent me down here to look for my sister."

"Ah. I guess she came here to be an actress, did she?"

"She did! How did you know?" Cal asked, incredulous.

"Oh, just an educated guess," he smiled at Cal – he knew his incredulity was absolutely genuine. Cal's innocent charm captivated him.

"She came chasing down here to find some fella who's in horror pictures. You know, that vampire fella?"

"Bela Lugosi? Is that who you mean?"

"That's him! Bela Lugosi! I forget his name, but I know it when I hear it. She says she's gonna be in a movie with him. I think she's all talk," Cal told him.

"What's her name?"

"Belladonna."

"She any good?"

"Oh, sure. Yeah, she's a good little actress. Been in showbiz since she was knee-high to a grasshopper. Her and papa used to have an act in the Wild West Show. She'd sing and dance and shoot."

"Well, I'll be!" James laughed. "Sounds like a fun act. I'll tell you what I'll do...hold on a moment..." James went to a roll-top writing desk across the room and sat down, started scribbling on a piece of printed personal stationery. He came back and handed an envelope to Cal. "Give this to your sister. It says to drop by my office at the studio and we'll give her a screen test. My next picture just happens to star Bela Lugosi. How about that?"

"Really? Dang! How about that indeed! Thank you. Thank you so much! She won't let you down, I promise. You're gonna love her!"

Cal swayed a little as he left James's house and tripped in the doorway.

"Oops! Careful there, Cal."

Cal giggled, regained his equilibrium, then tripped again. James, just as inebriated as Cal, stood in the doorway giggling back at him.

The driver grinned and playfully shook his head. He nodded to his employer as he helped Cal into the back of the car.

"He's a nice fella, your boss. Real nice fella," Cal said.

"He sure is, Sir. Best I've ever worked for. I've worked for a lot of these Hollywood types and he's a gem," the driver said.

"We had a great visit. We talked and talked and talked. Ate some good food, drank some golden colored stuff that made me a little tipsy. That stuff's worse than the moonshine back home."

As if to prove his point he hiccupped.

The driver smiled and drove through the darkened streets of Hollywood.

Rose was pacing the tiny apartment when Cal tumbled in. She was not amused at his drunken state, mainly because she was stone-cold sober and sorely in need of a drink herself.

"Look at the state of you!"

She made a disgusted sound at him, didn't even ask him how it went and if he was alright before asking him where the money was.

"Where is it?"

"Where's what?"

"The money, you idiot! Where's the money?"

"Don't be that way, Rosie. Why are you so sore at me?"

She lunged at him, started rifling through his pants and jacket pockets, looking for his earnings. She pulled out a huge wad of cash, complete with an engraved, gold money clip - *with love...James*.

Rose looked at it and laughed loudly at him. She spoke in a mocking voice.

"Ooh, a little gift from your new boyfriend, huh?"

She continued laughing while she put on her coat and headed out the door to meet her dealer.

Cal sat alone in the sparse room. The way Rose when he came in the door hurt him. He was happy, excited and eager to tell her all about his new friend, Mr. James. But he'd have to wait for that since she flew out the door after she found the money in his jacket pocket.

He's such a nice fella. It's a sin the way people treat each other. Guy like that shouldn't have to sneak around with strangers and give them money.

Cal had barely finished his thought when he drifted off into a boozy sleep.

Cal awoke with a start as Rose returned, carelessly slamming to door behind her. Seconds later, muffled shouting drifted down from upstairs, accompanied by old Mr. Smith hammering the floorboards with his size fourteen shoe.

"Oops! Sorry Mr. Smith," Rose hollered.

"Shh, Rosie; you'll wake the dead. You're gonna get us thrown out of here."

"Aww, you're all wet. We'll only be young once, lover-boy. We'll be old and gray...or dead and cold soon enough."

"Don't say things like that."

Rose was being a complete bitch. Not a rare occurrence, Cal had found out over the last few weeks living with her. He supposed it was the drink and drugs, or lack of them at times. She was hot and cold with him. Either all shit or all sugar. Unpredictable. You could never tell which Rose was going to emerge at any one time. And she could turn on him in a heartbeat. He loved her, but sometimes he didn't like her very much.

She was all smiles now, doped up and full of giggles. It didn't affect him that way. It made him feel good. Made him feel confident, as if nobody on earth could touch him. It made him fearless.

"Sorry I ran out on you before – you know how it is. Hey, got something for you!"

Rose tossed a tiny bag of white powder to Cal. His face lit up and for the moment his new friend was forgotten.

Cal lay back on the tattered red satin pillow-cases that had once been Rose's pride and joy.

"Gee, Cal, I didn't even ask you how it went with the Director guy. How did it go?"

"Oh, it was swell. He's such a nice fella. I was real surprised. He's not like all those pills you've told me about. He didn't even want to – you know – do *that*. He just wanted somebody to talk to, you know? He's even gonna set my sister up with an audition for his next picture. Bela Lugosi's gonna be in it. Wait'll I tell her – she'll blow her wig!"

Rose bolted upright as if she'd been electrocuted. Ever-so-slowly she turned around to look a Cal. His smile slid off his mouth as he saw hate contorting her face. She looked so ugly to him at that moment.

"He's gonna do what?"

Her last word was almost indecipherable and ended up more a scream than a spoken word. She was furious with him and for the life of him he could not figure out why.

"Rosie, what's the matter? What happened, honey?" Cal asked.

"Don't you honey me! How could you? How could you?"

Her anger was so potent that she couldn't even articulate to him what she was so angry about. She huffed and puffed. Gritted her teeth at him. Looked at him with contempt.

"Rosie, what did I do?"

"What do you think, genius? Are you really that much of a dumb country boy that you really don't know why I'm so sore?"

"No, I don't. And I'm not dumb. Country boy, sure, can't deny that. I'm maybe even unsophisticated and old-fashioned to you, and maybe I don't talk pretty like all these picture types you're used to, but I'm not dumb. Don't don't call me dumb, Rosie. Just tell me what I did to make you so mad at me."

"You arranged an audition for your fucking sister! What about me? Why didn't you tell him about me? You were in the company of one of the hottest names in pictures in this whole Goddam town and you didn't mention me? God, I don't believe you! How could you do that to me?"

She was screaming at him again, her face scarlet with anger, a bruised-blue vein throbbing at her temple in time with her thundering heart. Her eyes were mad, her rage, feral.

"But I thought you just wanted to be with me now. I didn't know you still wanted to be in pictures. It wasn't like that. I didn't even mention Bell was an actress. He guessed it. I don't know how, but he did. And he offered to give her a screentest, out of the goodness of his heart."

She looked around the room, searching, then rushed toward a heavy glass ashtray her eyes rested upon.

"Rosie, don't throw..."

She picked it up and with a grunt of effort threw it as hard as she could in Cal's direction. Cal flung himself to the side and it smashed against the heavy brass bedstead.

She was sorry it didn't hit him. She wanted it to hit him, wanted it to hurt him. She wished it had hit him in his stupid head and maybe knocked some sense into that simple bumpkin brain.

She wouldn't forgive him for this. She couldn't. He could not have done anything worse than this. This was the ultimate affront to Rose.

She'd been slugging it out in this God-forsaken place for nearly ten years now. She'd gone hungry. She'd begged, borrowed, stolen.

She'd sold herself to put food in her belly and allowed herself to be abused for the remote chance she might make it up there onto that silver screen.

If the likes of Clara Bow could do it – a dirt poor kid from the New York gutter with a crazy mother and a pervert for a father – then why couldn't she? *She* didn't come from the gutter but she was as near as damn it to it now. She knew her time was running out. It wouldn't be long before her lifestyle robbed what was left of her looks and sucked the rest of the life out of her. Some days, it was a chore just to get out of bed. Some days even breathing felt like hard work.

She sighed. Her shoulders slumped. All the rage seemed to drain from her leaving her limp. She raised her head and looked at Cal, a look that showed him she was defeated, a look that showed him her soul.

"Do you know what I've done to stay in this town? Do you? Do you know how fucking low I've had to sink, the men I've had to sleep with, the things I've had to let them do to me just so I could stay here? Well, do you?"

Cal shook his head, letting her know the answer to her questions.

"Why? I don't understand, Rosie. Why does it mean that to you?" Cal asked.

"It just does. I don't know if I can even explain it. It...just *does*. I don't ever want to leave here. Wild horses couldn't drag me away from Hollywood. Take me away from this place and I would wither and die. It's my life. And no matter how bad things are, no matter how low I have to sink, I will never leave here. It's home. I won't leave. I'll die here."

She paused. Wondering how much she should tell him, knowing it would leave her vulnerable, it would let him further into her life, further into her essence, than she had ever let anybody in before. But as she looked at him, his wounded gaze, the confusion on his boyish face, she decided to blurt it out, get it out there and maybe the Gods who grant Hollywood wishes would hear it and make her dreams come true.

"You see...if I'm here, here in Hollywoodland, then there's always a chance that my dreams will come true. If I'm not here, they never will. That's why I stay. That's why I will always stay."

There were tears in Rose's eyes; they made her irises sparkle like dark sapphires. She knew her dreams would never come true. Truth was, she had no talent and she knew it. All she'd ever had was her looks, her charm. And as the former faded prematurely, the latter became less effective.

She was only twenty eight years old but had already been here for a decade. And that decade had been hard.

But she would never give up hope; she would sooner give up breathing. And she would never, ever leave.

Now Cal understood. And he also understood his sister. He knew that Belladonna felt the same way.

Cal burst into the penthouse without knocking, startling both Belladonna and Vivant. He was grinning broadly and waving an envelope at Bell.

"Good grief! Where's the fire, Cal?," Belladonna asked.

"You'll never guess in a gajillion bazillion years what I got in here."

"What is it?," Vivant asked.

He thrust the envelope toward Belladonna.

"Open it! It's for you!"

She frowned, then smiled, her curiosity piqued.

She opened the envelope and pulled out the piece of crisp, neatly folded paper and began to read.

Cal grinned as he watched her reading and started shuffling from one foot to the other in excitement as her mouth fell open. A tiny squeak escaped from her throat.

"Is this...," she began, afraid to finish the question.

"What is it?," Vivant asked again.

"Is it..."

"Real?," Cal finished her sentence for her. "It sure is, sis – realer than a real thing in Real Town!"

She ran at him, hugged him so hard he almost lost his breath.

"How?...How?," she asked, incredulous.

"Mr. James. He's a friend of mine," Cal told her.

"The director James Walsh is a friend of yours?"

"Yup," he said triumphantly.

"I can't believe it! Oh, my God!"

"Will somebody please tell me what the Dickens is going on," Vivant demanded.

"I've got a screen test, Vivant. I've got a screen test!"

"How the hell did you swing that?" Vivant asked, impressed.

"Well, I didn't really do anything; I just talked about you and he guessed you were here to be an actress and he said he wanted to give you a screen test. H said he wasn't promising anything, but if you can act and the camera likes you, he said he'd hire you for his next picture."

Belladonna swallowed hard.

"His next picture?"

"Uh-huh,"

"Are you *sure* he said his *next* picture?" Bell asked.

"Yup, he did. Why?"

"His next picture...," her voice cracked and trailed off, her eyes filled with shining tears.

Cal was nodding. He took both her hands in his and squeezed.

"If I recall, James Walsh's next picture is to star that foreign horror hack," Vivant said.

Belladonna was not about to let Vivant rain on her parade. She started squealing and she and Cal jumped up and down, beside themselves.

Vivant rolled his eyes.

"*So* uncouth."

Belladonna's guts were eating themselves as she sat, rigid, in an extremely uncomfortable chair waiting to be called for her screen test.

Oh, my God. Maybe I'm delusional and I can't really act at all! What if I make a total twit of myself? Oh, Lordy. This is gonna be a trip for biscuits!

She was beating herself up so badly inside her own head she almost didn't hear her name being called.

"Belladonna Busto?," the casting director's assistant called.

She shot out of her chair and declared "That's me!"

"This way, please, Miss. Busto," the woman smiled and led the way, held the door open for her then closed it behind her. She felt like a Christian being thrown to the lions.

She wanted to run but her determination would not let her feet move, despite her flight instinct. *This* was the reason she was here, in *this* town.

This is what she had always wanted. And now, in the moment she'd been waiting for, she had to shine.

She remembered something papa would say to her before every show when they were on the road with the Western Extravaganza. Before they took to the ring, each time without fail he would say these words to her and she knew that they held magic. And she knew that she would always perform well. *Always*.

She knew if he were by her side right now, regardless of how he felt about what she was doing and where she was, he would say those words to her anyway, because he would know this was what she wanted.

Shine, mi chica, shine like gold.

And she did.

She ran all the way home, perhaps a little too fast for the amount of people there were on the streets, but unable to contain herself.

Her heart was fit to burst as she crashed through the door and into the apartment, almost knocking Vivant over.

"Vivant! Vivant!"

"Good grief, woman!"

"Oh! Goodness! Sorry!"

"Are you alright?"

"I got it! I got it!"

"Got what? What did you...you got the part?"

"Yes! I got the part!"

They clasped hands and jumped up and down together, Vivant totally forgetting how dignified and aloof he always was. He stopped and cleared his throat. Aloof and dignified once more.

"Ain't it keen?"

Vivant made a face like he was chewing a wasp.

"Belladonna; I wish you wouldn't use those out-dated colloquialisms. This is the 30s, you know. The 20s stopped roaring some time ago."

"Oh, don't be such a pill, Viv!"

"Now you're adulterating my name too," Vivant shook his head but couldn't help breaking out into a grin as Belladonna jumped around the room in celebration. Then she stopped abruptly. Composed herself, stuck her nose in the air.

"I have to go read the script. I'm not to be disturbed."

Vivant laughed as she turned back and winked at him, scurried off into the bedroom with the script clutched to her chest.

CHAPTER EIGHT : HELL HATH NO FURY, SUGAR

Rose was still sore at Cal. But she was pissed at James Walsh, even although she had never met him. But she thought of him as her dream-killer. He was the man who murdered the last shred of hope she had of becoming a movie star.

But Rose had never even come close to achieving success in all these years. But somebody had to pay for the death of her fantasy. She couldn't blame herself for it.

But just like he was connected in Hollywood, so was she. He was connected to all the movers and shakers in the motion picture industry. She was connected to all the scum, slime and low rent gangsters in town.

Giacomo 'Jimmy Scars' Scarlata – owed Rose a favor. A *big* favor. He had connections to all the local Hollywood gutter press and gossip rags, and she was cooking up the perfect portion of revenge against the man Cal called Mr. James.

Rose sat down and snorted the last of the stash up her nose.

"Time to make some plans."

She grinned to herself. This revenge was going to be legendary. It was going to be so huge she figured Mr. James would leave town and never, ever show his face around here again.

Maybe I'm being a little hasty. A little too hard on the fella. He didn't really do anything to me. I don't even know him. It's Cal I should be sore at.

But all doubt left her mind as Cal burst through the door and announced with gusto that Belladonna had wowed everybody at her audition, and Mr. James offered her the part on the spot, and she was going to be in Bela Lugosi's next picture.

She smiled, told Cal how wonderful the news was and how pleased she was for her old roommate and girlfriend. She just couldn't wait to see how her part turned out in the movie and she was going to be first in line at the theater to see it.

She was talking so fast her words were running together and she didn't even hear Cal telling her he was going to work on Mr. James, try and get her an audition and a screen test too, or that maybe even Belladonna, since she was *in showbiz* now, might be able to help her get a foot in the door.

She couldn't hear Cal at all now. Her blood was volcanic and roaring in her ears. She could barely see for the anger that hammered the back of her eyes and blurred her vision.

"'Scuse me, sweetheart, I have to go use the horn down the hall to make a call."

Rose felt her way along the wall to the phone, one hand flat on the rough, peeling paint, one at her side balled into a fist. She recited the number to the operator with a vibration in her voice, her throat tight, and getting tighter with every moment.

"Yeah," a sluggish, disinterested voice answered the phone.

"Let me talk to Jimmy Scars."

"Who's this?"

"It's Rose."

"Rose who?"

"What do you want, my life story? Just tell Jimmy Rose is on the horn, will you?"

"Alright, alright. Keep your panties on, lady."

Rose made a disgusted sound at the asshole on the other end of the phone.

"Rose, Jimmy. What can I do for you, dollface?"

"Hi, Jimmy. I need to call in that little favor you owe me. Got a little job for you."

"Hey, sweetheart, I owe you big time. You name it. It's done. Come by the piano club later and we'll have a little chat, alright?"

Rose bit her bottom lip, smiled seductively into the phone as if Jimmy Scars could see her.

"Thanks a bunch, Jimmy. I won't forget this. Thank you. Thank you!"

Jimmy Scars sat behind his desk, partially obscured by a blue haze of cigar smoke. Rose coughed a little as she entered his office. He apologized and waved his hand through the smoke, which only served to spread it further.

"Take a pew, sweetheart."

Rose sat down. Jimmy tipped his bottle of bootleg booze toward her.

"No, thank you."

"So, what's the story?"

"I wanna get somebody good, Jimmy. He's one of those Hollywood types. My fella's a friend of his – only knows him because of me, mind – and he gets his fucking sister an audition and a screen test with him! He's only the hottest director in pictures in all of Hollywood. He knows about *me*. He didn't offer *me* a damn thing. I've been here for years walking the street from casting call to casting call – wearing out the damn sidewalk – and I get squat."

"Your fella got an audition for his sister and not you? Holy cow, Rose. Sounds to me like you should maybe be sore at your man, not the other guy, no?"

Rose pouts for a few seconds, fearing that Jimmy Scars is going to refuse to do the deed.

"I *am* sore at him. I'm plenty sore. I mean, what would you do in his situation? I would get auditions for all my friends trying to make it in this business if I got somewhere."

Jimmy knew that Rose would forget about all her friends in a matter of minutes if she hit the big time. He knew she would forget all about him too. He knew that he would never see her again if she made it in pictures.

"Sure, sure. Of course that's what you'd do. I'd do the same thing. You gotta stick by your friends. Good friends are hard to find."

"Exactly. I'd pass some of my good luck on, you know?"

"So, what do you want me to do to this pill?"

"I want him ruined. I want him to be so humiliated he'll never want to show his face in this town again. I want his mug splashed on the front page of every rag in this town so everybody can see what he really is."

"See what he really is?"

"Yeah, see what he really is."

"Well, what is he?"

"He's a fruit"

"This is Hollywood, sweetheart – most fellas in pictures are that way, you know?"

"Well, I know that, but I know that the studios don't like it – you know who runs most of 'em as well as I do – they're all uptight immigrants. All the studios are starting to put those – oh, what do they call those things?..." she snapped her fingers, trying to pluck the phrase out of the air.

"Morality clause?" Jimmy offered.

"That's it! Morality clause! If it gets out, he's through. I know exactly what the studio will do – they'll fire him and bury his new picture so deep only people who might see it are in China."

Jimmy Scars was tickled by Rose's little joke and he laughed uproariously at it.

"I take it your fella's sister is in the picture?"

Rose nodded.

"Holy God, Rose. I hope I never get on your bad side."

"So, you'll do it then?"

"Sure, I will. I owe you a favor, you're calling it in. Besides, I'm too scared to say no!"

"Hell hath no fury, sugar," Rose said.

"Talking of sugar – I know I owe you a favor and all but this is a pretty big thing you're asking me to do. How about a little sweetner for your ole pal Jimmy, huh?

Jimmy Scars laughed and Rose smiled sweetly at him, even although the thought of letting him touch her again almost made her spill the contents of her guts all over his desk. But whatever she had to do she would do. She'd done worse. A lot worse.

"Sure, Jimmy, sure. Anything for my old pal," she said.
"OK, so gimme the details."

CHAPTER NINE :
SWANNING AROUND LIKE GRETA FUCKING GARBO

ON THE SET

After a decade here in Hollywoodland this was the first time Rose had ever set foot on a movie set.

After all the auditions and all the call-backs and all the old men she had to endure sex with, the one time it happened – the one time she was here with a real director and real actors and a real crew – she was only here because somebody else had got lucky and landed a part and invited her. Belladonna had asked James Walsh if Cal and Rose could visit the set. He was more than happy to oblige. Belladonna thought Rose would love it.

But what Belladonna didn't bargain for was Rose being a twisted fuck.

"Wow!" Cal said to nobody in particular about nothing specific.

Rose rolled her eyes at him. Everything he did was an annoyance to her. She resented every word he said, every gesture he made. She even despised him when he brought her flowers or candy and thought him a sentimental sap. He was no hep cat - that in itself was a crime to Rose. She never understood a man who was not abusive to her. She could not relate to Cal in any way, shape of form. She'd never been treated by a man the way Cal treated her and everything about him seemed weird to her.

But then Rose forgot herself; just being here on the sound stage surrounded by the cameras and the cables, the crew hustling and bustling, feeling the heat of the lights and seeing the microphones suspended from the ceiling made her feel like a star.

People ran around, doing their jobs, however menial or unglamorous, with smiles on their faces because they just loved to tell people that they were *in pictures*.

But Rose's star faded and lost its gilding as she caught sight of Belladonna waiting in the wings and realized that she was not part of this at all. Belladonna was.

She was beautiful. She shone from the wings as a make-up girl fussed over her and a hairdresser made sure there was not a single hair out of place. She smoothed her hands over her killer curves; her dress fitted like a glove and the sight of her tightened Rose's guts and changed her mood in an instant.

It turned the privilege of being allowed to stand here and be part of all of this for a little while into something spiteful and conspiratorial – Belladonna had done this to her deliberately, wanted to make her jealous.

Darkness fell inside Rose's head.

Belladonna would pay for this.

Something like grin but bereft of mirth or joy spread across Rose's face. She knew nobody would ever see this picture. She would make sure of that.

As she waited to go on and film her next scene, Belladonna caught sight of Cal and Rose; she waved to them, smiled. Cal waved back, excited and child-like about being here on the set. Rose turned away, pretending she had not seen her waving.

Why her? Why wasn't it me? I deserve it! I deserve it! I do! I'm the one who pounded these streets day after day, month after month, year after year. That little tramp's been here for five goddamn minutes and there she is swanning around like Greta fucking Garbo. This isn't fair!

Rage swelled in her chest and pounded the back of her eyes as she watched Belladonna talking to the director.

Rose imagined they would be talking about her scene – what was her character's motivation? What level of intensity did he require in her portrayal? She should definitely inject maximum drama into the scene.

What Belladonna was actually taking to James Walsh about was her good friend and talented actress, Rose.

Rose knew Belladonna could act. And she had the looks too. She had star quality, talent and determination. All of those tings wrapped up in one package were essential for *making it.*

All that Rose had ever wanted was to be a star. Her plans had never reached beyond that notion. She had never tried to hone any natural talent she had, if she really thought she had any. She had no love for the movies nor passion for acting. All she wanted was to be a star, to be adored, worshiped, and to reap the benefits of such a status.

Rose's face was a rictus of hatred. She looked at Belladonna as if she despised her – and at that moment, she did.

The swell of hate inside her was near murderous and she could see herself with her hands around her throat choking the life out of her, getting rid of her so she could step into her shoes, step into her life.

Jealousy rendered any bond they'd had meaningless to Rose. All that they'd been through together meant nothing now. Envy, rage, was all that was left. She had forgotten everything that had gone before; all the times they had worn a path in the streets of Hollywood from audition to audition, casting call to casting call. All the times they'd leaned on each other, cried on the other's shoulder. All the times they went hungry together to buy new stockings to wear to an audition – Belladonna would take them off and pass them to Rose in the bathroom so she could wear them when her name was called. They understood. They were close as kin. They both knew what it was like to stand in a line for hours on end with a hundred other girls only to be told *too fat, too old, too tall, too short, not pretty enough,* like they weren't even there.

Rose had been here for what seemed like forever and her first time on a movie lot is to watch somebody else take a part she thought should have been hers – if Cal had not been such an idiot.

Out of everybody both she and Belladonna knew in this town, Rose should have been the one cheering her on from the

sidelines instead of scowling at her telling herself Belladonna
didn't deserve it.

She was vaguely aware that Cal was at her side and yapping
about something and saying *wow* a lot.

But right now Cal did not even exist. All that remained in the
whole world was Belladonna and Rose.

Beauty and the Beast.

*How could you do this to me? You knew how this would
make me feel. How could you bring me here to see this? This is
all I ever wanted. It should be me. It should be me, you fucking
bitch!*

Rose felt even further away from it all than she ever had
before. She was an outsider. And she felt like an outsider.

And she realized for the first time that she would never ever
be a part of Hollywoodland.   She realized that her over-used
cunt wearing out the casting couch had not and would not ever
make her a star.

Cal was saying *wow* again and the sound of his voice made
her curl her lip. She knew that he would never understand how
she felt. And after today, she knew that she would never feel the
same again. Belladonna had done this to her. *She* brought her
here and made her feel this way. *She* did it.

Cal was sprucing himself up. Balming his hair. A splash of
cologne. His best shirt and jacket lay stiffly on the bed. Rose
walked in.

"Hiya, sweet cheeks!"

"Off to see your new friend tonight?"

"Yep! Hope he's got curry for dinner again. That stuff was so
good. Sorry to run out on you – gotta go! See you later and tell
you all about it."

Rose rushed to the window and the second the limo pulled
out, she fled the apartment and rushed down the hall to the
phone.

"Jimmy? Rose. He's on his way to that powder puff's pad."

"Sit tight, sweetheart. Your Uncle Jimmy's on it."

Click.

The limo pulled up to James's house. Cal was excited to see him again but something made him feel uneasy. He looked around and saw the same beautiful, tranquil surroundings with dense shrubbery and fruit trees that made the place feel like it was out in the country. He had an odd feeling, like a hand about to grab him by the neck.

"Cal! Hello again."

James stepped out the front door to greet him and hugged him affectionately.

Flashbulbs began fizzing and popping, blinding the two men as several members of the gutter press pounced on them from the bushes.

And in that moment of chaos James knew that his career, his life and everything he knew, everything he had ever worked for, was over.

Cal blinked rapidly at the flashbulbs as they blinded him, put his hand to his face to shield it his eyes in a classic *caught in the act* pose.

James just stood there. His mind was blank except for repeating *Oh, my God* over and over and over again.

He stared at the intruders as they snickered and jeered at the two of them. And Cal, in his innocence, thought it was just because James was a famous director, and maybe this happened all the time. He was one of those celebrities Belladonna had been talking about, ever since she was a little girl. This is just what happens to them.

But it wasn't because he was a famous director. James was not the Hollywood celebrity type who partied endlessly and loved having flashbulbs popping in their face twenty-four hours a day. He was a quiet, private man. And in a town of secrets, his was a dark one, one that would end his career should it ever be revealed.

He remembered the things that had been said about Clara Bow. Horrible, evil things, things he knew were not true. He remember how his skin used to crawl when he read ridiculous reports in local rags about her, about her sex life, about every aspect of her person. And he knew, right at that moment, he would never be able to live with that. He knew he was not strong enough to shrug shit like that off. He knew that he was not thick skinned enough to walk down the street and ignore the giggling and finger pointing and noises of disgust all aimed at him.

He had done nothing wrong. He had harmed no one. The only thing he was guilty of was being himself, being human, and needing somebody to talk to who didn't have an ulterior motive behind a kind word or a friendly gesture.

Sanjay was at the door in a few seconds after hearing the commotion. He pulled the two men inside and stepped out, ranted at the intruders in Hindi, and cursed at them in Urdu.

Suddenly, James was filled with rage, rage that brought him out of his fugue and made him reach for a walking stick in the foyer next to am Art Deco coat stand. He grabbed hold of it and raised it high above his head, made for the door, intent on doing some damage to the invaders outside his home.

"Mr. James! No!" Sanjay screamed at his boss.

He grabbed at the walking cane but James was too strong, too determined to hurt the men outside. He was insane with rage, couldn't even see straight.

James brought the silver-tipped cane crashing down on Sanjay's skull and didn't stop until his head was a broken, bloody pulp.

Cal backed away from James and into a corner.

This isn't happening

This isn't real!

Why, Mr.James? Why? Why did you do that?

Cal's mouth was open and he thought he was talking, but he was not. He was thinking the words, incapable of speech right now as his mind tried to deal with what he had just witnessed.

James just stood there, still, silent, now. He looked at Sanjay's body as if he had no idea why he was lying dead in the lobby.

Then he saw the bloodied cane in his hand, dropped it as if it were searing hot and jumped back.

Cal tried to collect himself, tried to get a grip on his own sanity.

He reached out for James, tried to put a comforting hand on his shoulder.

James screamed at his touch as if it hurt him.

"No! Get away from me! I killed him! I killed Sanjay. I killed him. He was my friend. He was my only friend."

James's head was suddenly filled with lucidity.

"How much did they pay you to set me up, you dirty wheat? Was it worth it? Did you have a good laugh at my expense? Did you?" James was screaming at Cal now, his rage reigniting. Cal backed away from him, scared that he was next. He stumbled in the slick pool of Sanjay's blood on the tiled floor.

"No, Mr.James. Its not like that! I didn't do anything! I would never do anything to hurt you, you're my fr...

The blood drained from Cal's face as the realization hit him.

"Oh, my God. No. Rosie. It was Rosie," Cal said, then put his hand over his mouth as if he was trying to force the words back in.

"Rosie? Your girlfriend? I don't even know her. Why would she do that to me?"

"She was sore at me for telling you about Belladonna and you giving her a part in your new picture, and all."

James slowly closed his eyes and reached into his inside jacket pocket. There was sadness in his eyes like Cal had never seen before. He handed him an envelope.

"Won't make any difference now, but give it to her anyway. It'll be more revenge than anything I could ever dream up."

"What does it say?" Cal looked shame-faced. "I can't read, Mr. James."

"It's a note I wrote earlier, inviting Rose to take a screen test for a role in my next picture."

Cal kept looking from the envelope to James and back again. He wished he could turn back time just a few hours and warn Rosie not to do anything stupid because you never know what's going to happen in the near or distant future.

He would tell her that something wonderful might happen later on today and that she could be in for a huge surprise, best surprise she could ever have. He would tell her to just stay in the apartment until he got home because he might have a little something for her that will change her life forever.

But he could not turn back time. And he could no more prevent Rose from doing anything than he could turn back the clock. She was wild, free, tempestuous. And her own worst enemy.

He probably shouldn't tell her about the letter. She wouldn't be able to live with it. She wouldn't give a fuck about Mr. James killing Sanjay, or about any of the rest of it, but she'd care about this, she'd care about the fact that she'd just shot herself in the foot, destroyed her last chance and her own wildest dreams. This knowledge would destroy her completely.

As he stared at the envelope he didn't notice James slipping away and into the library. He looked up as he heard the squeak of dry wood – Mr. James opening a drawer on his antique desk. Before he could open his mouth to ask him what he was doing, Cal heard the gun shot.

Then a *thud.*

Then silence.

Cal didn't know what to do. He was trapped inside a house with two dead bodies and there was no way, he thought, that he wasn't going to get the blame for both of them.

So he ran. Ran through the house searching for another way out. He tumbled out the back door and crashed into more photographers, was again blinded by flashbulbs.

Cal stopped in his tracks as he saw a police car pulling into the drive.

There was no point in running – that would only delay the inevitable and confirm that he had something to hide.

There was no escape.

Belladonna sat rigid in a horrendously uncomfortable chair at the front desk of the police station. The same man, a copper, she presumed, kept walking by every few minutes. He would stop, just for a second, and look straight at her.

She sat there for hours. The same cop must have passed by and looked at her a hundred times.

Finally, Cal emerged from the interview room; he looked haunted, exhausted. There were dark circles under his eyes and his hair looked dirty and greasy, his clothes disheveled. The sight of him was shocking to her. She had never seen Cal looking this way before. He looked at her and there were tears in his eyes.

"He's dead, Belle. He's dead and it's all Rosie's fault."

She reached out and touched his cheek with the back of her hand.

"What happened, Cal? Nobody will tell me anything. Where were you? What were you doing?"

Cal rubbed at his sore, tired eyes like a sleepy little boy. All he wanted to do was curl up in a ball and go to sleep. He didn't want to think about this anymore. Didn't want to talk about it anymore. Didn't want to hear the bang of Mr. James's gun anymore and the sickening thud as his dead body hit the floor.

"They let her go a couple of hours ago. They questioned her and everything and they said there was no crime. I think they think I did it and and tried to make it look like he did it himself. What she did, oh, my God, sis, what she did was..."

"Cal, this isn't making any sense to me. Who's dead? I don't know what you're talking about. Who did they let go? Are you talking about Rose? Here, come on home with me, OK? They said you're free to go."

"But Rosie..."

"Fuck Rosie!" Belladonna said in a forceful whisper. "Forget about her for one minute! I've no idea what's going on here, but I do know she's up to her neck in it. And I don't even want to hear her name again tonight."

"You just cussed! I've never heard you cuss. When did you start cussing?"

"When I started associating with degenerates like Rose."

Cal looked wounded. He didn't have all the details yet either, but he knew that this whole thing was down to Rose. But right now he didn't want to think about it. He'd been grilled by the LAPD for hours on end and he was a wreck. Belladonna held on to him as she led him away from the interview room he'd been sweating in all night. She could smell the fear rising off his skin.

The night air was cooler and fresher than in the room he'd just come from and Cal sucked in a lung-full.

They walked in silence as Cal patted his jacket pockets, looking for something. He put his hand in his inside breast pocket and pulled out the letter Mr. James handed to him before he blew the back of his own head off.

He began to laugh and cry at the same time but made no noise. His body shook with silent sobs as he remembered the letter's contents. And anger took over, anger at Rose and what she had done and a desire, suddenly, not to protect her or to see if she was alright.

She needed to see it. She had to read it. He wanted to watch the realization sink in that she had cut off her nose to spite her face. Yes, Mr. James was dead - her revenge was complete, his career over, his life over. But when she found out what she had robbed *herself* of, she would probably want to die. And right now, Cal decided that she deserved to share in his despair, even if her's would be for wholly selfish reasons.

"I have to go see Rose, sis. I have to do it. Just trust me. I know everybody thinks I'm some dumb wheat from the sticks, but I'm not. Well, when it comes to Rosie, maybe I am a dumb wheat. But I've got the message now. Just trust me, alright?"

Belladonna knew there was no talking him out of going to see Rose and there was no way she could stop him. He was adamant he was going to do it and nothing short of tying him up would deter him. She apprehensively let him go.

"OK, I trust you. But you come to the apartment when you're done, OK? We need to talk."

Cal took off at speed, racing through the streets as the sun set and darkness began to fall over Hollywood once more.

Cal walked into the room he shared with Rose. Rose was there, sitting still, silent, eyes cast downward. Neither of them knew what to say to each other but both of them knew there was so much to say.

Cal went to the sideboard and reached for the bottle of gut-rot bootleg gin. He stopped.

Not going to drink today. Need to be straight for this.

His mouth was parched and he didn't think he could talk more than a few words if he did not drink something. He put a squirt of soda water into his glass instead, took a slug and sat down opposite Rose.

"Don't you have anything to say to me?" he asked her.

"What can I say? What do you want me to say? *I'm sorry?* I didn't mean for him to die. I just wanted to hurt him. Embarrass him. You know, just make him pay for what he did? You know me, I'm not a bad old gal, honey."

"What did he *do* to you, Rose? You didn't even know him! How could he possibly have *done* something to you?"

Cal was angry; not just at Rose, but at himself for being so blind to what she really was. And that was a cheat, a liar, and a whore. The very sight of her disgusted him at this moment.

"Come on, Cal. You know what he did. He was going to make Belladonna a star! She's only been here for a few months. I've been in this damn place for nearly ten years now, never come close to catching a break, never got near landing a screen test for a Big Wig director. What's so special about her, huh?"

"There's lots of things special about Belladonna, Rosie. You're just jealous."

Rose sneered, twisted her face up and looked ugly again.

"Jealous! Why would I be jealous of that tramp?"

"Tramp! How dare you call my sister a tramp. If anybody's a tramp, it's you. She warned me about you and I wouldn't listen to her. And I *should* have listened. She knew you. She knew what you were. What you *are.* You're nothing but a user, Rosie. A low-down dirty user."

Cal *was* going to spare her the devastation of reading the letter. But he changed his mind. She deserved to feel as low as possible, she deserved to know that she had blown her last chance of ever being in pictures. She deserved to suffer. She deserved to know beyond the shadow of a doubt that her love affair with Hollywood was over and she could never, ever win back its affections.

Cal quickly packed his few belongings into two paper sacks. She knew he was leaving but she said nothing. She didn't care. He knew it. He knew that she did not love him and he knew he could never feel the same way about her ever again.

"I'm leaving now."

"I know."

"Oh," Cal reached into his inside breast pocket and pulled out Mr. James's letter.

"This is for you."

He closed the door softly behind him as Rose tore open the envelope. He smiled a little smile as Rose got exactly what she deserved – a karmic ass-kicking of immense proportions.   Her scream would have been blood-curdling to him in any other situation; he was sure people from all over the building would come running, thinking somebody was being murdered.

Rose threw herself onto the floor and pounded it with her fists until they hurt so bad she couldn't hit any more. She screamed. She cried. Neighbors from all over the apartment building came running in the direction of the screaming and stood outside her door, listening.   One old lady in a floral robe, hair curlers, and a half-smoked cigarette with a gravity-defying ash dangling from one corner of her mouth gingerly pushed the door open. Rose got up off the floor and started smashing and hurling everything in the room that wasn't nailed down or too heavy for her to lift.

Cal was almost a block away and he could still hear Rose screaming.

A siren wailed, got louder, louder still. It was heading his way and he was sure they were heading for Rose.

But they would find an empty apartment when they arrived. Rose was already gone when they got there. She was a woman on a mission now, and nothing would stop her from reaching *this* goal.

Rose stopped, exhausted, far from the top of Mount Lee where the Hollywoodland sign looked out over Los Angeles.

The muscles in her legs burned, her lungs burned – too many cigarettes, too much illicit booze and not enough upright exercise. She felt like she was going to die, right there and then on the hillside, far beneath the the sign she planned to throw herself off. She pressed on, making it twenty or thirty yards then had to stop again.

The Hollywoodland sign had always seemed so close. Now it seemed to be impossibly far away. She thought she would never reach it.

She was half-blind, her vision obscured by cascades of tears, and the back of her eyes being hammered by enraged blood. She pressed on. This had to be the one thing in her entire life she achieved. She *had* to do this.

When she finally reached the sign she was dry-sobbing, her tears spent already. She was utterly sorry for herself, feeling like the loneliest, most put upon, down-trodden, poorest soul on earth.

She looked at the sign.

She sighed.

How am I supposed to get up there?

She really had no idea the size of the sign until she got there. Looking up at it on the hillside from down below, it didn't really seem all that big. Just looked like little letters, sitting on the side of the mountain. But up close, standing there beneath it, it was overwhelmingly immense. Each letter towered above her and reached up into the heavens.

Telephone poles attached behind the sign buttressed it against the hillside, supporting each letter. She tried to shimmy up one of the poles and slid down again after making it a few yards up. She swore as she felt the splinters from the near-decade old wooden pole digging into the insides of her thighs. That wasn't going to work.

She sighed and testily put her hands on her hips. Looked around her for...something – *anything* - to help her get up there.

She squinted in the dark, walking carefully, slowly along, looking at the hillside, the sign, looking in the dirt for inspiration.

She found it.

The caretaker had left his maintenance ladder propped up against the second O.

She struggled as she tried to lift it – it was so high, so immensely tall that she almost lost her balance as she picked it up.

She huffed and puffed, made it a couple of yards and had to stop. Picked it up again, made it a few yards and lost her balance, crashing the ladder into the Y.

She heard a man's voice and threw herself into the brush as the door to the caretaker's cabin creaked open and he shouted out the door.

"Hey! Who's there? What are you doing up here?" the caretaker said.

She froze, not even making a sound as the dry brush scratched at her face and legs. She was sure he had not actually seen her, though. She lay still, barely breathing. She heard a shuffle of feet as he stepped out the door to take a look around. He saw nothing, shook his head and thought to himself that it was probably that damn cougar sniffing around again, coyote, maybe. He closed the door behind him and went back to bed.

Rose lay there for a few minutes, just in case he was still watching from inside. She didn't move until she heard him snoring and muttering in his sleep again from within the thin wooden walls of his tiny shack.

Once she was sure the coast was clear she crawled from the brush and squealed, clamped her hand over her mouth to stop any more noise emanating from it as she realized she'd been laying only inches away from a sleeping rattlesnake.

She tried moving the ladder again, struggled again. Committing suicide wasn't going to be as easy as easy as she thought.

Maybe it's a sign. Maybe there's still hope. Maybe I could still be a star if I just try really hard.

She sobbed, her body wracked with emotion, her head pounding with rage at what she had done to herself.

She knew that it was useless. She knew that there was no hope left. That was why she was up there, trying to scale the Hollywoodland sign and jump off it into welcome oblivion.

Determination gave her the strength to move the ladder and position it right where she wanted it.

Why didn't I just wait? This could have been it, I could have been the star I always wanted to be. All my dreams could have come true and I could have been walking down red carpets and sipping champagne in the back of limousines. Soon I could have been in the arms of some other rising star planning our bright future together, reading through scripts, deciding what our next picture is going to be...

She reached the top, her calf muscles aching, shaking with the effort of climbing up the thin rungs of the maintenance ladder.

The wind swayed her back and forth and she hung on to the top edge of the H. The individual sheets of metal that made up the letter, and the whole letter itself, moved back and forth as she clung to it. For some reason she'd always had the impression that the letters were solid, three-dimensional. On her way up she imagined standing dramatically on top of the H, gracefully diving off. That was not going to happen. The letter swayed on. She could not keep herself still as the wind breathed through the small holes in the individual sheets of metal that made up the sign. She felt like a marionette, like somebody else was pulling her strings and making her move against her will. She bowed her head, her vision obscured by the fresh tears that filled her eyes.

...Instead I'm standing here planning on killing myself and all I have waiting for me is a goddamn country bumpkin from the back of beyond who knows nothing, and owns nothing, who is nothing.

"He's worth a million of you."

Rose snapped her head up so violently in shock at the sound of the voice she almost toppled backward off the ladder.

"Belladonna, I..."

Her shock was so profound she wasn't even registering that Belladonna was impossibly standing on the top of the sign. She didn't even realize that she had not spoken out loud either, and that Belladonna's comment was in response to her own thoughts.

"You just couldn't stand it, could you?"

"What? What do you mean? I..."

"You just couldn't handle me getting a part and not you, could you?"

"Why, no, no, of course not. We're friends. I'm over the moon for you."

"Sure, you are, honey. Sure you are. That's why you're standing at the top that ladder, thinking about throwing yourself off - because you're so happy you just can't live anymore! God, you must be really hating yourself right now. Actually, I'd probably do the same thing if I were you. I couldn't live with that. I just couldn't carry on knowing that I'd completely destroyed myself and caused the death of an innocent man. Not to mention what you've done to my brother."

Rose's face burned with shame.

"But I know you don't actually care about what you did to them, you only care about what you did to yourself, don't you?"

Rose couldn't look at her, couldn't look Belladonna in the eye. Her shame burned deeper, and hot tears began to stream down her face. The main source of her shame was that Belladonna was right – she didn't really care what she had done to them. She was devastated only at what she had done to herself.

"I'll try to make it right. I promise. Please let me try."

"He's fucking dead!" Belladonna screamed at her. "How can you make that right, Rose? How? And I can see right through

149

you. You're not mourning for James Walsh, you're mourning for yourself."

Belladonna was so angry her pale skin was flushed red with rage and all she wanted to do was put her foot in the middle of Rose's forehead and push her backward off the ladder and watch her head split open when she hit the ground.

Belladonna knew the source of Rose's anguish was for herself, not for James's death, or for what she'd made Cal endure. She knew she had cut off her own nose to spite her face and there was no going back. Whatever happened now, she knew she was finished in Hollywood. Her name was already mud after what she'd done that actor. She should have gone home with her tail between her legs long ago. These realizations were what led her to this spot, to this moment, and the contemplation of her own suicide.

She was finished in Hollywood a long time ago – and her one and only chance – ever – was going to come from the man whose death she just caused.

Belladonna turned away from Rose, fighting hard to control the rage that burned inside her.

There was silence.

Or as close to silence as a vampire can get. She heard distant conversations, she heard the whistle of the wind as it made its way through the canyon, and she heard the throb of her own blood as it raged through her body. She had just fed; fresh blood and anger always made for a thundering heartbeat. When they fed, when they raged, when they were impassioned, the heart grew fiercer beat out a tattoo that would not end, that would not be quieted.

Belladonna took a deep breath and closed her eyes, willing herself to calm down so she could talk to the bitch behind her.

"Do you think...maybe...you could get me a part in a picture?"

Belladonna began to laugh uproariously and shook her head in disbelief without even turning to look at the wretched creature again. Rose took that as a *no* and in her own rage and hopelessness, grabbed at the hem of Belladonna's dress with her free hand and pulled her off the H.

Belladonna lay broken behind the Hollywood sign, her head burst open on a rock, every bone in her body broken.

Rose looked down at her, shocked at first by what she had done, then smirked at the death of her rival. She felt much better now that Belladonna was out of the way, lying dead, her body devastated by the fifty feet fall.

Rose started down the ladder behind the H, slowly and carefully, taking several minutes to get to the bottom. She was laughing to herself and calling Belladonna all sorts of names, inside her head, happy, giddy, that she had slain her.

She sucked in a shocked breath as she saw that Belladonna's body was no longer there.

A whistle in the wind from above.

Rose snapped her head up toward the sound.

She gasped as she saw Belladonna standing, unscathed, atop the H once more. Rose took off at speed, kicking off her shoes so she could run faster, not knowing what, exactly, Belladonna was, but knowing that she was not human. She knew that she had to get away from her.

It's not natural. You're dead! You're dead! I saw you! I killed you!

"No, you didn't, Rose; I was already dead."

Rose's horror froze in her throat and she couldn't even scream as Belladonna appeared in front of her and grabbed her by the throat; she moved so quickly that Rose had not even seen her move at all – she was suddenly no longer where she was looking and instead appeared before her. She lifted Rose off the ground effortlessly and flew her back up to the top of the sign.

"Who are you? Wha... *what* are you? Please, don't kill me! I don't want to die!" Rose pleaded.

"Well, I'm sure Mr. James didn't want to die either. You want to be famous, Rose? You want to be a household name and be splashed across every newspaper in California?"

"Yes! Yes! That's what I've always lived for!"

"Then I'll make you famous, bitch."

Belladonna dangled Rose over the edge; piss rand down her flailing legs and blew in droplets onto Belladonna as the wind howled. She curled her lip, looked deep into the eyes of her once-friend, and let go.

Her rage and fire were depleted now. She felt very little as she loosened her grip around Rose's throat and let her fall to her death on the hillside.

And anyway, she was sure, Rose would only have ended up another drugged-up, dead Hollywood whore before too long anyway. She'd think of it as a mercy killing. Belladonna couldn't help thinking that it was more kindness that she deserved after what she had done.

Belladonna was silent as she entered the house and sat down by the fireplace. By the fire was her favorite spot. Here, the farm, Gramama's house. This was where she sat to read, lose herself in the pages of a book, or listen to a radio play, just to daydream. Sometimes she sat there when she needed to work out a problem. Although no fire was burning, she still sat there by the cold, still hearth.

Both Vivant and Cal sat, watching her, waiting for her to say something.

Vivant could feel the remnants of her anger and knew how enraged she had been earlier. And he knew that she had killed Rose.

"Rose is dead," she said after a long silence.

Cal stood up, open-mouthed, trying to speak but unable to.

"She tried to kill me first. And she would have. If I wasn't dead already."

Cal laughed, a short, crazy little laugh.

"I don't think I can take any more, Bell."

"Would you rather it was me? She pushed me off the Hollywoodland sign!"

"Then you pushed her off it, I take it?" Vivant asked.

"No. I threw her off it."

"Oh, God," Cal said, his voice vibrating with distress and disbelief.

Cal was on the verge of a complete breakdown. He looked haunted. Belladonna could tell that he was imagining what both Mr. James's and Rose's bodies looked like as they lay dead – his friend with his head blown off by his own gun and his girlfriend, lying broken and twisted on the hills above Los Angeles. He couldn't have been any more disturbed if he'd actually seen them.

He wondered if Mr. James died instantly, or if the shot wasn't *quite* on target and he'd lingered before he expired, feeling the pain of his shattered skull, feeling cold seeping inside his head and into what was left of his brain.

He wondered if Rose died on impact with the hillside, or if she lay there, unable to move, unable to speak and nobody there to hear her if she did – except her killer. He wondered if she was being eaten by coyotes right now, if they were biting chunks out of her flesh, feasting on her cooling corpse.

He wondered what it would have been like if Rose had been an ordinary gal, one he could have taken home to mama and papa, settled down with on the family homestead in a little cabin made by his own hands. They could have had a couple of little ones and he would have worked the land whilst she made some extra money as a seamstress making the latest fashions she was always talking about, for well-to-do ladies of the county.

But that would never have happened, he knew, not with Rose. Rose wasn't built for *normal*. Rose was destined to be everything or nothing. Somebody or nobody. Starlet or common slut. But whatever she was, she would never have been a simple farmer's wife. Never.

"She probably couldn't even sew anyways."

"What?" Belladonna asked.

"Oh, nothing. I was just thinking. I want to be on my own for a while, sis, OK?"

Cal headed for the guest room. Belladonna took hold of his arm as he passed her.

"You alright, Cal?"

She studied him, terrified that he was going to be unable to cope with the loss of Rose and all that had happened over the last twenty four hours. She was scared he was going to do himself harm.

"I'll be fine. And I'm not going to kill myself, Bell. I know that's what you're thinking. I just want to sleep. I don't want to think anymore for a while."

Cal closed the door behind him. Belladonna's fears remained.

"He's not the type, don't worry," Vivant tried to reassure her.

"Not the type for what?"

"Suicide. That's what you're afraid of, isn't it? Like I said, he's not the type. That's not what he's thinking about."

"Well, I would have said he wasn't the type to take drugs either, Vivant. He's not the same person I grew up with. He's not the same at all. Under normal circumstances I would agree with you, but this...this is just *too* much."

"Don't worry; if he gets even close to thinking about that, I'll know, so don't worry, OK?"

Vivant kissed her on the forehead and pinched her nose between two knuckles, gave her a smile. It made Belladonna worry even more. Vivant wasn't overly-playful at the best of times, and she could see through his smile. He was worried, she could tell. Sometimes Vivant forgot that she had vampire senses too. And he didn't always cloak himself as well as he thought he was.

But she knew that there was nothing she could do if somebody was intent on killing themselves. You could watch them twenty-four hours a day and they would still find a way.

She remembered, some cousin of mama's, a farmer back east, just a couple of years ago, had his farm foreclosed on by the bankman.

He'd sold his equipment off bit by bit to try and make his payments, then his livestock, then everything else he owned until he had nothing left to sell.

Some local Big Wig bought it for cents on the dollar, wanted to charge him to stay on it and work the land, and then share in his profits at the end of the year - the old European feudal system alive and well in 20th century America.

He explained to the buyer that they made next to nothing, barely survived year to year – that was the farmers lot these days. But the knew this. He'd gone through the place buying up the repossessed properties and now owned over half the town. He didn't want to share his profit with a lowly farmer and he knew that they couldn't pay rent and a share of his meager profit at the end of the year. And why would he? He had men lining up outside his office - men he had thrown off their own land – begging him for a job that paid a pittance, working the fields they once owned.

And with the depression in full swing, the likes of him could clean up. He had money enough to buy up the whole town many times over and sit on it until the markets stabilized and property prices went up again.

Morag's cousin's shame was so profound he could not face his family or his friends in the town. And most of all, he could not face himself. He felt like a failure. Felt like he had brought a great shame upon his father, his whole family. He went to the barn that was no longer his and hung himself from the rafters. And there was nothing anybody could have done about it. He was intent on ending his life and no matter what, that was exactly what he was going to do. And he did.

Everybody thought that Cal was rough and ready, none too sensitive, not too bright. She'd never thought that was fair and had never thought that way about him. Yes, he was a country bumpkin. Yes, he was a little naive. Yes, he was a redneck. Yes, he loved illicit booze and a roll in the hay on a Saturday night. But he wasn't stupid. He wasn't a *dumb wheat*. She loved Cal and he adored her, he loved his family, would do anything for them, do anything to help *anybody*. She knew him better than anyone else. Even although he was only her half-brother, they couldn't not have been closer or had any more love for each other. The thought of anything happening to him made her want to weep.

"Vivant. What if he..."

Vivant placed a finger over her lips. He shook his head.

"I won't let any harm come to him, I promise you."

Belladonna trusted Vivant, but she knew that despair and determination were powerful partners.

Vivant held on to her. She was lost and in fear that what she had done would destroy Cal's love for her. She was terrified that things would never be the same between them again. She just didn't know what to do for the best.

And Vivant didn't know what to do either, or how, exactly, he was going to keep his promise.

Cal emerged from his room late at night the next day. He'd been alone for almost twenty four hours. Belladonna kept creeping up to the door to see if she could hear him moving around, or breathing, or crying. He made no sound and each time she grasped the door knob intent on going in there, Vivant stopped her. She needed to let him alone for a while, let him grieve for his friend and his girl. He'd come out when he was ready to come out.

Cal smiled a straight, feeble smile; it was all he could muster right now.

"You alright, sweetheart?"

"I'm alright, sis," he nodded, managed a slightly more convincing smile.

"I know what you're thinking, Bell, and I'm not going to do that. I would never do that."

"I wasn't thinking..."

"Yes, you were. But it's OK. I just don't want you to worry about me because I'll be just fine. You were right; Rosie was no good. I've always known that, but I still loved her. But if she tried to kill you, then she got what she deserved. And I don't hate you for it. You're my sister and I love you. You will always come first, no matter what."

"Oh, Cal. I'm so sorry."

Belladonna threw her arms around her brother. She was relieved that he seemed to be calm and rational, pleased that he didn't hate her for killing Rose and was lucid about the whole situation. But there was still a niggling, nagging worry at the back of her mind that would not leave. In light of what had happened over the last few days, he seemed *too* calm. Right now, he didn't seem like himself at all.

"I've gotta run. Some business to take care of. I'll be back later."

"Where are you going?"

"Tell you all about it later, gotta go!"

Cal grabbed his jacket and left.

Belladonna sat beside the fire with a book and tried to read but she could not settle. She   sighed.

"What's the matter?" Vivant asked.

"I'm worried about Cal. Where d'you think he went? Where could he have been going? Can't you tap into him or something, hear what he's thinking."

"Of course I can. You really want me to?"

"I can't read him or hear his thoughts for some reason."

"It's because you're blood – even although he's your half-brother, the blood is still strong enough. Maybe you'll be able to in a few years, when you're more powerful. But young vampires can't read family. It's annoying, I know. I don't know why that is, it just *is*. He couldn't have got far yet – I should be able to find him in a few seconds."

Vivant sat in his chair, closed his eyes and concentrated on tapping into Cal's thoughts. After a minute or so, Vivant's mouth fell open. He sprang from his seat and raced over to the sideboard, pulled open the top drawer where he kept his favorite pistol. It was gone.

"Oh, no. Oh, God, no."

"What? What is it?"

Belladonna ran to the drawer, knowing exactly what Vivant's alarm was all about. That was where he kept the Colt 1911. Vivant's reaction, she knew, was because he'd found the drawer empty.

Belladonna made a tiny squeak of fearful emotion in her throat.

"He's gonna get himself killed! He's going to try and shoot that low-life Jimmy Scars, isn't he? Oh, my God! Vivant! Do...!"

Before she could even finish her sentence, Vivant was gone and left her to fret alone.

Vivant found Cal skulking around the back of the piano store that housed the speakeasy owned by Jimmy Scars. He stood and watched him for a second, listening to the storm raging inside his head.

Goddam son of a bitch he ruined everything and now Rosie and Mr. James are both dead. Maybe I should just shoot myself instead.

"Cal," Vivant said softly.

Cal jumped, startled at Vivant's voice, so much so that he dropped the gun.

"I'll take that," Vivant said.

Cal didn't even try to beat him to the pistol. He knew it was futile. He knew Vivant could have picked it up and returned to where he was standing before he even detected a twitch.

"What are you doing here? How did you find me?" Cal asked, fumbling around on the ground for the gun.

"Firstly, I'm trying to stop you from getting yourself killed, and secondly, I'm a vampire, remember?"

"Oh. Well, just leave me be, Vivant. I have to do this. This is none of your business."

"It is my business, Cal. You're family. And offing Jimmy Scars isn't going to bring back your friend or Rosie. Why rot in jail for the likes of him? He'll get his, don't worry. Jimmy Scars is not long for this earth, believe me. I have my finger in a few Hollywood pies still – there's a lot of very, very powerful people not very happy with Mr. Scars. You understand me?"

"But I wanna do it myself. I want to watch that rat bastard die in front of my eyes! I want revenge! He has to pay!"

"Have you ever watched somebody die, Cal?"

"No. So what? What does that have to do with anything?"

"It isn't pleasant. Even as much as you hate him, watching him die will destroy you. You're not like him. You're not like most of the people in this town. And you don't *want* to be like them. Don't let him take any more from you. How d'you think she got him to do what he did? He knew there was a risk in doing it. What do you think he wanted in return?"

Cal's face paled and he slid down the wall, squatted in the back alley behind the club. The very thought that he had been inside her after Jimmy Scars's disgusting, greasy cock had been there was enough to make him vomit. He was lost. He knew that Vivant was right but his grief over the loss of Mr. James and Rose was eating at his gut and he ached for retribution.

He couldn't just sit idly by while Jimmy Scars went on with his life unaffected by the deaths he had just caused. He knew it was all Rosie's idea but she would never have been able to pull it off by herself, so, to Cal, the responsibility for the whole thing rested upon the fat, sweaty shoulders of Jimmy Scars.

And *somebody* had to pay for it.

"Cal," Vivant put his hand on Cal's shoulder. "He won't get away with it. You hear me? He won't. You need to remember, I know these people. I've been here for a long time. I promise you he'll pay for what he did if you'll just come home with me. You'll have your revenge."

Cal wiped the tears from his eyes. Vivant was right – he knew he could not carry on living if he felt any worse than he did. And he knew that guilt would eat him from the inside out if he murdered Jimmy Scars, no matter how big a scumbag he was, no matter how much he deserved it, he knew he wasn't like him. Vivant was right - he knew Vivant knew all about killing.

Vivant held out his hand and helped him up.

But he was still uneasy. He wasn't at all sure if he'd gotten through to Cal or not. There were so many thoughts, so many strong feelings running through him, it made him very difficult to read. And instead of his thoughts being calmer now, they raged even harder, more hate-filled, more dripping with confusion than before. Vivant hoped his words had hit home and he wasn't going to run off again and do what he originally planned. He hated not being able to read him sufficiently to put his mind at rest.

Vivant's concern wasn't entirely selfless; he was worried how this situation and anything that may happen to Cal would effect Belladonna, and ultimately effect himself.

After all, Vivant was still Vivant.

The days passed and turned into weeks, and Cal seemed no better. In fact, he got worse. He would never get over what happened to Mr. James and Rosie. Belladonna knew it. Vivant knew it. Cal knew it too.

Belladonna walked on eggshells around him, choosing every word carefully, afraid of triggering another fit of grief or rage in Cal. He was drunk all the time – or drugged – when he managed to steal enough money from Vivant and Belladonna.

Vivant knew what he had been doing. Then when he made sure there was no more money lying around for him to steal, he knew Cal was so hopelessly addicted that he would find the money to buy booze and drugs any way he could.

It was late, Vivant sat alone reading by the fire. Cal snuck from his room, mistakenly thinking that Vivant had neither heard nor seen him.

He gingerly opened the door – he knew just how far to pull it back before it gave a dry creak, a throwback to living on the farm and sneaking into the house, drunk on Bathtub Gin, not wanting to be yelled at by his mother for staying out all night and getting up to *God knows what*, she would always say.

Vivant followed him. Cal was oblivious, one-track-minded and determined to earn some money for booze and drugs.

He was done with cocaine and amphetamine. That was something he and Rosie did together when they were out having a good time. That wasn't what he was after now. He didn't want that sort of a high anymore. He wanted the opposite.

He didn't want to feel good or confident or invincible. He certainly didn't want to feel awake or alive. He didn't want to feel anything. He wanted to be numb. Sedated. He desired a stupor so deep he was incapable of thought or speech. He wanted to be unconscious. Unaware. The thought of being asleep forever, not thinking, not feeling, not having to *be* anymore seemed like the closest to bliss he would ever be again. His life was over. Unfortunately he happened to still be alive, even although most of him died the same night his Rosie did.

"Oh, God," Vivant said when Cal reached his destination.

Cal was on Sunset Strip. At this time of night there was only one thing he could be doing here. Vivant, age old Vampire who had seen it all and done most of it too, was shocked.

Christ, Cal, you cannot do this to yourself

Almost as if he had his own sixth sense, Cal turned around and saw Vivant standing there in the dark.

"Dang it, Vivant, what are you doing here? Do you have to fucking follow me every time I come out?" Cal frowned at him, annoyed that he'd tailed him again and he'd not thought to check after last time.

"What am I doing here? What the hell are *you* doing here? Are you insane? Do you know what goes on down here, Cal"

"Of course I know! What do you think I'm here for? You must think I'm stupid like everybody else does. Well, I'm not. Just leave me alone. Just let me do what I want to do and keep your nose out of my business."

"Oh, Cal. Cal, Cal, Cal. You know I can't do that. I can't let you do this. You have no idea what you're getting yourself into. This is not the life for you. You don't want to do this, trust me."

"Is that all you're ever gonna say to me – I don't wanna do this, I don't wanna do that? How would you know what I want to do? You don't even know me! I don't want to live anymore! I wish I was dead! You hear me, I wish I was fucking dead! And don't tell me I don't mean it, because I *do* mean it. This way I can get the job done quicker."

Vivant was at a loss for words. He didn't know what to say to him. There was nothing he *could* say that would make him feel better, that would make him want to live, nothing he *could* do that would end the poor guy's torment. The only way he could help him end the pain was to walk away and let him do what he came here to do. That way, at least, he wouldn't have to feel, even if it was only for a little while at a time. But he couldn't do it. He couldn't let him go through with it.

"I'll buy it for you."

Cal looked at him blankly.

"What?"

"I said I'll buy it for you, you don't have to do this. If you're intent on destroying yourself one way or another, I might as well make it easier and quicker for you. You don't have to go through with this."

He waited for Cal to respond, but he said nothing. He was suitably confused and that was what Vivant wanted – a little distraction that would buy him some time and at least get him off the streets for tonight. Save his soul for at least one more day. Tomorrow was another story. But he'd deal with it when it came around.

Tonight, at least, he'd managed to halt Cal's journey on the path of no return. And he made him swear on Belladonna's life that he would not sneak out again tonight. He was satisfied that Cal would not break his promise.

Vivant had seen the very birth of Hollywood. He'd been here since the movie industry first fled from the east coast to avoid being lorded over and litigated against by the tyrannical Edison company who owned patents on the film making equipment – the cameras and the projectors and monopolized other essentials, like film stock.

California was a motion picture-making haven. There were more hours of sunlight here and so more film could be shot in a day than on the east coast. And the Edison company were not there to file suit every time somebody spoke out of turn or did something they didn't like.

He'd been here since the movies were still silent and every star meant something different to every fan. They were unburdened by the timbre of a voice, didn't have to think about a grating accent or speech impediment or a voice that just did not fit the face, did not fit the legend. But not for long.

He'd been here right up to the recent excruciating birth of talking pictures – a technological leap forward that made the loftiest of screen stars pale at the mention of it, and whose inception slayed many a giant. He'd been here for the pain of Clara Bow, lovely, much maligned Clara Bow, who shook and stuttered at the mere mention of Talkies and eventually had a complete breakdown on the set of *Dangerous Curves* over the microphone dangling ominously above her head. Vivant had adored her – her beauty, her spirit, the sorrow that ran thorough her, right to her core, could make anyone – everyone – smile and laugh and weep and fall in love.

One day in January, 1929 a fire broke out on the Paramount movie lot. Clara heard the commotion of sirens and shouting, people running around like headless chickens.

She stood, half dressed on the stairs of her dressing room, looking down the lot. She heard cries of *Fire!*

"I hope t' Christ it's the soundstage," she said to nobody in particular as Vivant walked by with director Ernst Lubitsch. He winked over at Clara and she smiled back, fluttering her eyelashes at him.

He told her that it was and her face lit up. For a second she was happy to think that it meant the end of talking pictures. But, of course, it did nothing to slow down progress. All it did was made the process even more harrowing as the casts and crews stifled and sweated on the old stages, swathed in impromptu soundproofing of canvass blankets sewn together and attached to the walls and ceiling.

He'd been here when John Gilbert, Hollywood's darling and the heart's desire of every movie going woman in the nation, spiraled into suicide by alcohol after the inception of talking pictures. The invention of sound killed him. It wasn't just his plummy voice that had audiences rolling in the isles, but the clunky, unintentionally hilarious dialog he was made to speak. He went from sex symbol to laughing stock overnight.

Vivant knew what Hollywoodland could do. He knew that Cal was just another victim-in-waiting.

Few could escape her vice-like grip. She was a cruel mistress. A black widow. A femme fatale from a silent movie that nobody could resist. And her hooks were in Cal every bit as much as Rosie's had been.

Vivant had been here for every step forward, seen the birth of every star – and witnessed so many of them be swallowed up by this place, crash and burn, be consumed by the ravenous beast that was known as Hollywood.

And he fucking loved it.

Vivant sat drinking with Cal for as long as it took for him to fall into a stupor and carried him to his bed. He'd be out of it for hours, maybe even sleep until the next night. Precious time for he and Belladonna to attempt coming up with a solution. They had no idea what to do with him.

"You told him what? What did you do that for? What are you going to do when he comes asking for it? You going to buy it for him? God, Vivant!" If you don't, he's just going to go right out and do tomorrow what he was going to do tonight," she said, her voice vibrating with emotion. She fought back the tears and felt a sting of heat on her cheeks, a knot of anxiety in her gut. "What am I going to tell my parents? They'll blame me. They'll disown me, Vivant. First I get myself turned into a blood-sucking vampire and next my brother becomes a hop head and is one step away from being a...a... nelly!"

"Calm down, Bells. We're not gonna let him do that to himself, OK? That's not going to happen."

Belladonna shook her head in despair. It was all her fault. This would never have happened if she'd not come charging down here chasing a stupid dream. Whatever happened to Cal, she was responsible for it.

"No, you're not."

"What?"

"You're not responsible. Cal is a grown man, Bells. *He* made the decision to get involved with Rose even before you knew he was here. *He* made the decision to use drugs. How is any of that your fault? Because he came here to find you? You think this is your fault because he wouldn't be here if it hadn't been for you, yes?"

"Right."

"Nonsense. What happened, happened. Not your fault. If it's anybody's fault besides Cal's, then it's Rose's fault. Talk about a bad egg. But stop blaming yourself, sweetheart. You beating yourself up over it isn't going to help him. It can't change what's happened."

He took her face in his hands and stroked her cheeks with his thumbs.

"Is it?"

"I guess not. But I don't know what to do, Viv. I can't help him. But if I don't do anything he's going to end up dead, I know it. He's got a death-wish. He just doesn't want to be here anymore. And I don't know what to do."

She shrugged her shoulders, lost. Defeated. And she could feel Cal slipping away from her, more each day. He was not the brash, carefree brother she grew up adoring. He was not the rough-and-tumble country boy that could lift four times his own weight like it was nothing. He was no longer the bother that was always there for her and who would always fight for her, no matter what – even if she was in the wrong. He was loyal. He was caring. He was her big brother. And that man was gone now. Long gone.

Now he was just another lost soul in Hollywoodland. Another package of damaged goods. He was a bitter, hopeless shell of a man slowly dying from grief.

"Why did I have to kill her? I could have let her live and at least Cal would be happy."

"She tried to kill you! And she wouldn't have stayed with Cal for very long, you know that. Either way, he'd have ended up grieving for the loss of her - dead or alive. And besides, he deserves better than her."

Belladonna sighed heavily.

"I can't argue with that."

"*And* she was responsible for the death of a perfectly innocent man. A good man. I knew him a long time ago when he was starting out, way back in the beginning of the movies. He was no more than a kid. I can't believe that he's dead. And

Hollywood is a darker place without him. But the world's better off without that odious little slut walking around, if you ask me."

"But he loved her, Vivant. No matter what we think of her, he loved her, good or bad. And now she's dead. My brother is never going to be the same. Never. I'm sure one of these days we're gonna find him..."

Belladonna's words died off as a lump of emotion stabbed at her throat. She knew that she had to go home and take Cal with her. She owed her parents an explanation. Not only had they lost a daughter to a vampire, but they'd lost a son to the underbelly of Hollywood.

But if she could get him out of here, then there was still a chance that being back home with mama and papa, and away from the temptation that surrounded him here 24/7, would bring the old Cal. Maybe what had happened over the last couple of months could fade into a bad memory given time. But she didn't *really* believe that.

She knew that she was clutching at straws and most of it was wishful thinking. But Cal's life was worth saving and she would do everything she could try and make it better. She knew if he stayed here, he would be dead within a month, two at the most.

It was decided. She had to take Cal home. And Vivant was going with them.

CHAPTER TEN :
CONFESSIONS OF A HOLLYWOOD VAMPIRE

Rose's death was no more than a footnote in Los Angeles. The fame Belladonna promised evaded her, even in death.

The *Times* and the *Daily News* did not identify her by name. All she was was another Hollywood corpse. Only one newspaper mentioned her name.

Rose Marie McAllister was a common commodity in Hollywood – she was one of the many disposable population.

Rose was one of those who would always wait tables, pump gas, clean bathrooms, sweep the streets, collect garbage, sell sex – all the while dreaming that one day all of this would be left behind and their shot at fame would come along. One day it would be *them* up there on the silver screen and thousands of people would be sitting in the darkness gazing up at their image, wishing they could be up there too, praying that one day they would leave behind the drudgery and the grayness of their own lives.

But the chosen few were just that - *few.* So few.

Rose Marie McAllister was just another dead wannabe and the only one who cared that she was no longer here was Cal.

But Belladonna felt obliged to let the rest of the girls know. The girls both she and Rose had roomed with and shared the hopes and dreams of.

Belladonna bit her bottom lip as she climbed the familiar staircase. She climbed it slowly, in no hurry to reach her destination, gripping the one newspaper in her hand as if her life depended on it. She had no idea *how* to tell them that Rose was the corpse found at the bottom of the Hollywood sign.

Hi, girls. Sorry to tell you this but Rose is dead.
No, I can't say it like that.
I'm sorry to be the bearer of bad news – Rose is dead.
I have some bad news. Rose is dead.

She hesitated outside the door and jumped back as it opened before she even knocked.

"Belladonna!" Elizabeth shouted at her, a huge smile on her lips. She threw her arms around her nd hugged her tight. "Come on in!"

Belladonna stepped into the flat and all the girls flocked around her, including two new faces she'd never seen before – she and Rose's replacements.

"Where have you been?" Anna asked.

"We've been hearing all sorts of gossip about you!" Catherine said.

"I have some bad news," Belladonna started, but Elizabeth interrupted her rehearsed speech.

"You mean about Rose? Oh, we know. We always knew she would come to a sticky end. So, where have you been? We were worried about you," Anna told her.

"You know about Rose?"

"Sure, sure. Some cop came by at the crack of dawn and told us. It's too bad," Catherine said.

"What? Don't you care? Cathy? Anna? We all used to be roommates! How could you be so cold?"

Catherine shrugged.

"It was only Rose, Bell. You know what she was like. She was always gonna die young. She even said if she was ever gonna kill herself she would throw herself off the Hollywood sign."

"My God," was all Belladonna could think of to say. Her shock robbed her of any other words. She turned around and left the apartment for the last time.

"Hey! Where you going? Come back, Bell!"

Belladonna shook her head as she descended the stairs.

She'd forgotten what a bunch of bitches they could be. When she thought about it more later, she would remember how they were around other women and the vitriol that would spew from their lips. She'd been at countless casting calls with them and they had something nasty to say about anybody and everybody standing in line. Their desperation and their jealously could not be hidden. They would even talk about little girls standing in line with mothers who had tried and failed at this life themselves.

Belladonna wandered the streets of Hollywood as she always did when she needed to clear her head or ponder a problem. She's walk round the perimeter of the studio lots, catch a glimpse of the odd star here and there, watch expensive cars with black windows drive by and smile, wondering who was inside.

Now that the task of telling the girls that Rose was dead was over a lot more quickly than she anticipated, she turned her attention to something even more important - what the hell she was going to say to her parents.

Hi mom! Hi dad! I'm a vampire and Cal's a hop head!
Oh, brother.

What am I gonna to say to them? They'll both keel over and die! What am I gonna to do? God, help me, please. Everything mama said about this place was right. Everything. She told me people end up dead here. She told me people end up on the streets here. She told me the place was evil. And I know all of these thing are true. So why do I love it so much? Why do I know in my heart that I will always come back here?

Belladonna shook her head at herself and prepared to do a lot of walking.

She headed for the one place that was silent here, nothing but the noise of the wind whistling through the canyon and a coyote or two in the distance. It was the one place she could be pretty sure nobody else would be. She headed to hike up Mount Lee once again to her beloved Hollywoodland sign.

Although she was preoccupied with her own thoughts and hadn't sensed there was anybody else here, she began to hear her name said over and over again in an exotic voice, not out loud, but inside her head. Somebody at the sign was thinking about her and saying her name to themselves.

She reached the sign, knowing who was there before she saw him, his velvet voice unmistakable.

"Bela!"

Bela spun around with a gasp.

"Belladonna! My goodness! What are you doing here? I was just..."

"Thinking about me? I know."

She grinned at him and he threw her a bashful smile that was very unlike him.

"I come here to think. Clear the cobwebs out. This is my special place," Bela said.

"Really? I never knew. It's my special place too. I come here all the time for the same reason."

"I heard the terrible news. A young lady. - she fell from the sign."

"I know. It's horrible. Just horrible. So, how have you been?," Belladonna said, changing the subject quickly and thanking God that Bela could not read her mind the way she could read his.

"I'm wonderful! My new picture starts filming in a week. I have another straight after. How have you been, Belladonna?'

"I've been better," she said.

"Is everything alright?"

She had to tell him. There was no reason to keep it from him and if somehow he found out about it, then it would look extremely strange that she failed to mention her relationship with the dead girl.

"The girl who fell...she was my old roommate. She was my brother's girl too. And my friend...once"

Surprisingly to herself, her eyes welled up with tears.

"Oh, my dear. I'm so sorry. I did not know."

Bela put his arms around her and she melted into his embrace and wept. She was glad he was there to steady her. He knees were suddenly weak and threatened to give way beneath her. The strain of the last few days was wearing her down and had caught up with her all of a sudden.

"Oh, Bela. There's so many things I want to tell you right now. So many things. Everything is such a mess. All the things that have happened since I last saw you. You wouldn't even believe me."

Bela laughed softly and took her face in his hands.

"More incredible than you being a vampire?"

She managed to laugh through her tears. Her statement was quite absurd in the face of things. He had heard stranger things from her in the past.

"It's a long story. A very long story and I think you might hate me by the end of it. I did something..."

"Come. Come to my home and tell me your story, Belladonna."

She hesitated but did not resist the pull of his hand as he led her back down the hill toward his house.

Bela handed her a cup of strong hot coffee and sat down opposite her. She stood up and went to the window, peeked through the drawn curtains and looked out at the night.

"Holy cow!," she screamed and almost choked on her first sip of coffee.

"What's the matter?"

Bela rose and went to her side, looked in the direction of her gaze. She was looking at the Hollywoodland sign.

"Ah," he laughed. "You did not know you could see it from my home?" he asked.

"No! Wow. I'm sorry. I'm sort of in love with it," she giggled self-consciously.

Bela sat back down.

"Aren't we all?" He grinned knowingly at her. "So, are you going to tell me your story?"

Belladonna sighed, scared to tell him the whole thing but needing to unburden herself. And as a wise, worldly gentleman, she would listen to any advice he offered.

"Well, it started with the vampire thing. I stopped writing to my parents and after a couple of months not hearing from me, they sent my brother Cal down to find me, see if I was still alive. Rose, my roommate, you know, the one who's dead now, showed him some things he'd never seen before. He fell in love with her. Unfortunately, Rose wasn't a very nice person sometimes. She forced him into, um, keeping company with a big movie director. But he was a sweetheart and just wanted a regular person he could talk to and enjoy a meal with without them wanting something from him. You know how it is here. He gave me a part in your picture. I couldn't believe it – finally after all these months pounding the streets and going to casting calls and being pawed at and disrespected by dirty old men day after day, I got a real part in a real picture."

He smiled sadly.

"Ah. Our director - James Walsh. Such a tragic story. I did not know you were in it." Bela shook his head sadly. "But at least we have the picture! We *both* have the picture."

"But nobody will ever see it, Bela. They'll bury it. They'll never release it because of the scandal. When I think of all the low down, dirty goings on in this town that – let's face it – we all know go on, and they bury this picture so deep it'll never see the light of day again – and for what? Because of a friendly embrace? This is insane! I'm not going to give up. I know we didn't share any scenes in this one, but it was *our* picture, we were *both* in it – and *that* was my dream, the reason I came here. And I want us to be in another one, one that everybody will see, everybody all over the world. I won't let Rose kill *my* dreams too. I was so angry with her. I still am. Of course, Rose was all bent out of shape that I got a part. She went crazy. She decided that Mr. Walsh giving me a screen test and a part in his picture was a personal insult to her. And so she plotted her revenge against him. She knew a local hoodlum named Jimmy Scars and he set up the whole thing for her. Scars sent word to the gossip columns and they sent photographers to hide out in the bushes at James Walsh's house.This is the sort of story they would sell their own grandmothers for. When Cal got there and Walsh gave him a friendly embrace the flashbulbs started popping. It was completely innocent. I guess the shock of what happened sent him into a blind rage and his manservant got in the way.

Bludgeoned him to death right there in the doorway. Then he went into his study and shot himself in the head. This whole thing – all of it – was down to her."

"Good God! Hell hath no fury, as they say."

"I know. It's horrible. Just horrible. But that's not all. That's not the end of the story. Remember I said he was a nice man?"

Bela nodded.

"Well, he handed Cal a note before he went and killed himself. A note for Rose. Cal gave it to her and she took off running."

"What did the note say?"

"It was a personal note from James Walsh asking her to attend a screen test for a small part in our picture that hadn't been cast yet. It was just a tiny part – a walk on with one line – but it was a start, you know?"

"Oh, my God. I can see why she threw herself off the Hollywoodland sign."

"Well, that's really not the whole story. I don't even know if I should tell you this..." Belladonna chewed her bottom lip, afraid that Bela would think of her as a degenerate like Rose and never want to see her again. She decided to take the chance, needing to unburden herself. She didn't feel right about keeping the truth from him.

"...I went up there. I knew that was where she would go. I knew how she would want to kill herself if she had the guts to. I confronted her. She begged and pleaded with me to get her a part in a picture and said she would make everything alright again. I laughed at her and she pushed me off the H. The fall burst my head open and broke every bone in my body. She was happy she killed me. Or *thought* she'd killed me. If I were human I wouldn't be sitting here with you right now. I would be dead. I could hear her laughing inside as she climbed down the ladder. She was glad she killed me. We fought, she begged me not to kill her and I threw her off the Hollywood sign."

She waited for a response from Bela. She waited for outrage, for shock and disbelief, for disapproval.

"An eye for an eye," was all he said.

They talked long into the night sharing their recent adventures, everything that had happened in their lives since they last met. They were kindred spirits, these two.

As Belladonna and Bela parted ways again, he told her that they should not be strangers. He did not want to stay away from her; enjoyed her company too much, valued her friendship and he hoped that one day they would make another picture together – one that the whole world would see. He knew he had no sway with the studio but he said he would see what he could do.

And now there was a dark secret that bound them to each other. A secret that only three other people knew. And one of them was dead and gone.

CHAPTER ELEVEN : BACK TO THE BOONIES

Although the journey was half over, Cal had slept most of the way home. He'd been up for days. Hardly slept in a week, hardly eaten. He was exhausted and soon after they left Hollywood, the soothing motion of the car sent him off to sleep.

"I'm hungry," he said, rubbing his eyes like a sleepy child.

"Well, hello there, sleepy head," Belladonna said.

"Where are we?"

"We made Redding already, since Vivant drives like a maniac. We'll be home before you know it. This time tomorrow we'll be back with mama and papa and Quita and we'll be able to see gramama," Belladonna said.

Cal fell back asleep immediately and mumbled something incomprehensible. Belladonna watched him as he slept. She had the notion that each time he slept he wasn't going to wake up. She had a horrific picture in her head each day when she went to his room that she was going to find him black-lipped and open-eyed.

"You really ought to give yourself a break, Bells. He'll be fine. And stop beating yourself up! How long are you going to blame yourself? It's not your fault. None of it was your fault. If you want to lay blame somewhere, lay it on me. If anybody is to blame, I am."

"Oh, I don't blame you, Vivant. Me and Cal are both old enough to know better. Coming to Hollywood was a stupid idea and I should never have left home."

"Nonsense! What did you come here for?"

"To be an actress. A star! You know the old story. You've been here long enough."

"What did you come here for *exactly*?"

"To get a part in a Bela Lugosi picture."

"That's right. And you did. So how could it was a stupid idea? You achieved what you set out to do."

"Yes, I did, but unfortunately my ex-friend caused a scandal and the director committed suicide! Nobody will ever see the picture, you know that."

"Well, *that* wasn't *your* fault either."

"Vivant, what am I going to tell my parents? What *am* I going to say?"

"Well, the truth usually goes over the best, but in this case, I don't know, sweetheart. Maybe you should just play it by ear. Just wait and see what comes naturally when you get there. But I don't really see how you can tell them anything but the truth. Your father has Native blood, no?"

"Yes, but what does that have to do with anything?," Belladonna asked, brow furrowed.

"It means he should, at the very least, be more open to the supernatural than the average person."

Belladonna raised her eyebrows.

"I guess. But what about Cal? My mother will just die."

"She won't die. Look, if she's savvy enough to know what goes on in Hollywood and warned you about going, then she's probably sophisticated enough to not be at all surprised that it happened. And besides, she'll be overjoyed that her kids are actually alright."

She smiled and shook her head. Vivant never ceased to surprise her. But she only hoped that he was right.

"You mean apart from me being dead and all?" she giggled. It felt strange; she'd not done a lot of giggling lately, and immediately felt as if she were doing something wrong.

Vivant glanced sideways at her and grinned.

"It's only an hour or so until sun-up. We should stop for the day. Feed and get some rest."

175

The second half of the journey seemed to drag. It felt like they had been driving forever.

Cal *still s*lept and Belladonna *still* thought he was going to spontaneously die in his sleep. And she *still* blamed herself for everything.

The closer to home she got, the stronger the sick feeling in her gut became. She was terrified of facing her parents, telling them everything that had happened, what Cal had gotten into and what she had ended up doing.

The thing that she feared the most, though, was telling them that she was going back there, that Hollywood was her home now and no matter what happened, it always would be.

But whatever happened, however they reacted, she knew she had to tell them the whole truth. She owed them that. Sure, she could concoct some cock and bull story. But they knew her, they knew when she was lying. And when he wasn't sure, all papa had to do to get the truth out of her was utter three little words - "Say *I'll* die?" She had to tell the truth when he said that. *Had* to. It still worked even now that she was a grown woman. It always would.

She tried to nap but it was useless. She tried to read a book but she couldn't absorb the words. She chain-smoked until she couldn't stomach another cigarette. She turned on the radio but it didn't work here – they were going through the passes and radio towers were still few and far between outside the cities. Eventually she gave up and just stared out the window as the scenery became more familiar.

It was dark by the time they pulled onto the dirt track that led to the farm. Belladonna's guts were in knots. She felt like turning tail and heading back to Hollywood. This didn't feel familiar to her anymore. It seemed old. Faded. Alien to her. It felt like somewhere she had never been before. Or somewhere she *had* been and wanted to forget, like a bad memory resurfacing.

Oh, Bell, come on now. This is home. This has always been home. This is where you grew up. This is where everybody who loves you is. This was all you had ever known until a few months ago.

She knew she would be met at the door. Nobody got within five hundred yards of the house without him knowing about it.

Sure enough, he appeared at the door at the precise moment she thought he would.

Then he disappeared.

"He'll be going to get his old 30.06 since he won't recognize the motor."

"Well, that's comforting," said Vivant.

"Cal, we're home! Wake up now!"

"I'm awake, for goodness sake. No need to shout."

Rodrigo reappeared, one hand out of sight. Bell got out of the car and his face lit up.

"Bell!" Bell! Mama, it's Li'll Bell!"

She heard her mother screaming from inside the house.

They collided into each other's arms with such a force they almost knocked the wind out of each other.

"Papa!"

"Oh, God, my Bell. Mi chica."

Morag came screaming out of the the house, arms flailing as if the place was on fire.

"My wee bairn! My wee bairn!"

Vivant stood by, smiling. He could see that his Belladonna was very much loved. He felt that she could probably tell them anything and they would forgive her. He hoped that wasn't just wishful thinking.

"Mama!"

Quita dawdled across the field, schoolbooks dragging in the dirt behind her in Belladonna's old school satchel. She saw the crowd outside the house, stood looking, wondering what was going on and why so many people were standing around outside the house. She realized it was Belladonna.

She dropped the bag and took off at speed leaving her schoolbooks behind her.

Cal slowly and wearily got out of the car.

His parents ran to him now, fussing over him, hugging him, ruffling his hair as if he were still seven years old.

Morag broke down in tears.

"We thought you...we thought you were both..."

"Oh, mama. Mama, papa; I want you to meet someone," Belladonna said. Vivant knew that was his cue to be charming.

"Mr. and Mrs. Busto. I'm so glad to meet you both, finally. I've heard so much about you."

"This is Vivant. He's my...fiance."

Vivant smiled and raised an eyebrow at her, discreetly as he kissed mama on both cheeks and shook papa's hand vigorously.

"Oh, my goodness!" Morag said, utterly beside herself. She had obviously taken an instant shine to the charming, beautiful Vivant.

"Pleased to meet you, Vivant. Come on in the house. Getting a little cold out here."

Vivant was charmed by the house. He smiled when he saw the collection of miniature teapots Belladonna had told him about and couldn't wait to give Morag the gift he had for her – several pieces to add to her collection he had commissioned, just for her, from a very sought after Hollywood artist.

He hoped he and Belladonna could keep them talking about lighthearted things long enough for them to warm to him before the conversation turned to more serious subjects.

They ate good, old fashioned home cooking – fried soda biscuits, roasted quail, and home canned Chow Chow. The food reminded Vivant of the old Wild West days. He smiled as he thought to himself that not much had changed really – the west was *still* wild – one of the reasons he loved it so. He'd once been on a wagon train which made its way along the Oregon Trail from Missouri. Of course, he could have just flown there in a matter of minutes, but that would have been no fun. He liked to experience life, the way he did when he was human. Sometimes, he enjoyed living amongst ordinary people, live as regular a life as he could, considering his circumstances.

Back then, it was fairly easy to conceal his true nature. It was easy to spin a line, tell a tale and pull the wool over peoples eyes. They weren't nearly as suspicious or superstitious as the Europeans, especially the Easterners. They were perfectly willing to believe in devils and demons. And vampires.

Although sorrow and tragedy marred the path of the wagon train – there was an Indian ambush, a looting by asshole

Pinkertons and several deaths from fevers of various sorts, people killed by wild animals - Vivant looked back on that time in his life as one of the great times. He truly felt alive in the face of death and danger to a mere mortal. And nobody knew about him. To the wagon train he was a hero, he fought off wild animals and tended the sick. He was like a great warrior and always emerged from a fight unscathed.

He hoped telling Belladonna's parents about the vampire thing went well. He would love to talk with them about his life on the trail and about his love for Oregon. He only hoped

he didn't let anything slip too soon – explaining how he looked so good for his age might be a little tricky.

After dinner they all sat down and Vivant ended the few moments of silence after everybody settled down by giving Morag the present he'd had made for her.

"Oh, my, you shouldn't have," she said.

She carefully undid the ribbon and took the lid off the box. She was dumbstruck. She kept looking from the box to Vivant and back again and could not believe her eyes. Among the shreds of colored straw that filled the box were tiny little teapots, each one of them different, each one of them unique. If Cal smashed these, Vivant would kill him himself. They were horrendously expensive.

"Do you like them, mama?," Belladonna asked.

Her mother looked at her, her eyes filled with tears.

"I've never seen anything like them. They're so beautiful. I don't know what to say."

"How about *thanks,* mama?," Cal joked.

"Goodness. Where are my manners. Vivant, thank you so much."

"You're very welcome," Vivant said with a smile. One down. One to go.

The evening went so well and they all had so much fun that Vivant, Belladonna and Cal almost forgot what they'd come here for. Tomorrow, perhaps, may not be quite so enjoyable.

After breakfast the men went out quail hunting to bring home the meat for dinner. They took with them lunch bags of left over fried soda biscuits and hunks of homemade cheese. Vivant was looking forward to shooting. He hadn't shot anything except Belladonna in a long while.

Belladonna milked the cow. She was an old hand at it and hadn't lost the knack. She was sure the old cow remembered her, since each time somebody new milked her, she would fuss and end up kicking over the milk bucket. But she didn't fuss at all.

Quita pestered Belladonna all morning to do her hair in the latest style. She told her big sister that she had grown up a lot since she had been gone and she was not a little girl any more, even although it had been less than a year.

Belladonna relented and fixed Quita's hair amid disapproving looks from her mother.

Morag was a little tense. She knew that this was not just an off-the-cuff vacation. She knew her daughter too well to believe that.

"So, how have things been down in California, then, darlin'?," Morag asked her.

"Oh, you know. Ups and downs. There's good and bad everywhere, mama."

"What did you come to tell us, Bell?"

Belladonna furrowed her brow at her mother.

"What do you mean, mama?"

"Don't be coy, now, child. I'm your mother. I gave birth to you. There's never going to be another person on this earth who can sense things about you the way I can."

Belladonna grinned involuntarily – that wasn't actually true any more. Maybe it was at one time but now there was somebody who could read her mind – literally.

"Everything's fine. Don't worry so."

"You may think you're better than us now, but don't ever think that we're stupid, Belladonna. I know there's something not right about that young fellow of yours. I can sense it."

Belladonna suddenly felt panicked.

"What do you mean? I thought you liked him."

"I never said I didn't like him, Bell. I think he's perfectly charming. Good looker too. But there's something not right about him and I want you to tell me what it is."

"Maybe he's a vampire, like Count Dracula!" Quita blurted.

Belladonna looked at her little sister, horrified. She looked to her mother and even as insane as it sounded, she knew that what Quita said in jest had struck some sort of nerve in Belladonna.

She swallowed hard, tried to force out a laugh at Quita, tried to tell her not to be silly. But nothing came out. She had no words. Hearing her sister say it, say that Vivant was a vampire like Dracula was just too much of the truth for Belladonna to deal with.

She needed Vivant by her side to help tell this story. She just couldn't do it on her own. The only thing she could do was run. She could not stay here right now. Her mother's accusatory glances had been setting her on edge all day. She decided to wander around until the boys came home. If she did stay, she knew that her mother would get the whole story out of her somehow. She could just never, ever lie to her successfully.

Belladonna ran out the door and smacked head-on into Vivant, shattering his cheekbone with her forehead, in the process.

Vivant clutched is cheek momentarily, but by the time Morag reached him to help, he was already healing. There was only one way to explain it and that was to tell the whole truth.

"Well, I'll be darned. I thought that was a hard enough smack it was going to be broken for sure," Morag said, eyeing Vivant very suspiciously.

"Oh, it's nothing, don't worry. Just a scratch."

"Nonsense. Your skin was broken. Your shirt front is bloody, laddie. And by the way, I'm foreign, not stupid."

She was right. There were blood spatters from his shattered cheek dotted all over the front of his shirt. But he had healed already. There was no mark on his skin. No scar. Nothing but quickly drying blood and no indication left of where it came from.

"Alright you two. Actually, you three. You were there as well, Cal. Sit down. All of you. You lot have some explaining to do."

Rodrigo came inside the house carrying two braces of pheasant and wondered why Cal, Belladonna and Vivant were sitting there like three errant children with Morag standing over them.

"You need to hear this as well. You sit down too,'" she instructed her husband. He obeyed, sat down, wondering what the hell was going on.

"Mrs...," Vivant tried to speak.

"Never mind Mrs-ing me, young man. Out with it. I want the truth. What are you?

"Mo, what's this all..."

"Just let me handle this, darlin'. You didn't see what I just saw."

"You want the truth?," Vivant asked her.

"Of course I want the truth! Tell me!"

"I'm a vampire," he told her. "And so is Belladonna."

Morag staggered backward in her usual dramatic way and landed on the sofa. Rodrigo went to her side, took the dish rag from her clenched fist and fanned her with it.

"What in the Sam Hill is going on? Morag! Mayka skookum, uptsêh?"

Rodrigo asked Morag if she was alright and called her sweetheart. Whenever he was stressed or in a rage, he would automatically revert to talking the Chinook Jargon he was brought up speaking.

He stopped in his tracks and turned to Vivant, his words suddenly sinking in, but not quite sure if he heard right.

"What did you just say?"

"I said, I am a vampire. And so is Belladonna," he repeated.

"If this is your idea of a joke on what you think are local yokels, then I have to tell you it's not funny."

"Am I laughing?," Vivant asked.

"Please tell me this is a bad dream and I'm going to wake up soon, papa," Morag said.

"Don't worry, mama," Rodrigo said. "They're just making fun of us."

"No, we're not. Look, I'll prove it to you," Vivant said.

"Vivant, no. Not that. Mama will die of fright."

"OK, I'll just show you then, Rodrigo," Vivant headed outside and turned back to Belladonna's father. "Take a gun with you,"

Vivant headed for the barn, shouted back to Rodrigo to come on, but Rodrigo didn't seem to be in any great hurry. He knew the man was afraid. Very afraid.

Vivant was sitting on a bail of hay waiting when Rodrigo finally got there.

"Injure me any way you can. Try to kill me. Shoot me, stab me with that pitchfork over there – anything, whatever you want."

"Are you crazy? Why would I want to do that? Why would *you* want me to do that? You know, I worried about my little girl going to Hollywood and mixing with all those crazy folks and all, but you take the cake. And I really liked you. I thought you were good for Belladonna."

"I am. You just have to trust me for a second, OK? This isn't a joke. I'm not making fun and I don't look down on you because you're country folks. I admire you, actually. You just have a persecution complex."

"Maybe so. What are we doing out here, Vivant?"

"I told you; I want you to injure me in any way you desire."

"Don't tempt me," Rodrigo said, his patience faltering.

"Then I guess I'll have to just show you myself."

Vivant grabbed the 30.06 from Rodrigo, racked a round into the chamber and blew the back of his own head off.

Rodrigo screamed, rushed to Vivant who was crumpled in the dirt. The back of Vivant's head was completely gone, the exit wound in the back of his skull big enough to insert a big man's fist.

Rodrigo gasped and backed away as he watched Vivant's ruined head begin to put itself back together again.

Rodrigo's golden skin paled.

And by the time all the color drained from Rodrigo's face, Vivant was good as new again and the two men stood looking at each other.

Rodrigo had no idea what the thing standing before him was, but he knew that it was no ordinary man. Not even human. And trickery or magic of some sort was not a reasonable explanation either. He was right here in front of him. No slight of hand or trick of the eye could be responsible for this.

When all other explanations have been exhausted, the one which cannot be explained and remains is usually the answer. The only other option Rodrigo could see, the only one that made any sense, was that this thing in front of him was something supernatural.

And whatever this *thing* was, Belladonna was one of them too.

Rage suddenly swelled inside Rodrigo. His vision blurred and his temples throbbed with anger. He drew his fist back, ready to strike Vivant square on the nose then stopped, mid-swing. There was no point in hitting him. He could do him no harm. No matter how hard he hit him, no matter what he did to him – even if he pounded on his skull with sledgehammer for hours - he would suffer no lasting effect from the assault.

I want to kill you for what you've done. You took my little girl and turned her into...into...

"I turned her into an extraordinary creature."

Vivant reading his mind seemed to make him even more angry.

"*Creature* is right! She's not human anymore! She's not my Belladonna!"

"Nonsense. She's better than she could ever have been as a human. She is an exceptional vampire. She's full of fire, full of life. You should be proud of the woman you and your wife raised. And she is still your daughter. She still loves you – in fact, she will love you even more because she *is* a vampire. We love like no other being that ever walked the earth. You are still her father. Nothing else has changed except that now she will never grow old, never be sick, never suffer from the human condition, and she will never die. She will be young and beautiful forever. How can anybody view any of those things as bad? They are wonderful things. Miraculous things. And she can give those things to you too. If you want them."

Rodrigo didn't have an answer. As he looked at Vivant, looked into the eyes of a being that was so beautiful, a creature whose eyes held the knowledge of centuries, he felt the tension drain from his muscles. There was no fight here that he could win. There was no crime to punish and even if there was there was nothing that Rodrigo could do to the perpetrator.

For his own peace of mind, he knew that he had to live with this and find acceptance. He could not change what had been done. He could not transform Belladonna back into a human.

Tears began to spill down his face. Vivant put his hand on Rodrigo's shoulder. He tried to shrug it off, not wanting the touch of such a creature. But Vivant held on harder.

"You need to be strong. Morag may take this even harder than you. And you have to convince her that everything is alright. Belladonna is happy. We have a wonderful life together. There is no reason to worry about your daughter. Who you need to worry about, however, is Cal."

"Cal? What's the matter with Cal?," he asked.

"Well, we should go back inside and talk things over and see what we can do."

Rodrigo wiped his eyes, took a deep breath and headed back to the house to see what the next bombshell was going to be. There was nothing he could do for Belladonna. Perhaps he would be able to help Cal.

Vivant and Rodrigo returned to the house. Belladonna and Morag looked like they'd not moved a muscle or uttered a word since they left.

Then tension in the room was fierce.

"Mama," Rodrigo said, "don't worry, OK? Our baby is fine. There's no need to fret about her. She's just the same as she always was. Just remember, she's your daughter. Our daughter. And all you need to know is that you love her and she loves you."

"But she..."

Rodrigo put a finger gently to Morag's lips.

"She's just Belladonna," he told her.

"Mama..." Belladonna got up and started toward her mother but her mother shrank away from her, a rictus of fear on her face.

"Oh, mama, please don't be afraid of me."

The pain on Belladonna's face broke Rodrigo's heart and he went to her, suddenly aware that nothing he'd learned had changed the way he felt about his daughter. And if Morag didn't face this now, this minute, she might be lost to them forever.

"Morag, come here, sweetheart. Give your baby a hug," Rodrigo said.

He pulled firmly on her hand to make her stand up, and pulled her to their daughter.

Morag's love for her was stronger than her fear. They threw their arms around each other and held tight.

"Oh, Bell. My wee Bell. I love you. I'll always love you no matter what. Nothing could ever stop me from loving you."

"I love you too, mama. I've not changed. I'm still your little girl, no matter how grown up I pretend to be."

There would be questions. There would be tears and anger. There would be shouting and screaming, they knew. But blood is blood – vampire or human. And nothing could break that bond.

THE STORY ABOUT CAL

"I guess we better hear the story about Cal, now," Rodrigo said.

"There's no need to worry about me, papa. Honestly. I'm home now. I'll be fine. Nothing to worry about."

"Maybe so, but let's hear it anyway. So, what's the story?" Morag asked.

Cal pleaded for help from Belladonna with his gaze.

"Cal got into a little bit of trouble down south. Wasn't really his fault though. Got in with a bad lot, you know how it is. He...started taking drugs," Belladonna said.

Cal cast his head down. He was ashamed. He thought they'd be more sore at him for being a hop head than they were at Belladonna for being a blood-sucking vampire.

"Oh, Cal. No. Tell me it's not true."

Morag commenced more weeping and wailing. She really wasn't an hysterical woman, she was not prone to fits of girly drama, but when it came to her children, the slightest thing wrong with them sent her into apoplexy.

"It's alright, mama. Please don't cry. I'm over that now. I won't do it again. I'm home now...if you'll let me stay," he said.

"Let you stay? Of course you can stay! This is your home! We should never have sent you to that God awful city in the first place. This is all our fault. All of it, you, Belladonna

– everything is our fault," Morag said.

"No, it's not your fault. It was my own fault. I'm a big boy now, mama. I made my own bed and I laid down in it too. But I'm home now and you don't need to worry anymore. I'm not going back there. I want to work the land again, work here with you and papa and help out where I'm needed. Old Man McDuff'll probably need help with his orchard, since he's getting on and all. Maybe I'll take a walk over there tomorrow and have a chat with him," Cal said, not even convincing himself that he didn't want to go back.

"There's a lot more to the story, but it's all water under the bridge, wouldn't you say, Cal? I don't think we really need to go that deeply into it, do you?," Belladonna asked him, hoping that he could read her and realized that she really didn't want to go into the whole suicide/murder/prostitution story.

"It's OK, Bell. I want them to know. I want them to know about Rosie," Cal said.

Belladonna's guts tightened. She had no idea how far into the story he was going to go.

"Rosie? Who is Rosie?," Morag asked.

"She was my girl, mama. She's dead now. Bell killed her," he said.

Belladonna gasped as if hearing the shocking detail of the story for the first time and her mother shot out of her chair like it was on fire.

Vivant slowly closed his eyes. He knew Cal was going to do that. He'd been listening to his internal dialogue for hours, debating with himself on whether or not he was going to bring up the whole sorry mess or not.

But if I tell them that then it means I've gotta tell them about the whole thing, tell them about Mr. James. And then I would have to explain how I knew Mr. James, how I met Mr. James and everything. Don't know if I wanna do that though. Don't know how they'd react to that. They'd be mad. They'd be ashamed of me. I don't know what to do.

But then Cal blurted it out. And there was no going back. The whole sorry story would have to come out.

"What?" Morag said, "Cal, what are you talking about? Bell wouldn't hurt a fly," she said, a nervous laugh punctuating her words.

"It's a long story," Vivant piped up, trying to calm Morag with a disarming smile.

"Well, if it's that long a story, kids, you better make yourselves comfortable and get to talking," Rodrigo said, sitting down wearily and waiting for the next bombshell to drop.

Vivant, Belladonna and Cal were silent, none of them wanting to be the narrator of this story. Belladonna and Cal looked at Vivant.

"Oh, no. No you don't. I'm practically innocent in this whole thing," he said.

Everybody looked at him.

"Well, maybe innocent isn't *quite* the right word, but this story, the Rose and Cal story, really wasn't anything to do with me at all. Yes, I know, I turned you into a vampire and if it wasn't for that all the rest would never have happened, I know, I know...," Vivant said.

Belladonna looked at him with Silent Movie eyes, a look he could never resist. He rolled his eyes, more at himself than her.

"OK, you win. I'll tell it."

It took the best part of an hour to go through the whole tale from start to finish. He tried to play down Cal and Belladonna's roles. It was not hard to vilify Rose and make her the star of the show - she was a hard case, a lying, cheating, dirty little whore whose jealousies consumed her, filled her with hate, even for somebody who had been her friend and would have made sure Rose was OK if she had *made it*.

Morag and Rodrigo were shocked at the story, horrified that the jealous Rose had tried to kill Belladonna. But the worst part, the part that got everybody - even Belladonna and Cal, who had been there, who had both been her victims, both been wronged by her - was the note.

There were so many if onlys in the tale.

If only she had waited a little while.

If only she had tried to cool off a little before she sought her revenge.

If only she could have been happy for Belladonna instead of consumed by envy.

If only.

All of Rose's dreams coming true were in the palm of her hand. Everything she had longed for, everything she had ever wanted, was within her reach if she was just willing to put in the work, start at the bottom and work her way up. And she threw it away in one vicious act of revenge, one that there was no return from.

And now she was dead.

It was a harrowing tale. Shocking. All the more shocking to mama and papa since it was their own children who were players in the drama, their own babies who had been wronged by Rose, been hurt by her.

And again, gratitude that they were alright, that they had come out of the sorry mess, *seemingly* with no lasting effects was enough for them.

They visited gramama. Nobody mentioned a word about any of the troubles. But the old lady knew they were keeping her in the dark about something. She knew she would find out eventually. She would weedle it out of her daughter, Morag, somehow. She always managed to get the truth out of her, even when she didn't *want* to tell her the truth about something.

The rest of the visit was uneventful - the conversation was kept lighthearted, trivial, even. Everybody seemed scared to broach either subject again.

But Morag was so full of questions she was fit to burst. She wanted to ask her daughter so many things about her new life. She wanted to know what it felt like to be a vampire, if she had killed anybody, if she liked being a creature of the night. And she wondered what it was like to drink blood. But she didn't ask any of them. She would leave that for another time.

Rodrigo had accepted what he had been told. He was so relieved that his daughter and step-son were alive and well, he told himself that nothing else mattered except that. Then he remembered that Belladonna was a vampire and she *was*, in actual fact, dead. He laughed, a slightly manic laugh and looked around the yard to make sure nobody was around to hear it.

As Vivant and Belladonna said their goodbyes to Morag, Rodrigo and Cal, and hit the road to head back to Hollywoodland, Belladonna had a sinking feeling in her gut that Rose wasn't done causing trouble yet. Her keen sixth sense – something she's always had but was now even more pronounced because she was a vampire – told her that something was brewing back in the land of dreams and nightmares.

CHAPTER TWELVE : SHE FLEW

The two cops hiking up to the Hollywood sign were not happy. It was the third time this week they'd been called up here because some bum had gone nuts. They were particularly bemused since it was probably the same crazy bum as the previous two occasions. Their patience was running out. This time they were going to take him in and let him cool off in the drunk tank.

The caretaker of the Hollywood sign had came down to the station to complain that some old drunk living in the brush near the sign had gone nuts – was shouting and screaming about a girls corpse and the undead fiend who murdered her.

They spied said crazy bum hanging around near the sign.

"I knew it! It's him! How long are we gonna have to babysit this loon?," Officer Richter said.

"For cryin' out loud. I'm too old for this baloney," the other cop, Muldoon, said, stopping to lift his hat and wipe his sweaty brow with his necktie.

"Too old? You're only 32. You're just fat and outta shape; you're not too old."

"Hey, who you callin' fat? I ain't fat – I'm just big boned."

"Big boned? Musta borrowed them bones from a elephant then."

Muldoon looked at him, hurt; he was mad at himself that he lacked a snappy comeback. But there was really nothing he could say – Richter was younger, good-looking and fit.

"Alright, you. Let's go. We're taking you down town this time," Richter said.

"We got a cozy little jail cell for you, pal."

"She didn't jump. She was thinking about it, I know, but she didn't jump. She didn't jump. The other one threw her off. But *she* did it first. And the other one got up after *she* fell and she pushed *her* off the H. I had some of her brains and blood on me," the old man said.

"What the...? What are you talking about this time, fruit cake?" Ritter asked.

"Same thing I was talking about last time. They were both dead. Both of them. But one of them got up."

"Say, have you been on the giggle juice?," Richter asked him.

"Never! How dare you insult me! I never touch the stuff."

"Alright. That's it. Let's go, pal," Richter said, cuffing the old man's hands behind his back.

"I'm so sorry, detective. I don't know what to say. Mea culpa," the coroner said, raising his hands in submission, thinking this was probably bad enough to lose him his job.

Flint just nodded. The coroner stood shaking his head and was about to speak again but Flint spoke first and told him he could go now. Thanked him for the note.

Detective Flint sat staring at it lying on his desk. The coroner had explained to him what happened.

The note had been concealed in Rose's clenched fist and when the rigor mortis wore off, her hand opened enough to let the small, multiply-folded up piece of paper fall from her palm and onto the floor where it had been kicked around the mortuary for days. The coroner's assistant picked it up and was about to throw it in the trash, but instead opened it first to see what it was. The ashen assistant took it to the coroner who gave it to Flint.

Something unsettled him about the note. It was too perfect a scenario – woman wrongs man, man kills self, woman kills self out of remorse. The end.

That wasn't how life was, he knew. And he knew from bitter experience – never, ever to ignore his gut. It wasn't that he thought the note was phony, just that there had to be so much more to it than just a simple suicide. It was just *too* neat. Flint never trusted anything that seemed *too* neat.

He walked out into the hall, got some bad black coffee and strolled around the station. Thinking.

What's the story here?

There's more to it than this. I know it. It's too damn neat.

He walked by the drunk tank just as a commotion broke out. Richter and Muldoon were trying to put the old man from Mount Lee in a cell.

He didn't want to go in a cell.

"Get your filthy hands off me!"

"Settle down! Get in the goddam cell!"

"I will not! You have to listen to me! She didn't jump! She didn't jump! The other one threw her off the H!"

Flint stopped dead in his tracks. Then ran to the drunk tank.

"Hey, hold up there, fellas."

They unhanded the problem prisoner.

"What were you talking about?"

"I was talking about the girl on the Hollywoodland sign. She didn't jump. But nobody will listen to me."

"Have you been drinking?"

"No, I have not. I never touch the stuff."

"You sure? Come on, now, don't tell me any stories."

"I may be crazy, sir, but I am not drunk. Now, can you ask these two buffoons to leave me alone? I need to talk to a detective."

"I'm the detective in charge of the case you're talking about. You can talk to me, OK? Come on, I'll get you some hot coffee and we can have a little chit-chat."

The old man looked at the two officers as if they were dirt, and stuck his nose in the air and dusted himself off dramatically as he made his way past them.

"So, tell me your story. From the beginning. I'm listening," Flint said, lit a cigarette.

"I've been camping up on Mount Lee for a while. I saw two girls up there. A blonde and a brunette. They were fighting. The dark haired one was standing on top of the H on the Hollywoodland sign. The other one was at the top of the maintenance ladder. The dark one was screaming at the other one – she was saying the the blonde didn't care and that somebody was dead. You can't really hear very much – the wind , and so high up, you know? But I could pick out the odd word here and there."

"Go on," Flint said.

"Then the blonde one – the *dead* one – pulled the other one off. She landed practically at my feet. Her head burst open and I got splattered with brain tissue and blood. It was horrible. Then the dark haired one threw the blonde off the H."

Flint raised an eyebrow.

"You say the blonde, - uh, the *dead* one – pulled the dark haired one off the sign?"

"That's right."

"And then she got up, climbed back up the ladder and threw the blonde one off?"

"No."

"No? But you said..."

"No, I didn't say she climbed back up the ladder. The rest is correct, but she didn't climb back up the ladder."

"Oh? How did she get back up there then?"

"She flew."

"She flew. OK. Time to go, old man."

Flint stood up and gestured toward the door.

"Detective, please. Listen to me! I don't know what they were arguing about, but that one girl should be dead and she isn't. And the dead one isn't innocent, not by any means and I dare say she maybe even deserved her fate. From what I heard she was no good at all, but I saw what happened and the one with he dark hair should be the one in the morgue. She got up after being smashed on a pile of rocks just feet away from me. I'm telling you the truth. I am not a drunk. I am not a – what's that charming term? - a hop head. I am completely lucid. You may think I'm some crazy old man whose seen better days – and I won't deny that, I may very well be slightly off and I've most definitely seen better days - but detective, I've told you not one word of a lie. I saw everything I said I saw."

"Those letters are what? Forty? Fifty feet high?"

"Fifty, I believe."

"You don't walk away from fifty foot fall, mister."

"I didn't think so either, until I saw somebody do it. Look, the blood and brain matter is still there, where she fell. Go look. You will be able to tell that the tissue is not from your dead girl in the morgue. A simple ABO test will tell you that."

Flint raised an eyebrow again, surprised that a crazy old hobo knew about blood typing. The old man saw his surprise.

"I was a doctor. A long time ago."

"Ah," Flint nodded. "OK, take me there."

The closer they got to home – each mile – made Belladonna's sinking feeling increase to the point where she felt sick. The whole Rose thing was not over. She knew it.

"What's wrong? There's so many things going through your head I can't even read you."

"It's not over. I can feel it. There's something waiting for us back home."

"Ah. Well, I won't lie to make you feel better – I've been feeling the same thing."

He was right – that wasn't what she wanted to hear. It intensified her fears. If Vivant felt it, then that confirmed her fears and wasn't just paranoia on her part.

"D'you think somebody saw you that night."

"I don't know. Maybe. Normally I would have been able to sense somebody watching us, but I was so angry, I was distracted. I knew the Hollywoodland sign's caretaker was asleep in his little shack – I could hear him snoring and mumbling in his sleep – but I wasn't really paying too much attention to anything else. I have to stop doing that. The other night I went up there and I bumped into Bela. I didn't even sense him there."

"You bumped into Lugosi up there? You didn't mention it."

Vivant frowned, not pleased that she hadn't told him about it and that he hadn't sensed it.

"I forgot. With Cal and the whole Rose thing, it just slipped my mind, that's all. I wasn't keeping it from you. If I was, I wouldn't have mentioned it just now, would I?"

"I guess not. It's not important. I'm not mad or anything. I was just curious."

Belladonna curled up into a ball and pulled her coat over her like a blanket. She wanted to sleep. Needed to just switch her brain off for a while. Her thoughts were exhausting, draining her energy. She just didn't want to think anymore, at least for a little while.

Flint and the old man headed up the hill to the sign. The old man lead the way, familiar with each rock and rut all the way up. The detective was out of breath, his leg muscles burning, even although he was at least thirty years younger.

The old man went straight to the spot and pointed to the stains on the ground.

Flint crouched down, took off his hat and stared at the mess in the dirt.

"Well, sure looks like what you say it is," Flint said.

"It is what I said it was," the old man said. "I was standing right here..."

He stepped back into the brush, showing him where he was when the whole thing happened.

Flint stood and looked up at the sign, went to it, touched it.

"You said the dark one was standing on the H," Flint said.

"Yes."

"Standing. On top of the H."

"That's right."

"How in the Sam Hill could she have been standing *on* the H?" Flint lifted the brim of his hat and scratched his head.

"That I don't know. And I don't know how she fell fifty feet and got up again either..." the old man paused. "...Oh, I remember something else too; I've seen one of them before – the brunette – she was at the station - same day the other one was killed – but before it happened. You saw her too, I know you did – I saw you watching her as she sat beside the front desk.

"Oh?" Flint said.

"Yes, certainly you did. She was stunning. Like one of those silent picture actresses. All dark dewy eyes and mystery. She seemed..."

"Seemed what?" Flint asked, feeling a red flush painting his cheeks.

"She seemed...I don't even know how to describe it. She was...just *different*. Had this air about her. I can't really describe her any other way. But you *do* know who I'm talking about, don't you, detective?" the old man said with a grin.

Flint broke eye-contact with him and cleared his throat.

"Uh, maybe. Maybe I do. Not sure."

He knew exactly who the old vagabond was talking about. He was talking about the woman he could not banish from his thoughts since the moment he'd laid eyes on her.

"For the life of me I can't remember what her name was but I know it began with a *B*," the old man said.

"Belladonna. It was Belladonna. Belladonna Busto."

"Ah, Belladonna – from the latin; *beautiful woman*. And a beautiful flower. And a deadly poison."

When he'd hiked up the hillside to Rose's body a few days ago, he had a bad feeling about this case. It looked like a plain and simple case of suicide on the surface, but cases like that – one's which looked neat and clean and easy, seldom were. And he didn't like them at all.

It had been bugging him ever since. And with the discovery of the note – something that made it even neater, even cleaner, ate away at his gut like acid. Add the old man to the scenario and there was most definitely some back story to this case.

What it all meant he didn't know, but he was going to crack this case if it was the last thing he did. Besides, his curiosity about the mysterious raven-haired beauty would not allow him to rest. He wanted to see her. Watch her. Feel again what he felt when he was in her presence. It was something he had never, ever felt before. Like her namesake, she was like a drug. He craved her. He wanted more. He needed more.

"Home sweet home," Vivant said as he opened the apartment door.

The two caretakers Vivant employed to maintain the building followed with the luggage and waited for a tip.

One of them cleared his throat when he realized he was being ignored.

"I'm sorry; are you waiting for a tip?"

They both grinned.

"Never sit down with a light bulb in your back pocket," Vivant said. "Off you go."

Vivant waved them off with his hand, a cold, dismissive gesture. As they made it to the end of the corridor Vivant heard one of them speak.

"Well that was a trip for biscuits," the tall, spotty-faced one said.

"Tight-fisted Gunsel," replied the other.

Belladonna gasped, her eyes wide and clamped her hand over her mouth. Vivant grinned and whistled at them to come back. They turned on their heels and ran back the whole length of the corridor. He handed each of them a hundred dollar bill.

"Don't spend it all at once," he said.

Their jaws dropped in unison. They left slowly, both of them staring at the bills they had in their hands. Neither of them had ever held a $100 bill before. Probably never would again, unless it was from Vivant.

Belladonna laughed.

"Did you hear what he called you?," Belladonna asked him.

"Of course I heard. I like to play with people, you know that. I especially love to make people feel ashamed of themselves. And I suspect they're both feeling pretty ashamed of themselves right now. The hundreds I just gave them should ease the pain though."

Flint pounded the pavement, checking out all of Rose's known haunts, talking to people, trying to piece together a better picture of her and why she ended up broken at the bottom of the Hollywoodland sign.

OK, so what I know so far is, this dame, Rose, is shacked up with this fella, Cal. Cal makes friends with some fag in pictures. Cal gets his sister – the dark haired one – a part in the guy's picture. Rose gets all bent outta shape, plots her revenge, it all goes wrong and the picture fella ends up dead of a self-inflicted gun shot wound. Cal gives Rosie a note from the pansy telling her she's got a screen test for his new picture and she can't take it, takes a header off the Hollywoodland sign. The end. No, no, no. Too neat. Way too neat. Something's rotten in Denmark – I can fucking smell it. Now we got my pal up on the mountain; says there was somebody else there – Rose didn't commit suicide, says she was thrown off the damn sign after she pulled the other gal off it and killed her. Sure. Sure. That makes a whole lotta sense.

"Bell, don't panic, but there's a cop on his way up here who knows you were there that night," Vivant said.

He heard the detective's internal dialog before he entered the hotel.

"Oh, my God! How did he find me? Who saw me? There was nobody else there except the caretaker, and he was asleep, I heard him snoring. But even if there was somebody else there, how did they know who I am or where to find me. Christ, Viv; what are we going to do?"

"Calm down. He's just human. If he gets out of line, we'll just kill him," Vivant said, throwing her a disarming grin. She laughed but the noise sounded like panic. "Just stay calm, OK? Everything'll be just fine."

Belladonna jumped as she heard the loud rapping on the door and gave a frightened little squeal. Vivant threw her a gesture, letting her know she needed to hold it together right now. This was not the time to fall apart.

"Go into the bedroom; I can stall him a minute or two and let us think."

Vivant straightened his clothes, ran a hand over his smooth black hair and opened the door.

"Yes?" Vivant said, radiating youthful innocence.

"Detective Flint. LAPD. I'm looking for Miss Busto," he said.

"Yes, she's here. Is everything alright?" Vivant asked, super innocently, stepping back and gesturing for the policeman to come inside.

"Well, not really. A woman was found dead up on Mount Lee, about a week ago. I have a witness who says he saw..." he looked down at his notebook as if he didn't remember the name of the woman he couldn't get out of his head from the moment he set eyes on her, "...Belladonna Busto, arguing at the scene with the dead woman."

"Oh, my goodness! Well, you better sit down, Detective. I'll get Belladonna for you. I'm sure we can clear this up quickly."

"Why would you say that? You know something about it?"

"No, no. I just meant that, obviously, you're here because Belladonna is a suspect of some sort, and I'm sure we can set the record straight for you. She wouldn't hurt a fly."

"Well, we'll see, son. What was your name?"

"Just call me Vivant. I'll get Belladonna for you. Excuse me for a moment."

Vivant went to the bedroom where Belladonna stood shaking.

"What the hell am I going to tell him?," she asked.

"Just stay calm, OK? I think we can talk our way out of this. He doesn't seem overly bright to me. Just don't show him fear. Cops are like dogs – they can smell it, and if they get the scent, they won't give up."

"That's comforting, Vivant; thank you."

"You're an actress, Bells – act. I'll direct. You can handle him. Just take a minute or two to calm down before you come out, OK? Don't worry. You'll be fine," he said, and smiled before leaving her alone to try and calm down by herself.

"She'll be out in a second, Detective. Can I offer you some coffee? I just brewed some fresh."

"Sure. A little sugar, lots of cream."

Belladonna took a deep breath. Smoothed her dress and prepared to face the detective. She was panicking inwardly, but she was confident that she could appear calm on the outside.

Viv's right. I'm an actress. All I have to do is act.

She made her entrance.

"Detective," she said in her best seductive voice and extended her hand to him. It was like a scene from one of those bad B pictures she'd auditioned for so many times. She just hoped she didn't *actually* have to seduce him to get her ass out of this mess. But at least he was handsome – maybe it wouldn't be so bad. The look Vivant shot her told her he'd read her thought and disapproved.

"You don't seem at all surprised to see me, Miss Busto," Flint said.

"Why should I be? Rose was a friend of mine. It's customary for you to interview everybody who knew somebody who died in strange circumstances, no?"

"Why, sure; but why would you say strange circumstances? You know something I don't?"

"I probably know many things about Rose that you don't, detective. Like I said, she was a friend of mine. And some of her other friends were...well...let's just say they were less than salubrious."

Vivant turned his back on them and grinned to himself. Belladonna had him hooked.

"She was in with a bad crowd?"

"Oh, goodness, yes, detective. Won't you sit down?"

"I'll get that coffee," Vivant said. She was a natural. She didn't need his *direction.*

"You know who she was running with?"

"Yes, I do; a low-life named Jimmy Scars. Do you know him?"

"Know him? Boy, do I know him! I've been trying to lock up that crumb for years."

Vivant returned with two cups of coffee, handed them out and sat down.

"So, tell me the story, Miss Busto. Tell me everything. How did that pretty young gal end up dead on top of Mount Lee and what's the connection between her and Jimmy Scars?"

"Didn't my brother tell you everything you needed to know, detective? You grilled him for long enough. The poor thing was a mess when I came to get him."

"He told me everything he knew, I'm pretty sure. Kid was beside himself. But there's more to this story. And it ain't got nothing to do with your brother. All he did was fall hard for the wrong dame. We've all done it. That's no crime."

"Well, I don't know how much more I can add. Except maybe fill in a few blanks for you."

She was cool. Collected. Surprising herself at how well she was handling the situation. And she was confident.

"So, start from the beginning. Refresh my memory," the cop smiled; he had his Mr. Nice Guy act down to a T.

Belladonna sat down, took a tiny sip of her coffee.

"Well, I assume you know that my brother is a drug addict and that Rose was too, yes?"

She jumped in with both feet, stealing his thunder, not wanting the cop to throw anything at her he thought she might not want him to know. He nodded, yes. She wanted to keep a firm hold on the situation, stay one step ahead of him.

"Well, they were destitute and needed drugs. Rose was also a prostitute as well as an aspiring actress. She had some dubious acquaintances. Somehow she had the contacts to arrange for my brother to spend some time with James Walsh, the motion picture director. All they did was talk. He was a nice man and all he wanted was somebody to talk to. Somebody who was ordinary. Somebody who would talk to him like he was ordinary too, without an ulterior motive. And that was Cal. So, when Cal told him about me, just in casual conversation, Walsh guessed that I was here to be an actress, Mr. James trusted his own judgment that he wasn't being taken for a ride and decided that he wanted to give me a chance. He arranged a screen test, liked me, and offered me a part in the movie he was casting for. Rose was jealous. She wanted revenge. And she took it. She set Mr. James up for a scandal with the help of Jimmy Scars and his gutter press goons. And then she threw herself off the Hollywoodland sign because Mr. James had actually arranged a screen test for her too. She would have had her big chance if she'd just waited for a little while. Instead, Mr. James is dead and she's dead and my brother is falling apart. And that's the whole story. But you knew all that anyway, didn't you?"

"Sure, sure. I knew all that. But there's something else bothering me, see? There's this old bum who camps up there on Mount Lee, near the Hollywoodland sign. And he came to me the other day with the craziest story I ever did hear in my entire life in the LAPD, and lemme tell ya, I've heard some stories!" Flint said, with a little chuckle.

"And what was the old bum's story, detective?" Vivant asked, a little irritated because he knew the cop was playing games.

"It's the damnedest thing; the old fella says the blonde wasn't alone up there. Says she didn't throw herself off the sign at all."

He studied Belladonna intently, looking for the slightest twitch or flinch, the tiniest flicker of fear or recognition in her eyes.

"And, I assume, that you think that person was me?," Belladonna said.

"I have no reason to really suspect you did anything, except that my witness *said* it was you. I'm just doing my job, Miss. He was at the station at the same time you were, when you were waiting for your brother to be released. He'd been arrested for vagrancy, was sitting there waiting to be booked and get a nice comfy jail cell and three squares for a couple days, when lo and behold he notices you. Said you were stunning, looked like something out of a silent pictures. I saw you there too and I knew exactly who he was talking about. Said he could never forget such a face. And he didn't. Neither did I. I knew he was talking about you. He said he saw you there that night, arguing with Rose McAllister under the Hollywoodland sign."

"Well, what can I say? I could call him crazy, but that would be unfair. I don't know him. So, I'll just tell you that he is mistaken and that he didn't see me there at all," she paused, then said, "Oh, I may have an explanation for his confusion. I do visit the Hollywoodland sign on a regular basis and if he's living there then he may very well have seen me on more than one occasion and confused the two things."

"Well, could be. But that wasn't all he said. Gets crazier that that. But I'm sure a nice young lady such as yourself could never have done the things he said you did. Like I said, some of his story was just nuts."

"And what did he say I did, *exactly*?" Belladonna asked, going where she knew the detective was trying to lead her.

"I'm sure we can clear all this up if you would just give us some of your blood," Flint said.

"My blood? Why would you want my blood?" she asked, his mere mention of blood made her pulse kick in and her face feel flushed, but she knew it would be imperceptible to him.

"One of the things the old man said was that you...uh...had a fall and hit your head. Says he saw you hit the ground and your head split open. There's blood on the ground right there where he said you landed. There's brain tissue too. Darnedest thing."

Belladonna laughed.

"Well, detective, I can assure you my entire brain is in my head still. Would you like to examine my head? Surely if I had an injury serious enough to spill my brains out into the dirt, I would have a wound or a scar of some sort, wouldn't I?"

"I would assume so, yes. Pretty big wound, I'd guess."

"Indeed, she would. Even although she's a very fast healer I'm sure she would still be showing some signs of such an injury," Vivant chimed in. He was enjoying the show.

"Yep, I'm sure that's true," Flint said, running out of things to say with out venturing into the realm of crazy and repeating what the old man said. But he needed more time. He did not want to leave.

He was enthralled by Belladonna. There was something about her – she wasn't like everybody else. He was instantly fascinated to the point that he'd even made himself look foolish by constantly walking by her every few minutes when he saw her at the station. There was something unusual about her, something that made you feel different when she was in the room. The old man had felt it to.

And he could feel the same vibe coming off Vivant. There was no other reason to hang around here. And he could not leave them. He wanted to be there, with both of these beautiful, mysterious people.

"If that's all, detective..."

"Well, there's a couple more things I should mention..."

"And they are?" she asked.

"He said you were dead and you got up again. And you flew."

Great now she's gonna thing you're some sorta nutcase!

"I died?... *and* I flew?" Belladonna laughed. Flint's face turned scarlet and both Vivant and Belladonna could smell his blood as it rushed to the surface of his skin. "Well, you can see I am very much alive, detective, and I'm not aware of having wings of any sort. Would you like to check?"

"That won't be necessary, Miss Busto," he said, and paused to clear his throat. "Just passing on what my witness told me. I didn't say I believed it. Just doing my job."

"Of course, detective. I'll see you out, shall I?"

Belladonna lightly laid her hand on Flint's arm and led him to the door.

"I may need to call on you again, Miss Busto. The investigation is still open."

"Sure, detective, sure. Drop by any time. I'll be here."

She closed the door and she knew he was still standing there when she walked away. She smiled at Vivant and he grinned back at her.

"Damn, you're good," he said, pulling her violently against him and kissing her hard.

"He's gonna come back, Viv," Belladonna said, turning over on her side and resting her head on his alabaster torso.

"Of course he will. I was listening to what he was saying inside his head all the time he was talking. He wants you. Bad. He's fascinated by you. Actually by both of us. I know he doesn't look it, but he's sensitive. He can feel that we're different. He didn't want to leave. He wanted to stay with us. I was quite touched by his thoughts, actually."

Belladonna smiled. The thought of being able to read everybody's mind the way Vivant could would come with age. The ability to home in on somebody, no matter where they were, the gift of being able to tell what a person was thinking, at will, both thrilled and terrified her. For now, it came to her in fits and starts, and heightened emotions could either enhance or impede her abilities. With age would also come control over it. Right now, sometimes it drove her crazy.

"You don't think they'll be able to prove anything, do you? I mean, what if they find out it's my blood? I know I managed to stall him and divert him earlier, but...they'll arrest me, won't they."

"I suppose they could, but you can easily manipulate him. I think he'll do anything you ask him to. He's the one in charge of the investigation. And you know how corrupt they are. There's police chiefs in that department who sell positions. I know somebody who bought one a few years back."

"Why would anybody do that?"

"Lots of reasons. Revenge. Power. Money."

"Revenge. There's that word again. Seems everybody's out to get revenge for something or other."

"Well, right now I'm gonna get my revenge on you!"

Vivant flipped Belladonna over onto her back and pinned her wrists against the bed. She squealed with delight as he teased her, dipping his head down as if to kiss her and pulling back at the last moment. It was a delicious torment but one that never lasted long – he couldn't resist her any more than she could resist him.

Belladonna stepped out on to the balcony, lit a cigarette and inhaled deeply. She paid no attention to the man standing in the darkened doorway across the street until she felt a swell of emotion coming from him and with it, his thoughts.

I know you did it, Belladonna. I know you did it. I don't know what you are but I know you're not human. You should be dead. That girl killed you and you got up again. What are you? What the hell are you? Oh, my God, I want you.

Belladonna flicked her cigarette down into the street below and slowly stepped back into the bedroom.

"Vivant! He's outside. I just read his thoughts and he knows it was me. He knows I'm not human."

"He doesn't know. He just thinks he knows. If he repeats that to anybody he'll be thrown off the force. Anybody would think he's touched in the head. He's infatuated with you. I wouldn't worry about it too much."

"I am worried, though; how could I not be? Everything is upside-down and wrong-side up! I don't think he's gonna go away that easy. I think he might be obsessed with me."

"I know the feeling," Vivant said, grinning at her salaciously and lifted up the hem of her silk slip with his toes.

"It's not funny. I'm scared."

"What on earth do you have to be scared about? You're a vampire! You could crush him with two fingers!"

"I know that. I just know that he's not gonna go away. I can feel it. He's thinking about me right now."

Vivant easily tapped into Flint's thoughts.

I have to know what you are. I have to know how you would feel under my hands, how you would feel beneath me, our hot skins connecting...

"Good Lord!" Vivant laughed. "He's quite the poet for a copper! Did you hear what he just said about you?"

"I heard," she said, bemused.

"Quite excitable, isn't he? I'm not cleaning the mess off the sidewalk in the morning."

"Oh, you!" Belladonna picked up a pillow and threw it at Vivant.

CHAPTER THIRTEEN : KILLING JIMMY SCARS

A loud rap came at the apartment door rousing both Vivant and Belladonna from their sleep. Vivant threw on a robe and opened it, no too happy his slumber had been interrupted.

"What is it?" he asked, his voice sleepy.

"Telegram, sir. Sorry for waking you, but it said URGENT.

"That's alright. Not your fault. Thank you."

It was addressed to Belladonna but Vivant unfolded the message and read it anyway.

CAL MISSING STOP BELIEVE HE IS HEADED YOUR WAY STOP PLEASE LET US KNOW HES OK IF HE TURNS UP STOP WE LOVE YOU BOTH STOP MAMA & PAPA STOP

"Oh, God. Stupid little bastard," Vivant muttered through gritted teeth.

His face was grim and Belladonna knew that there was something wrong.

"What is it? Is it Cal?" she asked, knowing that it was, indeed, Cal.

"It's from your parents; Cal's gone walkabout. They think he's headed back here."

"Oh, no. I knew he was gonna do this. I knew it! I should have warned them before we left that he might try to come back.

I knew he didn't want to stay home. I should have talked to him. I should have...done something."

"Bells, you're not responsible for every single little thing that goes wrong in Cal's life. He's a big boy now. He's old enough to make up his own mind. And if he was hell-bent on coming back here for whatever reason, then there was probably nothing you could have said to change his mind."

"Maybe so, but I knew he wasn't going to stay there and I lied to myself. I told myself everything was gonna be OK and he was gonna go back to normal, back to being the old Cal again. And I knew he wouldn't. I knew he would never be the same again and I didn't do anything!"

"Sweetheart, calm down. We don't know that he's come to any harm. Let me see if I can find him, alright?"

She nodded, her eyes filled with fear and water.

Vivant sat still and silent, concentrating on tuning in to Cal. His brows knotted with effort and his breathing labored slightly.

He stayed like that for several minutes, determined not to let Belladonna down.

With violence, Vivant's eyes sprang open and alarm rang all over his face.

"Oh, shit," was all he said.

Cal's head hung limp, his hair plastered to his face with sweat and blood. His hands were bound behind his back, his feet tied to the front legs of the wooden chair he sat in.

A big, ugly thug stood over him polishing the blade of a flick-knife with a black handkerchief. He couldn't wait to get the thing wet and dirty again. The blade had seen a lot of flesh, tasted much blood.

"Bring him round," Jimmy Scars ordered his goon.

The goon looked disappointed; he thought he was going to be allowed to play some more. A couple of punches and a few slaps just didn't do it for him. He threw the pitcher of water into Cal's face with such a force he immediately came round, sucked in a huge lung-full of air. The goon threw the water with such force it hurt; he was displeased at not being allowed to torture Cal.

"What the hell you doin' here, kid?," Scars asked him.

"You know what I'm doing here. You have to pay for what you did," Cal said, without fear, or even so much a quiver in his voice.

"For what? What did I do? I did a favor for an old friend and it got outta hand. Hardly my fault."

"A favor? Mr. James and my Rosie are dead now because of you. Maybe you should've have told her *no*." Cal said.

"Oh, sure; you ever try saying no to that broad?" Jimmy Scars laughed uproariously.

"She was my world. She was everything to me. And you took her away. This is all your fault. If you hadn't agreed to doing what you did, Mr James and Rosie would both still be alive. You put the whole thing together. You made it happen. She could never have done that on her own. That makes you responsible, you...you...," Cal fumbled for an appropriate insult to hurl at Jimmy Scars. He found it. "...underworld lowlife!"

Scars chuckled.

"Listen, kid; the whole deal was Rose's idea. All I did was call on a few...associates. But the whole shebang was her idea. And if that little whore was your whole life, fella, maybe you oughta be a little more choosy about your women in the future," he said.

"Rosie may have been a lot of things, Mister, but she loved me. She wasn't perfect, I know that. But I know she loved me," Cal said, his face rigid with anger and hatred, his eyes moist at the thought of Rosie. But even he didn't believe his own words.

"You shittin' me? Rose McAllister didn't love you, you sap. She wasn't capable of loving anybody. She was so full of fuckin' bitterness about how bad her life was she had no room in her black little heart for anything or anybody. All that dope you two did musta addled your brain. I knew her for years. Years and years. I knew her when she was still a kid. In all that time I never heard Rose say a good word about anybody or anything. Ever," he paused, then snapped his head up, suddenly remembering something he needed to say to Cal, hoping it would shock the shit out of him. "Oh, by the way, did you know your lovely Rosie tried to kill your sister?"

"How do you know that?" Cal asked, shocked that anybody else knew.

"I have my sources – I'm a...what was it?...*underworld lowlife*, remember?," Jimmy Scars delighted in the epithet and seemed proud of it. He and his goon chuckled. "This town has ears. Nothin' happens in Hollywoodland that Jimmy Scars don't know about. Nada," Jimmy Scars sighed. "What am I gonna do with you, kid? You think this is like some gangster picture? Think I'm gonna go all soft and let you go 'cause you're just some dumb kid and you didn't really mean no harm?"

"No. I did mean harm. If he hadn't caught me, you would be dead now. I was going to kill you. So, if you're going to kill me, just do it. I won't struggle. I don't care anymore," Cal said.

Scars and his goon exchanged raised-eyebrow looks.

"Oh, I get it. You want to commit suicide by gangster, right?" Scars was tickled and laughed hard.

"Call it what you want. I don't care. I just don't care."

The goon adjusted his pants, his cock hardening a little at the thought of being allowed to kill Cal. He hadn't tortured anybody to death for a while. He could almost feel Cal's blood on his hot olive skin already. He ran his tongue over parched lips in anticipation, rubbed the sweat from his palms on the front of his stale, almost-white shirt.

The front door of the piano store was locked. That wasn't a problem for Viviant. He just pushed it open, splintering the door frame, but hardly making a sound, save for the crack of the wood. He headed straight for the concealed door and opened it, slipped through and descended the stairs without making a sound.

They were in a room off the main tunnels, door ajar and voices filtering through it to him. He was going to smack Cal for his stupidity if the poor guy lived through this.

Viviant knocked gently on the ajar door. He could sense all three of them were startled by the unexpected visitor and could smell the scent of their adrenaline surges.

Viviant could feel the vibrations of the goon's heavy footfalls coming toward the door. Even although no harm could come to him, Viviant still enjoyed the little thrill that violent confrontations gave him. He was old – old enough to remember when people were still primitive, old enough to remember when people would fight to the death for what they believed in. He was old enough to remember a time when people still believed in an eye for an eye. And Vivant had always been very much in touch with his primitive side.

The goon opened the door.

Without thinking, without even asking Vivant who he was or what he wanted, he grabbed him by his shirt collar and dragged him into the room.

Vivant was pissed. But he kept a calm, affable exterior. For now.

"Who the fuck are you?," Jimmy Scars asked the vampire Vivant. Before he could answer, a flicker of recognition crossed the criminal's face. "Wait. I know you. Don't I know you?"

"I believe we've met, yes. Perhaps I've sang at one of your salubrious establishments?"

"That's it! My pansy club on Sunset. I thought I knew you," Jimmy Scars said.

"That's right."

"What the hell you doin' here? Club's closed right now."

"How the fuck did you get in here, twilight? I locked the front door," the goon said.

"Never mind that. Mr. Scars, I'd really appreciate it if you wouldn't kill my friend," Vivant said.

"You know this schmuck? Why should I spare the sap? He came here to fuckin' bump me off. If I'd been here all on my lonesome he might've succeeded. Gimme one good reason, faggot."

Vivant was dying to rip his face off, but he resisted, for now.

"Firstly, I'm not a faggot, as you put it. But even if I was that would be none of your business. I'm bisexual, for your information. But that's none of your business either. Secondly, if you kill him, I'll kill both of you next. Your move, Mr. Scars," Vivant said.

Cal's mouth hung slack. He'd never heard of bisexuality before but quickly figured out what it was.

Both scumbags laughed.

The thug unsheathed his beloved blade again.

"Kill them both," Scars instructed.

"Sure, boss."

Before he could even move toward him, Vivant whipped out the Thompson concealed under his long, black trenchcoat. Both gangsters stared at it, both fully aware of what the piece could do and struck by its beauty. They both looked at it like it was a woman.

Vivant's 1921 model had a blued barrel and custom-made furniture. The stock and foregrip were lacquered, jet black and shone like jewels. They had no idea what they were made of. He'd spent an obscene amount of money on it.

Vivant grinned; he was proud of his beautiful baby. And it was an historic firearm. He stole it from a young thug who worked for Johnny Torrio in Chicago. The thug stepped out of line with a dancer, named Alice at a club Vivant was singing at on one of his few breaks from Hollywood. He set him straight and took his Tommy gun from him. The young thug's name was Al Capone. Vivant named it after the young chorus girl.

Vivant opened fire on Scars's goon.

The noise was deafening in the confined space of the office and the sulphurous smell of gunpowder, heavy in the air, mingled with the scent of blood. It was like an aphrodisiac to Vivant and he roared with delight.

The big tough psychopath was now a pile of bones and bloody meat, felled by a beautiful woman named *Alice*.

Scars opened his mouth as if to scream but no sound came out. He tried to heave his fat ass off the chair but his legs failed him and the momentum his girth gave him as he moved made him land heavily on the floor.

"Good Lord! They don't call them 'choppers' for nothing, do they?" Vivant said and laughed uproariously.

The goon's body was ruined.

Suddenly Jimmy Scars found the will to move out of the way; he'd never seen anybody control a machine gun like that before, and he was more than familiar with them. He didn't think it was even humanly possible. Most of the slugs would usually hit the top of a wall or the ceiling. But every slug hit the Scar's guard dog square in the torso and the head. It was a bloody mess.

Jimmy scars gagged and choked as the smell of his henchman's innards hit the back of his nose.

"I'm pretty mean for a pansy, don't you think?"

A hot, dark patch spread across the front of Jimmy's light blue pants as Vivant made his way toward him.

"Give me your gun," Vivant told him.

"You're gonna shoot me with my own gun?" the gangster asked, incredulous.

"Goodness, no! That would be very rude of me. I just like guns. Give it to me."

"You're not gonna kill me?"

Vivant said nothing, just held out his hand waiting for the piece.

Scars slowly pulled up the right leg of his pants, his eyes never leaving Vivant's face. There was something strange about him - something about his eyes – he couldn't quite put his finger on what it was but it was unmistakable.

Something wild.

Was all he could think to himself as he looked at Vivant.

Something wild.

Jimmy Scars slowly removed his pistol from his ankle holster and handed it to Vivant.

He smiled and ran his fingers over the blued barrel.

"Ah. Savage 1907 model. .45. Six shot. Good choice – and rare. I figured you'd be a .45-man. Original walnut grips too. She's beautiful."

Vivant smiled at him, a disarming, charming smile.

"You're not gonna kill me?," Jimmy Scars asked, hopefully.

"I didn't say *that*. I just said I wasn't going to kill you with your own gun. I'm going to use my bare hands."

Scars started screaming, pleading for his life as piss ran into his expensive shoes.

Vivant grabbed hold of his windpipe and sank his fingers deep into Jimmy Scars's flesh. He ripped it out in one smooth motion. For some reason the noise that came from his gaping wound horrified Cal more than the bloody scene. It was a wet, airy, sucking noise, a noise that made the hair stand up on the back of his neck, a noise that came from inside Jimmy Scars's body, noise that nobody ever heard. Or should ever hear.

Vivant opened his mouth and let the torn arteries rush into him. He gorged on the dying gangsters blood, covered in it from head to toe.

In less than a minute, Jimmy Scars was dry.

Cal was suddenly aware of his own guts. He concentrated hard on not spilling their contents, tried to breathe deeply to calm himself down but realized quickly that was a bad idea as he inhaled the scent of the criminal corpses' insides. He could smell blood and bile and shit.

Cal lunged over to his right as far as he could, trying to reach the small trash can at the side of Jimmy Scars's desk. He vomited as elegantly as his restraints would allow and didn't spill a drop on the deep shag or on himself.

"Get me out of here!," Cal screamed at Vivant.

Vivant untied Cal and helped him stand, his feet numb from the tightness of the ropes the goon had secured around his ankles.

"You OK?"

"I'm fine, I'm fine! Let's go!" Cal said

"Wait in the hall – I have to shoot the shit out of Scars to cover up his...injury."

Cal didn't hang around in the room to argue and instead stumbled as far down the dingy tunnel as he could.

It was cold down there – in the underbelly of Los Angeles, deep underground.

It was fine down here when there were dozens of beautiful Jazz Babies sucking down bathtub gin and Bolivian cocaine like greedy infants. But now, deserted, dark, it was creepy in its echoing desolation. It had a cold that seeped into the bones, chilled the blood.

He jumped when he heard the crack of the Thompson again and a few seconds later Vivant was right beside him. Before he could form words to speak, the pair of them were back in the penthouse apartment, like nothing had ever happened. Except Vivant was red from head to toe.

Nothing would look amiss that the scene in Jimmy Scars's office. Everybody expected him to go out that way anyhow. He was an underworld scumbag. Nobody would miss a low-life like him and his thug. The police certainly wouldn't shed any tears over his demise. They wouldn't waste too many resources investigating the crime. Most of the cops would be yucking it up, calling the hit a public service. And they wouldn't ask too many questions if an anomaly or two about the percentage of on-target shots seemed incredulous, or the devastated state of the bodies was more extreme than they had ever seen in a gangland hit.

Most people would be glad to see the back of him.

Some of the cops knew that Hollywood movers and shakers would breathe a sigh of relief.

Vivant told Belladonna all about his adventure with Cal and showed her his new toy – the Savage pistol he got from Jimmy Scars. Belladonna cood over it like it was a new born baby. Cal sat quietly, the inside of his head still echoing with the sounds of the murders he'd just witnessed, the stink of their viscera still in his nostrils. He wasn't sure he would ever be able to rid himself of the memory.

"Bells, you wanna come with me on a mission?"

Belladonna knew Vivant wanted to return to the scene of his crime and poke around, get rid of the bodies, and clean the place up. She was the only one who could help. She knew Cal couldn't take much more. Thankfully he'd passed out on the sofa.

It was after dark. Late Sunday night. The streets were quiet. Those who were out were deep underground in the damp, smoky speakeasies that lived in the belly of Los Angeles, knocking back bad homemade liquor that could kill you or make you blind. The air would be wet with the sweat and exhalations of the revelers that would go on drinking and dancing hour after hour.

Vivant turned down a side street off Sunset and headed for the piano store. He wasn't overly concerned about discovery of the corpses, but a couple of simply disappeared scumbags was much easier for the cops to gloss over and be nonchalant about than a pile of undigested gangster hamburger in the guts of LA.

And the second Flint got word of it, Vivant knew they wouldn't be able to get rid of him.

"Uh-oh," Vivant said.

They ran smack-bang into a cop fest. Police and cars everywhere, coroner, detectives.

Vivant killed the headlights and backed up as discreetly as he could hoping to avoid the attention of the LAPD crawling all over the place like flies on a shit pile.

"Who found them, for Christ's sake?" Vivant asked.

"Delivery man. I saw a van, Back open. Two pianos in the middle of the road. But what was he doing here at this time of night? And what did he need to go way down there for?"

"He was probably delivering other goods, if you know what I mean," Vivant said.

"You mean liqour?"

"Liqour, guns, drugs – whatever Jimmy was in the market for. He had his fat little fingers in a lot of pies."

"What in the Hell are we going do do now, Vivant?" Belladonna asked.

"Look, don't worry about it. They didn't see us. They'll never be able to prove anything anyway, I promise you. You were fabulous last time Flint turned up to interrogate you, by the way."

"Yes, I was, but what about Cal? He's a mess. Look how it went when we were talking to my parents – he just blurted it out, everything about Rose, about me and you. He'll crack in a heartbeat if that cop questions him. He's just not cut out for this."

Vivant frowned.

"Ah, but, he won't know that Cal's even in town, will he? He only just got here. He headed straight for Scars when he arrived. Just try and stay calm. Don't panic. If Flint's that much of a problem, I'll just kill him. Simple," Vivant said with a shrug.

Belladonna rolled her eyes.

"Is that your answer to everything? Just kill this one. Just kill that one. God, Vivant."

Vivant grinned.

"It's all part of my charm. Look, I said don't worry. So don't worry. I'll take care of it. Anybody stops us and asks questions, we're just out for a romantic Sunday drive, OK?"

"In the middle of the night?"

"We're night owls, aren't we?" He grinned at her and winked, and she just couldn't help but smile.

Cal had woken up and was panicking when they got back to the penthouse. He looked like trapped wild animal pacing frantically to and fro behind bars. His eyes were wide. He was shaking.

"There was somebody at the door!," Cal blurted at them before they even got inside.

"Who was it?," Vivant asked him.

"I don't know. I didn't answer it. But I bet it was the police!"

"Nobody knows you're here. Just calm down. We need to talk, OK."

"Did you get rid of the bodies?"

"Uh, no. No, we did not," Vivant said.

"What do you mean, no? What happened?"

Cal ran his fingers through his sweat-drenched hair.

"When we got to the club there were cops everywhere," Belladonna said.

"Oh, God. They know! They know!" he howled.

"They don't know a damn thing, now pull yourself together, Cal. Enough of the hysteria. Now sit down, shut up and listen to me," Vivant said.

Cal did what he was told and sat down. He tapped his heel rapidly on the floor and chewed on a thumb nail.

"Look, there's nothing that can tie you to Jimmy Scars except Rose. Rose is gone and you're up north, anyway, aren't you? That's what we're going to tell the police if they come. OK?" And if they have a search warrant, or if they check up on you in Oregon, I can slip you out the window and have you home and be back here before they even know I've gone.

Cal frowned and looked at Vivant as if he was completely insane. He was not confident that Vivant could do what he claimed. Nothing calmed him down and he was getting on

Vivant's nerves. He tried to hold his temper while he explained to Cal that the detective would certainly be back – they knew that – since he had taken quite a shine to Belladonna. Him coming back would not come as a surprise and, indeed, they were expecting it.

But nothing helped. Cal continued pacing. Wringing his hands. Chewing on his thumb nail.

LATER...

"Listen, the detective is on his way over here. I can hear him rehearsing what he's going to say. He suspects there's a connection between us and the terrible untimely death of Jimmy Scars and his goon, but he's got nothing on us. Nothing but his gut feeling about it. And he doesn't know you're here, Cal."

"Wow," Cal said.

"I know; I'm impressive, aren't I?"

Belladonna rolled her eyes and shook her head, but couldn't hide her grin.

"I guess I'll go slip into something more...stunning," she said.

Vivant smiled. He was proud of her. In a few short months he'd taken a pretty country bumpkin and watched her bloom into a sophisticated, articulate, talented, manipulative bitch. He was Pygmalion in love with his own work of art. To Vivant, she was just what a woman should be. And just what a vampire should be too.

It wasn't long before the expected loud rap on the door broke the silence.

Vivant ushered Cal into the bedroom and told him to stay there, not even move, until he came back to get him. He was fine with that. He knew himself well enough to know that he would spill his guts to the cops in a second. He just couldn't master lying. It wasn't in his nature.

He pulled a chair up near the door and sat down, took the key out of the keyhole and spied through it. He could actually see the whole living room area they'd all be in pretty well. He cocked his head and pressed his ear to the keyhole and listened. He could hear their voices filtering through the air. He didn't realize he was holding his breath until he started to feel light-headed.

He listened.

"Sorry to interrupt, Miss Busto; but there's been a new development in the case."

"In Rose's case?"

"Yep. Jimmy Scar's...he's dead. Murdered," Flint said.

"Jimmy Scars is dead?" Belladonna said, wide-eyed and innocent.

"Yes, last night. God-awful mess. You wouldn't believe what a Tommy gun can do to a human body. I've never seen anything like it. One of his employees was found dead too," Flint told her, shaking his head a little to try and dislodge the image of the carnage still burned into his retinas.

"My goodness! That's horrible!" Belladonna said, touching her hand to her chest. "Who would do such a thing?"

"In this town? Take your pick. Jimmy Scars had enemies a-plenty. Could be an one of a hundred people. Thousand, maybe. Your brother around?"

"My brother? No, he's back home, up north. Vivant and I took him there ourselves."

"Actually he's not. Apparently he went AWOL. Your parents sent a telegram to the LAPD. They seem to think he's headed back here."

Vivant stepped in.

"Detective, this whole thing has been very, very hard on Cal. He's probably just taken off into the woods somewhere. He's a country boy; that's where he goes to get away from it all. I'm sure he'll turn up. I'm afraid Mr. and Mrs. Busto may have been a little premature in contacting you."

"You think so, huh?" the Cop asked.

"I do."

Belladonna felt a knot of panic tightening in her gut. She felt sure that the cop knew Cal was in the apartment. She was terrified that guilt – guilt about everything – was written all over her and seeping from her pores. She thought he could see it, thought he could smell it coming off her skin. She was so agitated and afraid, she could not read his mind.

But Vivant could. Nothing could phase Vivant or put him in a flap - except Belladonna.

She looked at him and he could feel her panic even although she maintained a cool, calm exterior. He winked at her, a slow, tiny wink that could have been an involuntary twitch of the eye had the detective seen it. But Belladonna knew what it meant - Vivant could read him even if she couldn't.

Don't worry Bells he knows nothing. He's just a dumb gumshoe.

She trusted him, but she couldn't shake the feeling that something was going to happen. She was waiting for Cal to have a meltdown and come crashing out of the bedroom confessing to everything from the Ripper Murders in London over forty years before, to the Chicago *St. Valentine's Day Massacre* in '29. But for the sake of her own sanity and safety, she had to trust him and believe he would do what he was told and stay put.

"So, what happened to Jimmy Scars, Detective?" Vivant asked, feeling a deafening silence developing between Belladonna and the copper. He knew silence would make Cal nervous. He was wishing he'd knocked him out before he let Flint in.

Vivant wanted rid of Flint now. He could hear Cal freaking out in the bedroom. The guy was ripping himself apart, shaking, screaming inside. He didn't want to talk to him telepathically in case that made him lose it completely and start screaming out loud.

Right now, Vivant just wanted Flint out of the apartment. He was going to have to take Cal back to Oregon before Flint came back. And he would, he knew.

"Well, somebody musta been real sore at Jimmy. Somebody turned the pair of them into chopped liver," Flint said.

"My goodness," Vivant said, and shuddered dramatically.

Flint studied him, eyes narrowed searching him, willing him to slip up and implicate himself. He knew these two were in it up to their necks. He knew the dumb kid couldn't have done what he saw in Jimmy Scars's club earlier. He knew he didn't have the stomach for it.

He'd nearly cracked up under questioning about James Walsh's death, even although everybody knew he didn't kill him, and he was never a suspect.

You did this you son of a bitch I know you did it I know you did it.

Vivant smiled, a slight, barely-there smile he knew was ambiguous to the cop but Belladonna could see clearly.

"I don't know how we can be of any help, Detective. None of us actually knew Mr. Scars – we don't associate with people like that. I've been to his *piano store,* but I've never met him, not that I know of, anyway. We only knew *of* him because of what Rose did," Belladonna said.

"Actually," Vivant butted in, "I must correct you there, darling; Jimmy Scars *was* an acquaintance of mine. I wouldn't say I knew him exactly, but I have sang in a club or two he owns. So I've seen him around."

"Oh, really?" Flint said, looking like the cat that got the cream.

Vivant could tell from the gleam in Flint's eye that he thought he was on to something.

"Like I said, I didn't actually know Jimmy Scars. Can't even say that I ever had a conversation with him, to tell you the truth," Vivant said, playing down his acquaintance with the scumbag.

Belladonna had a feeling there was something Vivant wasn't telling her. He was blocking her from reading him. She was starting to think that maybe Vivant knew Jimmy Scars a lot better than he was letting on.

"Is there anything else we can be of help with, detective?" Belladonna asked, politely, calmly.

"No, I guess that's all for now. But don't you two go leaving town without telling me, alright?" he said.

"Of course," Belladonna said, with a sweet smile on her soft lips and a flutter of her eyelashes.

Vivant saw the cop to the door and Belladonna was waiting for him, hands on hips, when he came back.

The sweet smile and the fluttering eyelashes were gone.

"Alright, Viv; out with it," she demanded.

"Out with what, sweetheart?"

She laughed.

"Innocence doesn't suit you, Vivant. You knew him, didn't you?

"Who, Scars? Yes, I told you both – I've sang in some of his clubs."

"Yes, I heard you say that. Did you know him before?"

"Before?"

"Did you know him years ago?"

Vivant chuckled.

"Damn vampires; can't hide anything from them," he grinned at her, giving her that irresistible one-sided grin of his.

"Never mind trying to distract me by being cute. I want you to tell me the truth," she told him in earnest.

Vivant sighed; he couldn't lie to her successfully any more that she could lie to him successfully. Even if he blocked her from reading his mind, she still knew when he was lying.

"Alright; I confess! Yes, I knew him long ago. He recognized me but he didn't know from where. I don't think his recognition was of me as a singer. I *have* sang in his clubs, but I've never run into him in any of them. It's always the club manager I deal with. Anyway, back in the beginning, when Hollywood was just being born, just when all of us in the picture business were moving west to get away from that pill Edison and his damned lawsuits, I knew Jimmy Scars," Vivant said.

"Well, go on. Let's hear it."

Vivant explained how he knew Jimmy Scars.

Jimmy Scars had been a small-time crook in Brooklyn who somehow – through a friend of a friend of a friend, ended up working as player for one of the motion picture companies in New Jersey.

That was when the movies were still silent. They made mainly one reel comedies. Jimmy Scars had done grunt work and stunt work. He worked building sets and then did the stunts that would inevitably end up in the destruction of most of what he had just built. He did walk-on roles and played corpses and villains, fleetingly seen bad guys on the run from the cops.

But Jimmy Scars wasn't satisfied with that. He'd heard about some of the guys and gals he knew going out west and becoming famous, earning big money. So he headed out there.

But Jimmy Scars's sordid, violent past caught up with him. He wasn't quite as small-time a crook as he appeared.

He was wanted in connection with a murder in New York City. An innocent bystander – a little boy – got caught in the crossfire when Scars and his hoodlum buddies had a shootout in the middle of downtown, in broad daylight. Scars gunned the kid down right in front of his young mother. She hung herself a few days later, consumed by grief and unable to live with the horror of being covered in her little boy's blood,

Even the film-makers who came west and founded the studios – some of them with dubious pasts themselves - balked at what Jimmy Scars had done.

Nobody would touch him – his reputation preceded him. He couldn't even get a job taking out the trash and cleaning bathrooms for any of the studios.

So, Jimmy Scars flitted around the periphery of the movie industry, always needing to be near it, close enough to see everything that went on, but always *just* on the outside.

And he hated them all.

But he still wanted to be one of them.

They didn't mind using him if they needed anything illicit that they didn't want to dirty their own hands with procuring, anything that they didn't want to risk transporting themselves.

Jimmy Scars'll do it – just don't tell anybody you know him. Shit sticks.

That was why he jumped in with both feet and was so willing to destroy one of them, one who had done him no harm but could play the role of his victim perfectly.

"...So, he probably saw me at swanky parties when he was delivering coke or heroin or opium, or little boys to silent movie stars, just before he got the door slammed in his face. I was in pictures too, remember? A lot of people look at me with recognition. And it was a smaller town back then. He probably saw me here and there and everywhere. But all those people I fraternized with are all wizened and debauched now. Or dead. And I'm still fresh as a daisy. That's why he recognized me, and yet couldn't *quite* place me. I shouldn't look like this after - what? - got to be twenty years or so," he said. "God, those were the days! Sometimes – rarely - somebody does recognize me from the old pictures. They tell me I must have a seething, festering portrait in my attic," Vivant laughed. "If only they knew!"

He was totally unfazed by the detective, but Belladonna couldn't shake the feeling that Flint was going to be a problem.

Vivant heard her thoughts.

"Bells, look; what do you think he can do to us? We're fucking vampires! I could kill him in a heartbeat. If it'll make you feel better, I'll rush Cal home right now for a couple of days and he can get his Keystone Cops up there to check in with your parents. They'll see him there. They'll leave. And Cal can come back down again if he wants to. See? Easy."

She smiled a little at him but couldn't not rid herself of the feeling.

Cal gingerly came out of the bedroom, resigned to Vivant shuttling him home to Oregon.

But no matter what, he was not going to stay there.

This was home now. This beautiful, God-awful, sordid and glamorous place that managed to get so far under your skin in ended up in your blood.

Just like Belladonna, and most others who made their way here, he could not bear the thought of leaving and not coming back.

Cal the country boy, the wheat, the bumpkin, the rube, was just as dead as the old Belladonna was.

Vivant took Cal back to Oregon. He told him he'd come back for him in a few days and to just be patient, wait for all of this to blow over.

He reassured him that nobody would really care about the death of Jimmy Scars and his goon, and the only reason that Flint gave a flying fuck was because there was a connection to Belladonna.

He made Cal promise to stay put until he came back for him. He knew the police were going to check up on him real soon and not to worry – just don't tell them anything. Don't crack up. Be calm – they really don't know a thing.

The next morning the farmhouse was awoken by loud knocking at the door. Cal was already up and practicing what to say, how to act.

And he played it expertly.

This acting thing must run in the family.

And he couldn't wait for Vivant to come back and get him.

He couldn't stand it here anymore. He was a different person now. The old Cal was gone. He didn't want to hunt anymore. He didn't want to crash around in the boonies in his beat-up old Ford pickup anymore. He didn't want to go rolling around in the hay with the local gals anymore and getting drunk on old Grampy Zeke's corn mash moonshine. All that was kid's stuff now.

He thought of home as somewhere he had always been a child. A place he would always be thought of as a child. And he didn't want that anymore.

In Hollywood he could reinvent himself. In Hollywood, the world's capital of make believe and wildest dreams, he could be anybody he wanted to be. Or at least pretend to be somebody else.

Everybody there lies all the time anyways.

He loved mama and papa, and his little half-sister, but he'd outgrown the outback. He was a man now – not the overgrown boy everybody saw him as.

Shortly after the police left, Vivant appeared. His desire to return to Hollywood was so strong, Vivant heard his longing, all those miles away.

Back in the apartment Cal just had to ask a question.

"Vivant?"

"Mmm-hmm?" Vivant looked up from his book at Cal.

"How come you've never been caught flying?"

Vivant laughed.

"That's a good question; the reason is that I prevent anybody who may be in the vicinity and watching, from seeing me," he said.

"But...how?"

"Mind control, Cal. It's really not that hard. It's a basic vampire skill."

"Oh."

"What would you say if I wanted to be one?"

"What?"

"You heard me – what would you say if I wanted to be a vampire?"

Belladonna walked into the room just in time to hear Cal's question.

"Cal! You don't want to be a vampire, trust me," she said.

Cal protested, told her that she seemed to like it just fine and Vivant obviously loved it. Why shouldn't he be a vampire? He'd been a great hunter – he would probably make a fantastic bloodsucker.

Cal had learned well in the time he'd been here. He decided to try some emotional manipulation.

"But if you make me a vampire, sis, then the drugs won't be able to kill me."

Vivant grinned and shook his head. The kid was learning. He was learning how to *be* Hollywood.

He was mastering the skills of how to lie and cheat and manipulate, just like the rest of the population.

Cal's fear wasn't that he would die from taking drugs.

Cal wanted to be a vampire so he could go on taking drugs forever and not have to worry about dying from them.

There was nothing for him back home anymore. Being back there just for a day made him feel like a stranger. He felt like he was visiting a place he had never been before. He knew that he could not stay there. Not now.

Rosie had changed him, just as much as Vivant had changed Belladonna.

And he was going to stay forever in the place where the new Cal was born, the place his Rosie died tragically and loved so much.

"Are you out of your mind?" Belladonna asked.

"No. Not anymore. I'm fine now. And I know what I want," Cal said.

"You don't know what you're saying. I can't believe you're saying this to me."

"Why not? If you make me a vampire, you don't have to ever worry about me again. I won't be able to die. And I can take as many drugs as I want for as long as I want and I'll be just fine, sis."

"That's what you want out of life? You want us to turn you into a vampire so you can take lots of drugs? What an ambition. You're better than that," Vivant said.

Cal sat down heavily and sighed. He explained to Vivant that he was not better than that, that he didn't care anymore about anything. All his hopes and dreams died with Rosie.

She was all he had ever wanted. She was the love of his life – no matter how short a time they had been together – and he would never be able to love that way ever again.

And she had been taken away from him. Belladonna had taken her a away from him. She was responsible. If she wasn't going to be made to pay for her crime, then she should at least try to make amends for it.

Belladonna was horrified.

"Cal! You don't mean that. How can you say that? She tried to kill me! If I hadn't already been fucking dead, she would have. I don't even know you anymore," Belladonna said, her vision blurred by the tears that teetered on the brink of her lower lids.

"You killed my Rosie, Bell. You murdered her. And if you don't do what I ask, then I'll go to the police."

Before he could even wait for a reaction, Vivant was on him and picked him up out of his seat by the throat.

"You listen to me, you drugged-up little bastard, you'd already be dead if it wasn't for me saving you from your own stupidity, God knows how many times. You dare to sit there and blackmail us? I could kill you without even touching you! And if it wasn't for Belladonna, I probably would have already. You're pathetic," Vivant said.

Vivant's face was scarlet, a very, very rare occurrence that only happened when he was utterly enraged.

He turned away from Cal, the mere sight of him making his lip curl in disgust. And he felt betrayed. He'd taken Cal into his home, looked after him, indulged him, protected him. And he repaid him with blackmail.

"Anybody would think you were born here. Congratulations; you fit right in with the rest of the degenerates," Vivant said, his expression akin to tasting something unpleasant.

Belladonna couldn't even speak. She was crushed by Cal's words and the way he was acting.

How could you love that dirty whore more than your own sister? How could you?

Vivant answered her, out loud.

"Because dope fiends don't care about anything except their own addictions...oh, and dead whores, apparently."

Cal leapt from the chair and attached himself to Vivant's back. Vivant grabbed hold of him by his shirt collar, plucked him off like a leech and hurled him across the room.

Cal's skull shattered as he hit the wall.

Belladonna rushed to his side, screaming; he was barely alive, gargling and wheezing noises escaping from his throat.

"He's dying! Vivant, do something!"

"Oh, for the love of God," Vivant said, rolling his eyes.

He picked up the dying Cal by the scruff of his neck like an errant cat, and sank his fangs into his throat.

He tore open the skin on his own wrist and held it to Cal's mouth. Cal gagged and struggled at first as Vivant's blood began to slide down his throat.

Then a light came on in his eyes.

He sucked harder.

Drank deeper.

He kept drinking as he felt the bones in his skull start knitting back together again.

Vivant's wound healed in moments, but before he could make another Cal tore it open with his own teeth. He sucked feverishly; each second the pain became less and less until finally, after a minute or so, he was good as new.

Then his knees buckled beneath him and he lost consciousness.

Belladonna knew what was coming – Cal would experience the worst physical pain he would ever feel.

Vivant picked him up and laid him on his bed and waited for the screaming to start.

Cal was a vampire now.

He got what he wanted.

Now he was going to have some fun.

"I'm gonna take more drugs than any one person on the face of the earth has ever taken, " he announced.

"What happened to you, Cal? I don't even recognize you any more. You don't even sound like yourself. You're like a stranger," Belladonna said, looking hurt.

She missed the old Cal, the innocent country boy with a taste for moonshine and milkmaids of questionable character. Everybody loved *that* Cal.

Cal didn't answer. It was as if he'd woken up the day before with an intense hatred for Belladonna. Overnight, he'd forgotten what Belladonna and Vivant had done for him. And forgotten what Rose had done to *all* of them.

"Your plans are fine and dandy, Cal – except for one thing..." Vivant said.

Cal was looking smug. He was enjoying his triumph over smarty-pants Vivant, enjoying the fact that he'd got what he wanted out of making Vivant react violently.

"Oh, what's that then?" he asked, displaying an attitude neither of them had seen before.

"What I was going to tell you just before you made me slam you into the wall, was that you're a vampire now. Vampires are not affected by chemicals, pharmaceuticals or alcohol."

Instantly Cal was like a balloon with a loose knot. He was deflated. He visibly sank down toward the floorboards. He wasn't quite so smug anymore. He'd just lost the one reason he had left for living. And now that he was undead and could not die, the fact that he couldn't even get high was like being in Hell.

Cal moped around for days feeling sorry for himself. He wouldn't come out of his room and just sat there, staring out the window, or staring at the floor, or staring at the ceiling.

But he could not settle. There was no quiet anymore. He could hear voices, hundreds of voices – people laughing, crying, fighting, screaming.

He could hear music, but it was dozens of songs all running together in a one chaotic noise.

There was the sound of machines and vehicles.

Everywhere there was noise.

He stuck his fingers in his ears but all that seemed to do was trap the noise inside his head. It was driving him insane until finally he kept repeating stop...stop...stop over and over and over in his head.

And it did stop.

He had the power to turn it off.

And with that, he realized that he needed Belladonna and Vivant more now than ever. He was a new vampire and he needed the benefit of their experience, just like Belladonna had needed Vivant when he took her over.

But what Cal really needed right now was to get high. Any way he possibly could.

Finally, he emerged.

"There must be something!" he said, in desperation.

"Something for what?" Vivant asked.

"Something to get me high."

Vivant rolled his eyes. He couldn't believe this whiny pain in the arse was now an immortal. He knew he should have just let him die on his imported French parquet floor with his skull in pieces. But he knew Belladonna would never have forgiven him.

So, now, Cal would spend eternity with the two people he blamed for all of his misfortunes.

And, he couldn't even get high.

"There is something that can get you higher than you could ever imagine, Cal," Vivant said.

"There is? What is it? Tell me!"

Vivant grinned at him.

"Blood," he said. "There's not a drug on earth that can compare."

"How would you know? You've never felt what cocaine feels like. Or what opium feels like, or amphetamine or heroin," Cal said.

"I don't need to. I know how it feels when I drink blood."

"Well, I didn't feel anything like that when I drank your blood."

"You weren't a vampire yet when you drank my blood."

They looked at each other.

"I wasn't?"

"No, you didn't become a vampire until after the pain hit. You've not even fed yet. You've been sulking for days. Why don't you let me take you out and we can feed?"

Vivant had a horrible feeling he was about to create a monster.

It was late and the three vampires sat around the fire talking and sipping blood-red wine from old ornate chalices.

"Oh, for Heaven's sake," Vivant said.

"What is... Shit. Flint's here." Belladonna said.

Vivant went to the door and waited for the inevitable knock.

He paused a moment before opening the door.

"Detective; what a lovely surprise. What can we do for you," Vivant said.

"Can I come it. I have some news."

"Certainly. Come in and have a seat."

"Can I offer you a glass of wine, Detective Flint?" Belladonna asked, her sweetest voice immediately in place.

"Well, I don't usually when I'm on duty, but it's kinda late, so, yes."

She handed him the glass of wine with a smile.

"So, what's the news, Detective?" Vivant asked.

Flint took a long sip of wine and savored the heat spreading through him.

"The case on Jimmy Scars and his goon has been closed."

"Oh, really?" said Vivant.

"So, you arrested who did it then?" Belladonna asked, pretty sure of what the answer was going to be.

"Well, no, actually. But the chief says it was a gangland hit, perps unknown. And we don't have the manpower to investigate two dead hoodlums nobody's gonna miss," Flint said. "So, I just thought I would let you know you're in the clear."

"In the clear?" Vivant said. "What do you mean by that?"

"I mean, I know you three are involved, but you don't have to worry – you're in the clear; case is closed. I think some powerful people in this town don't want shit stirred up, if you'll pardon my French, Miss Busto."

Vivant looked at the cop and read his mind. He had nothing on them, nothing but a finely tuned gut and years of experience.

Vivant smiled.

But Belladonna was not smiling.

"Detective, I don't know what you think we did, but we had nothing to do with it. I'd never even met either of them."

"Oh, I don't think you had anything to do with that, Miss Busto. But I know you had something to do with Rose McAllister's header off the H. I'm sure of that."

Belladonna stood up, indignant and afraid.

Flint held up his hand.

"Don't worry, I can't prove that either. That was the other thing I came to tell you. Rose's case is closed too. Ruled a suicide. She's already forgotten. She's been stamped and filed and thrown on a shelf to gather dust. It's like she didn't even exist."

"Detective Flint, you sound sentimental about her. With all due respect, you didn't know her. She was a God-awful cunt. Sorry, Cal, but it's the truth. I think you're a sucker for a pretty face and a sob story."

Flint looked at him but said nothing.

"Detective, why do you think I had something to do with Rose's death? She committed suicide. You just said so. She was despondent over what she did, I guess. Who wouldn't be? And if you're looking for people with motives to to Rose harm, well, that's probably quite a long list. She was no angel," Belladonna said.

She wondered if he actually had any evidence against her apart for the old man who lived in the brush.

Cal was starting to fidget.

Then he started to laugh.

Vivant took him by the arm and led him toward the bedroom.

"You'll never guess what I did tonight, Detective!" Cal said over his shoulder as Vivant shunted him through the door.

"I'm sorry, Detective Flint; he's not been the same since Rose died," Belladonna said.

Flint looked at Vivant who tapped his temple as Belladonna spoke.

"He looks a little pale," Flint said and drained his glass.

Vivant almost laughed but bit his bottom lip instead. He listened to Flint's internal dialog.

Goddam I need another drink and I don't want to leave her and I want her. I want to touch her and hold her and kiss her and fuck her.

"Another glass of wine, Detective?" Vivant asked.

Flint said nothing but held up his glass.

"Thanks."

"You seem on edge. Is there something else you want to tell us?" Vivant asked.

Yeah that I'd like to kill you and have Belladonna all to myself you pansy little fuck.

Vivant had had enough of this asshole.

"Well, that's not very nice, Mr. Flint."

"What?" Flint said, confused.

"That you'd like to kill me and have have Belladonna all to yourself."

"What?" Flint bolted out of his seat and knocked over his glass of wine. He was drenched in panic.

"Is something the matter, Detective Flint?" Vivant asked.

"You just read my mind," he said, breathlessly. Flint had always thought of himself as pretty close to being a mind reader, so accurate were his instincts.

"I'm sorry, what?"

"You read my mind!"

"Are you alright? You're not making any sense, Detective." Belladonna played along. Vivant didn't need to use telepathy to let her know what he was doing. She was sharp.

"I knew there was something fishy about you two. You're not...you're not...right."

Vivant suggested that Flint was tired and that maybe he should go home and get some rest.

Flint's eyes darted around the room, looking for something solid that would prove him right that there was something wrong with these two. But there was nothing. It looked perfectly normal. They looked like a young couple in love. An extraordinarily beautiful young couple. *Unnaturally* beautiful.

He knew there was something different about them. He'd known it from the start, sensed it, *felt* it. But once again, he couldn't prove it and only had his gut as a guide. But he *knew* it.

The very air around them felt different when one of them was near, and with both of them here it was almost like the room was full of electricity. He could almost hear the buzz and crackle in the air around him, almost feel it crawling over his skin.

He ran his fingers through his hair. He was sweating and tilted his head to the side to stretch the tight muscles in his neck.

He couldn't take not knowing any more. He had to know what it was about these two that obsessed him so.

Then he decided to go for broke.

"What the fuck are you?"

Belladonna and Vivant looked at each other.

Cal didn't want to miss out on the fun. He burst through the doorway and made the announcement.

"Vampires! All three of us!"

"Cal..." Vivant said, trying to stop him from running his mouth. But the cat was out of the bag and there was no putting it back in.

"I gotta get some sleep; I could swear he just said you were all vampires."

"He did," Vivant said.

234

"You people are crazy. Fortunately for you though, that ain't a crime...and fortunately for me, cause I must be crazy too," Flint said.

"So, now you know. What are you going to do?" Belladonna asked him.

"What am I gonna do? I'm gonna go home, get drunk and pass out."

Flint picked up his hat, covered his sweaty hair with it and left.

Even although there were in the clear on the two cases Flint had been investigating, all three of them knew they had not seen the last of Detective Flint.

CHAPTER FOURTEEN : WANDERLUST

1932

The tragic suicide of aspiring actress Peg Entwistle brought memories of Rose flooding back to Belladonna.

It had been a year but the wound reopened easily as she read about the twenty four year old falling to her death off the Hollywoodland sign, despondent over her stalled career.

1947

January 15th.

Belladonna would never forget that day.

A young mother strolling along on a crisp winter's morning looks over on to a vacant grassy lot. She spies a shop mannequin, the two halves just dumped there among the dewy grass.

But as she gets closer she realizes with abject horror that the lower and upper body are not that of a mannequin, but that of a young woman, bisected at the waist. She rushes to get help.

Elizabeth Short was a twenty-two year old wannabe starlet from back east who came to Hollywood with a dream, like so many others.

Some things never change.

And on that day was born the infamous crime that would be known throughout the world as The Black Dahlia Murder.

Belladonna was shocked by the revelation that Elizabeth Short was obsessed with her, dressed like her, talked about her incessantly – and she'd been in the wrong place at the wrong time and became the victim that was supposed to be Belladonna.

1949

Belladonna watched with sadness as the years went by and the Hollywoodland sign fell into terrible disrepair.

The H had long since fallen to pieces.

She was glad the Hollywood Chamber of Commerce decided to repair the sign, even if they were going to fell part of the sign and it would never quite be the same again.

Belladonna stood at the bottom of Mount Lee watching, as the last four letters of the sign were demolished.

Tears streamed down her face as she watched HOLLYWOODLAND die.

Although the sign would still be there, something would always be missing for Belladonna. That sign had been part of her life, like a family member that she adored. She felt as if she was standing at an open grave, mourning the loss of a loved one.

Hollywoodland was no more.

RIP.

1956

August 16.

Belladonna awoke sobbing. She was in pain, almost as excruciating as the pain she felt since the night Vivant made her a vampire. She was inconsolable. Mute with grief. She couldn't answer Vivant when he asked her what was wrong.

It took her a long time to calm down and regain her power of speech.

With a heart filled with sadness that would never quite leave her, she told Vivant that Bela Lugosi was dead.

Decades came and went.

People grew old and passed away in what seemed like a heartbeat to those who cannot age and can never die.

Hollywood changed and it stayed the same.

It grew, got bigger, louder.

With each year more and more hopefuls got off buses from the boonies.

And still some of them wound up whoring, drugged out, dead.

Hollywood changed.

Hollywood stayed the same.

She loved it. She always would and she would always call this horribly wonderful place home.

But there was more to see. There was an entire world out there that she had never explored. And, when she chose, Hollywood would still be here to come back to. Always.

Belladonna had been a computer geek from the start. She loved computers and electronics and gadgetry of all sorts.

And she was an internet junkie. She drank up information about the rest of the world, obsessively watched webcams around the globe and delighted in simply watching people from other parts of the world go about their daily business. She loved all her books and atlases and had studied them over the decades, but the internet took her places the other things could not.

She watched any and all foreign films she could get her hands on, watched news programs, watched news in languages she didn't speak, just to see the rainbow of people and hear different tongues.

There were so many places to go, so many countries, so many people to see, cultures to enjoy.

She *had* to get out there and see it.

But Vivant had seen it all, done it all, hundreds of years before she was born. He was jaded.

He could never understand the thrill that the thought of traveling gave her.

And she hardly saw Cal. He was a wanderer. Last time she heard he'd sent her a postcard from Rio. He was drinking his way through the entire carnival and having the time of his life. He told her Brazilian cuisine was the bee's knees. He'd never lost that Jazz Age slang. Even if he *had* learned it when it was going out of fashion in the first place.

Mama and Papa were both gone. They lived a long life and even came to visit here in Hollywood many times and eventually they were persuaded to move nearer. Vivant bought them a little house in Southern California. Both of them were in their nineties when they passed away.

Belladonna wanted both of them to come over to *the dark side*, as Morag called it, and live forever.

Morag would have none of it.

Rodrigo would have done it if Morag had agreed to it. But he didn't want to spend eternity here on earth without the love of his life. He always told Belladonna he would rather spend it with mama in Heaven.

Even little sister, wee Quita, was dead and gone. She would never come over to the dark side either.

Only she and Cal were left.

Belladonna had itchy feet.

And she was going to take off and explore the world, with or without Vivant.

NOT LONG AGO...

Vivant sat in his usual chair by the fire reading. He knew what Belladonna had come to say before she said anything.

He could not look at her. If he did he knew that he would beg and plead with her to stay and he was not about to do that. Not his style.

"I'm leaving now, Vivant."

"Leave your key on the sideboard by the door," he said, eyes boring through the pages in his book.

His vision blurred with tears and he was afraid to move his head in case one fell.

He did not want her to see his sorrow. But she was a vampire. He knew that she could feel it, even if she couldn't read him quite the way he could read her. She could read him enough, no matter how hard he tried to keep it from her.

Just about anybody in the whole world could feel the weight of his heart at this moment. Any mere mortal would be able to feel it.

"I brought you something. It reminds me of you. If I didn't know better, I would swear she knows you."

She offered up something in a blood red gift bag, but Vivant didn't look up, didn't take the present from her.

"Just leave it there with your keys. I'll get it later. Thanks."

"I'm not leaving because I don't love you, Vivant. Don't be that way. I've explained this to you. Why can't you just set me free, for a little while?"

He looked up and a Judas tear ruined his stony facade.

"Set you free? Set you free, Belladonna? Have I ever chained you to me? Have I ever kept you prisoner?" Vivant asked her, a feeling of deja vu flooding through him.

"No. No, you haven't. But there are some things I need to do. For me. Just for me. I asked you if you would come with me and you said no. We have forever, Vivant. We have lifetimes. I just want to see some of the world. It's so different from the one that we knew, the time I came from. Just think what there is out there to explore!"

"I hate to tell you this but they have the same shit in other countries that we have here, Belladonna."

She sighed. She guessed that he had seen it all. Done it all. Nothing in the world held any interest for him any more.

"You're so jaded, Vivant. I feel sorry for you."

"Comes with old age, sweetheart."

He went back to reading his book.

"Well, if you're not going to give me a goodbye hug, I guess I'll get going."

She turned to leave and he looked up at her with a look so profound, if she'd seen it she would not have been able to walk out the door and out of his life, even if it was not forever.

He instinctively reached out for her, caught himself and buried his nose back in his book in time enough for her to turn around and see him in exactly the same stance as before, as if he had not moved, as if he had not reached out to her, shown her his soul, his truth through a simple glance, a simple gesture.

But she missed it.

And it was gone.

"See you around," she said.

Vivant heard the clank of her key as she dropped it on the sideboard by the door, just as he had asked her to.

The sound was so final for him. Worse than the sound of the heavy door closing behind her, the noise of her footfalls becoming fainter and fainter.

He broke down. Wishing he could do something to himself that would remind him of this pain, wishing he could do something to mark the occasion, something that would leave a permanent scar. But he could not. It would heal in seconds and he cursed his nature.

He picked up the present she left for him and sat back down in his chair. He reached into the gift bag and pulled out a book.

Vampire Red by Lily Transyl.

He turned the book over and saw a picture of the writer – he raised his eyebrows. The girl in the picture was a dead ringer for Belladonna. She had that timeless Silent Star look - dark hair and dark eyes and a soul that shone from behind them.

"I may just have found your replacement, you little bitch," he said, knowing he meant not a word of it. Nobody could ever replace his Bells.

With a smile Vivant opened up *Vampire Red* and settled down to read.

END OF BOOK ONE

GLOSSARY OF TERMS

Pitch woo - to make love
Snow bird - cocaine user
Crumb - a loser
A swell - wonderful, a rich man
Gunsel - derogatory term for a young homosexual
Mrs. Grundy - a prude, a kill-joy
Running with - hanging out with
All wet - no good
Rubes – money
Trip for biscuits - a task that yields nothing, a wasted journey
Blow your wig - go crazy about something, become excited
Whacky – crazy
Horn – telephone
Wheat - a country bumpkin
Nelly / Pansy / Twilight Boy - a gay man
Pansy Club – a gay club
Hep cat - a cool person
Gumshoe – detective
Okies – migrant workers from Oklahoma / mid-west migrant workers in general
Chopper - Thompson machine gun
Dollface - endearing term for a woman, normally when a man is looking for forgiveness.
Chase the dragon – smoke heroin / opium / morphine

ABOUT ALEX SEVERIN

Alex Severin was born and raised in Scotland and transplanted to the US in 2005. And she freakin' loves it!

A full-time writer since 2011, Alex earns her living writing things she will never admit to in public. She writes under many pseudonyms and in a diverse range of genres including paranormal romance, children's stories, horror, post-apocalyptic & dystopian, erotica, romance, and genres you didn't even know existed, nor would you even want to. Seriously.

She writes short stories, novels, screenplays, and loves to write about things that both repel and fascinate.

Her debut novel is the first installment of the *Vampire Vintage Series*, *Belladonna in Hollywood*, kicking it off with a Golden Age Hollywood Noir.

Vampire Vintage Book Two : The Ministry of Lilly, and *Vampire Vintage Book Three : Blood & Celluloid,* are due for release in 2012.

You can contact Alex via her online haunts at -

FACEBOOK -
Facebook.com/SeverinVampireErotica

BLOG -
AlexSeverin.BlogSpot.com

TWITTER -
@AlexSeverin